Deadly Challenge

Trish Kocialski

Quest Books
a Division of
RENAISSANCE ALLIANCE PUBLISHING, INC.
Nederland, Texas

ISBN 1-930928-76-9

First Printing 2002

9 8 7 6 5 4 3 2 1

Cover design by Mary D. Brooks

Published by:

Renaissance Alliance Publishing, Inc.
PMB 238, 8691 9th Avenue
Port Arthur, Texas 77642-8025

Find us on the World Wide Web at
http://www.rapbooks.biz

Printed in the United States of America

Acknowledgements:

There are many people who have encouraged and supported my efforts, and I would like to thank them. Carol Stephens, my partner, who is always there to save the day when I inadvertently hit the wrong key and send my draft into cyberspace; Daylene Petersen, my editor and beta reader, for her guidance and editing skills; Linda Daniel, the Director of the Quest Division, Barb Coles, President, and Cathy LeNoir, CEO of Renaissance Alliance Publishing, Inc., for their continued faith in my stories; and Mary Brooks, Graphics Division Director, who designs my nifty book covers. Lastly, I would like to thank my readers for their support of the Dean and Katie series. The many emails I have received from them provide the encouragement and confidence to continue writing the series.

— Trish Kocialski

Dedication:

This book is enthusiastically dedicated to Linda Mullen. The best ex-secretary, friend, and devoted fan I could possibly have. Thanks for all your support, encouragement, storyline requests, and most of all, your spirited sense of humor.

Chapter
1

26 November, 1030 Hours

The ride to Walter Reed Army Medical Center took longer than expected, due to the large numbers of holiday shoppers clogging the highways at every mall entrance along the way. Lieutenant Colonel Deanna Peterson and her partner, DEA Special Agent Katie O'Malley, were on their way to pick up Tracy Kidd, a good friend who was to be discharged from Walter Reed that afternoon.

As they neared the military hospital, a silent reminder of injuries incurred during their recent encounter with terrorists, Katie shivered at the thought of the last few weeks. "You know, we were pretty lucky on that op. It could have ended a lot worse."

Nodding, Dean concentrated as the traffic became more congested. "I know what you mean. This country could be embroiled in turmoil right now if Gentry had been successful in taking over those warheads."

Katie shivered again. "If even one of them had gotten through..."

Dean considered the targets chosen by Gentry. "It would have been pandemonium, no matter which one got through. Taking out the President and Vice President would have plunged this country into political chaos, not to mention the damage and loss of life Pensacola Naval Air Station would have sustained."

"And if the one targeted Havana had hit...the retaliation would have had world-wide effects."

Dean nodded her agreement. "I hate to say it, but probably the least comprehensive damage would have resulted from the warhead that was aimed at the Red Stone Arsenal. There'd have been a lot of collateral military damage—loss of life and such—but the civilian casualties would have been minimal."

Katie looked over at Dean as she drove through the rush of traffic. "Jeez, when you think about it, it's amazing that the only injury our team sustained was the bullet Tracy took."

"And, the loss of a perfectly good helicopter!" Dean began laughing as she remembered Tracy's words when she'd rescued her from the sinking craft.

"What's funny about that?" Katie inquired, failing to see the humor in the crash that could have taken both the lives of her lover and their very good friend.

"Do you know what Tracy said to me when we surfaced from that sinking helicopter?"

Curiosity piqued, Katie turned toward Dean. "No. You never told me she said anything."

Dean controlled her laughter long enough to say, "She said, 'Damn. You sure know how to show a girl a good time!'"

Both women broke out in smiles, then chuckles, and finally belly-shaking laughter as Dean eased the SUV into the entrance for Walter Reed and managed to find a parking space fairly close to the entrance. "Well, here we are, at last," Dean commented, removing the key from the ignition and wiping the tears from her eyes. Glancing at her watch, she sighed. "Hope the discharge papers haven't been processed yet. I know how impatient Trace can get when she wants out of some place. She'll be having a cow if she could have left by now."

"Oh?" her young blonde companion drawled, wiping the tears from her eyes too as she exited her side of the SUV. "You mean she can be worse than you?" Katie smiled at the frown Dean shot her as the two women walked toward the hospital entrance.

"What do you mean? I'm not impatient at all," Dean bantered good-naturedly, holding the door for her partner.

Katie looked up into Dean's twinkling sapphire eyes and smiled back knowingly. "Okay. You just remember that the next time you have to go in for your annual physical." Katie waggled a finger at the taller woman as she passed inside. "I don't want to hear one word of complaint from you."

They headed for the first bank of elevators, pressing the button for service as they waited. Dean stood facing the elevator, hands clasped behind her back, rocking on her heels as she waited. Katie was mentally counting off the seconds, certain that before she even reached twenty, Dean would make a comment about the slow service. Her count was interrupted by the arrival of Colleen Shore, Tracy's partner.

Colleen spied the two women as she came out of the coffee shop across from the elevators. "Hi, guys! Nice tans. Glad you were able to get something nice out of that so-called vacation."

"Hey, Col! Thanks for the use of the condo for the week. We managed to wind down pretty good on that island. Of course, Tom and Tiny were excellent companions and guides." As the elevator doors opened, Dean added, "Has she been released yet?"

"Nope. The doctor has to come up to give her a final once over before he'll sign the paperwork for the discharge. He was quite intrigued by the story of her injury," she teased.

Katie began chuckling. "Yeah, I'll bet he was! Did she tell him it was her first time actually flying a helicopter?"

Colleen nodded, trying to stifle her laughter. "You should have seen his face when I told him that she had only flown one in simulation and had crashed every time she tried to land!"

"Oh, I bet that was rich," Dean added, chuckling. "I would have loved to have been there."

The three women entered the elevator along with several hospital staff, who just looked at them wondering at the source of their mirth. "Yeah, his mouth really dropped open as she told him how she nearly bought the farm until you released her seatbelt." She grimaced wryly. "He doesn't seem to have had much experience with the military, but he seems really nice. He's young, but quite competent."

"That's right, General Carlton was going to assign someone special to her case. What's his name?" Dean asked as the elevator stopped on their selected floor.

Colleen answered the question as they arrived at Tracy's room. "Captain O'Brien."

Stepping through the door, they noted that the privacy curtain had been pulled around Tracy's bedside, but they could hear a male voice giving her instructions for the home recuperation period.

"Now make sure you get those stitches out on Friday. You can just come to the outpatient clinic, and one of the PA's will take care of it. Then you can start on some therapy next week," the voice instructed. "And no more flying!" he added with a chuckle. "At least not until you take some hands-on flying lessons. I'll send your therapist my orders today. That way, they can line up your treatment schedule so you can start on Monday." He paused before continuing. "Now, any questions before I go sign those discharge papers?"

"Um, none I can think of right now," Tracy began, "but if something comes up, I've got your number. Thanks, Captain, and good luck to you."

"Captain......hmm, I don't know if I'll ever get used to that," the doctor muttered softly. "Thanks for being a model patient, Tracy. Now, just do what we talked about for the next few days, and you'll be fine. I'll go get your paperwork started. A corpsman will be here in about an hour to escort you out."

The curtain slid back along the ceiling track, allowing the young doctor to exit the area. As he turned, he noted Colleen and the two other women standing by the door. "She's all yours..." He stopped speaking as he recognized the two women. "Hey, Colonel Peterson...Agent O'Malley. What are you two doing here?"

"Pete?" both women mouthed together as they recognized the young doctor.

"Yeah, it's me. What a surprise, eh?" He beamed at the slack jawed women who were just staring at him in disbelief.

"What...how..." Dean stammered.

"Long story," Captain O'Brien noted. "But the short of it is, your general is a pretty fast talker and an even faster paper pusher. I've been here for ten days now. Tracy was my first patient." He looked over at Tracy who was now redressed and interested in the conversation. "I take it you know these two?" He pointed at Dean and Katie.

"Yeah, Doc. That tall one over there is the one responsible for my getting in the way of that bullet," Tracy quipped, as she walked over to Dean and gave her a hug. "But I don't hold it against her."

Dean looked over at Tracy and gently poked a finger into her chest. "Hey, you're the one who said you could fly the damn thing!"

They all laughed and then proceeded to get a quick rundown on Pete's new commission as a medical corps officer. Ten minutes later, Captain O'Brien excused himself so he could get Tracy's discharge in motion.

"Wow. That's pretty cool of the general," Katie admitted. "Pete can get his residency finished and get paid well in the process. No more crummy jobs to provide for his family." Dean nodded and smiled, making a mental note to thank the general.

As promised, the corpsman showed up within the hour, providing a wheelchair for Tracy's departure. Tracy eagerly sat in the chair for her ride down to the lobby, telling her friends that she was not about to spend any more time than necessary in the hospital. Regulations were regulations, after all, and she knew she would have to give in to the ride sooner or later anyway. As soon as the corpsman came into the room, Dean left to get the SUV. Parking by the curb, she helped as the corpsman got Tracy settled into the back seat. Once they were all in, Dean cautiously pulled out and headed the SUV back to Occoquan.

"You're sure you guys don't mind us crashing with you until Friday?" Colleen asked for the third time. "We could get a hotel room."

"No way!" Katie declared. "There's plenty of room, and the cats will love to have company for a few days. Besides, we got to use your timeshare while you were up here, so let's just call it even."

"Even, it is," Tracy agreed. "How was the rest of your vacation, anyway?"

"Fantastic! I can see why you guys go there every year. It's so laid back and restful," Dean contributed.

"And the beaches are great, too," Katie chimed in, a bit too eagerly, which elicited a wide grin from Dean.

"I hope you guys remembered the beach blanket!" Tracy teased, which caused them all to burst into laughter. The ride continued in relaxed companionship as the women exchanged information from the past week, and they were soon pulling into the driveway at Dean and Katie's new home.

* * * * *

A small, camouflaged body crept stealthily through the trees surrounding Dean's property. At a distance of fifty yards, it stopped and slid into a prone position behind a series of small evergreen shrubs that had been planted in a random pattern along both sides of the property. Across from the deck that extended around three sides of the house, the intruder could now see directly into the kitchen where the foursome was gathered. A gnarled right hand pulled a pair of binoculars out of a backpack, the magnification allowing the voyeur to feel as though they were sitting amidst the four laughing people.

"So, that's the grand tour," Katie pronounced as she led Tracy and Colleen back into the kitchen before taking the tray of snacks out to the living room.

"Nice place you've got here Dean, but aren't you worried about privacy? There's not a curtain in the place." In testament to her statement, Colleen gestured at the undraped floor to ceiling windows.

"Hey, just take a look outside, Col, do you see anyone watching?" Dean joked, then turned serious. "Not to worry my friend. Besides all the trees between here and the next property, I had this little item installed." Dean walked over to the main control panel for all of the electronic toys she'd added for security, and pushed a series of buttons. Instantly, the windows went from a clear view of the outside, to an opaque view, allowing light, but no sight, to filter through.

"Awesome!" Tracy and Colleen chimed in together. Dean pushed the buttons once more, and the windows returned to their clear view mode.

"I saw this at a home show up in Philadelphia. I thought it was the coolest thing ever devised. Saves a lot in window dressings, too," Dean explained. "Of course it was a bit pricey to add, but I think it's worth it." Dean led her guests to the living room where Katie had put out the tray of cheese, fresh fruit, and crackers, along with some hot cider. They chatted on for nearly an hour, reliving their experiences of the past year.

Turning to the subject of their invitation to the White House and their upcoming visit there, Colleen asked, "Have you ever been asked to the White House before, Dean? I mean, it's a bit unnerving and...well, what should we wear and all?"

"Well, that's an easy one for me, I'll be in uniform; you guys can just wear something casual," Dean snickered.

"Casual? To the White House? To meet the President?" Colleen objected.

"Yeah, Col, you know me. Best I'll do is a pair of slacks and a jacket," Tracy admitted.

"Sure, that'll be fine. It's a private meeting, no press or anything," Katie offered. The general said he just wants to meet us, and thank us...again." Katie's mind whirled back to nearly a year before, when she'd first met the President in Dean's hospital room after her partner had come out of surgery. *Now, that was an interesting experience. Watching the President thank Dean for saving the day, even though she was acting on her own initiative and technically against orders. I don't know who was more intimidated in that brief meeting, the President or Dean. My gut, though, tells me it was the President—for not taking her warnings seriously.* Katie returned from her thoughts to be greeted by a knowing smile from her lover. "Speaking of the general, shouldn't she be here soon with our feline brood?"

Outside, beneath the evergreen shrub, the silent figure continued a vigilant watch, listening to the conversation through the small transmitters that had been planted earlier in the week. "You're getting really good at saving the day, aren't you?" the camouflaged body whispered. "Well, we'll just see how good you are, won't we." Then the phantom packed the binoculars back into the backpack and slipped away into the silence of the night.

* * * * *

Bidding the general goodnight, then giving Sugar her evening medication, Dean and Katie finally and thankfully made their way to their bedroom. After brushing their teeth and washing up for the night, Dean doused the lights before the two naked women exited the bathroom. "I think I need another vacation, just to rest up," Katie moaned as she crawled under the fluffy comforter.

"Mmm, me too," her tall lover replied, following Katie into the bed. "Nice to be home, though."

"Yes, it is. And the cats seem to be glad to be home, too." Katie had no sooner finished the sentence, than Butter jumped up on the bed, stalking her way over to her mistress and eliciting an "urf" from the woman as the cat plopped down all sixteen of her pounds on Katie's chest. Sugar quickly followed her sister and took over the lower section of the bed, purring with contentment. "Gotta put these cats on a diet," Katie gasped, as she moved Butter from her chest.

"Looks like you were missed," Dean stated as she stroked the calico that now took up residence between them.

"Umhm. And it looks like she wants to keep an eye on both of us." Katie looked around the room in anticipation of Spice joining them. Not seeing her, she shrugged her shoulders and rolled over to face Dean. "I guess Spice is still angry about being left behind."

"She's probably down with Tracy and Colleen," Dean offered. "Colleen really does attract all sorts of animals. If there's a stray animal around, she'll find it. Just like those puppies in the woods outside the resort. Remember how they took right to her?"

"Yeah, they just swarmed over her like ants over melted ice cream." Katie giggled at the memory and was about to make another comment when the two women heard something slide across the hardwood floor and bounce off the molding, followed by the sound of a cat pouncing on her prey.

"Meow!" Bat...slide...crash-thump. "Meeooowww."

"Good grief! What has she got now?" Katie threw off the comforter and grabbed her robe, slipping it on before turning on the lights. Scanning the room, she found the source of the noise crouched in the corner, tail smacking heavily back and forth on the wood floor, eyeing an unseen object under a chair. Going over to check out what treasure Spice had conjured up this time, she bent down and reached under the chair and came up with a totally unexpected surprise.

"Dean...you'd better take a look at this." Katie took the object over to Dean's side of the bed, offering it to her lover as she sat up. "I think Spice may have gotten into some of your techno toys."

"What the..." Taking the small item in her hand, sapphire

eyes darkened. "It's not one of ours." Dean looked at the tiny transmitter, turning it over in her hand several times. "It's a European model, maybe a NATO issue."

"Are you sure?"

"Positive."

"Is it working?"

"Not now." She pointed to fresh teeth marks in the small object. "Spice took care of that." She looked up into alert emerald eyes as she got out of bed, slipping on her nightshirt. "But I'm sure there are more where this came from," she added in a barely audible whisper.

Silently, Dean headed for the exercise room, flipping on the light as she entered. Katie followed, knowing that Dean was heading for her secured closet where she kept a variety of high tech equipment on hand for short notice assignments. Dean entered the ten-digit combination, turned the handle, and entered the closet, emerging in a few seconds with an electronic "bug" detector. The item was not much larger than a portable tape player, but had an eight-inch tube protruding from one end. She turned the instrument on and began a thorough sweep of her entire house, inside and out. Katie, in the meantime, went to Tracy and Colleen's room and silently apprised their guests of the situation. Within thirty minutes, Dean had found fifteen other transmitting devices, bagged them, and relegated them to the freezer, before joining her friends in the living room.

The tall woman sat heavily in the chair by the fireplace. "Okay, it's safe to talk; I've got them all."

"Just a typical night in an intelligence officer's life?" Colleen queried as she took in the exhausted look on her friend's face.

Dean sighed. "Guess you could say that."

"Any ideas?" questioned Tracy as she readjusted herself on the couch, careful not to aggravate her injured shoulder.

"Not a clue." Tired blue eyes looked up at the three people staring at her. "We'll have to wait for daylight before I can check the grounds more thoroughly. Until then, I suggest we try to get some sleep."

Chapter
2

Dean was up before daybreak, sitting in the dark kitchen while she waited for enough daylight to start her search. Katie woke as she felt the presence of her lover fade from her side. Deciding that she wouldn't be able to sleep anymore, she got up and slipped into her sweats, ready to help in the search. She quietly entered the kitchen, taking up a position behind her lover who was staring out the wide expanse of windows. Gently placing a hand on Dean's shoulder, she greeted her partner with a soft kiss to the top of her head.

"Morning, love," Katie whispered as she removed her lips from the shiny black hair. "Couldn't sleep, huh?"

"Nope. Just trying to figure out who could have bugged us." Dean turned in her chair, sapphire eyes searching emerald ones. "And how the hell they got in here past my security. I checked the entire security program when we got in Saturday night, and there were no discrepancies, no unauthorized breaks in the code, no indication of anything being amiss." Dean stood and shook her head. "Maybe there's something missing in my program. I'll ask Colleen to check it out tomorrow." She took her tea mug from the table and downed the last of its contents before placing it in the dishwasher. "It's getting light enough now. I'm going to start around the house and garage first, then make my way out to the perimeter. Care to join me?"

"My thought exactly. Maybe you can teach me some of the tricks of your trade along the way." The two women walked to the laundry/mud room and slipped on their jackets to insulate them against the cold morning temperature. Dean disarmed the security alarm, grabbed a flashlight from the shelf, and softly closed the door, not wanting to wake Tracy and Colleen. They turned to the right and circled the house in gradually expanding circles as they checked the foundation, shrubs, and garage. By the time they reached the outer reaches of the lot, they were becoming frustrated and about to give up on finding any indication of something out of the ordinary, until Dean spotted the depression under the shrub.

"Look there, hon. See the depression under the shrub?"

"Yes. But couldn't it have been made by an animal?"

"Not that big a depression. And the boughs of the bush are too close to the ground for a larger animal like a deer to use this as a resting place." Carefully going around the shrub, Dean inspected the rest of the area. Pointing to a depression in the leaf bed, Dean explained that someone crawling under the shrub and then backing out the same way had probably caused it. She followed the faint trail into the woods, noting that it followed the roadway into her property. When the trail finally came to the roadbed, Dean was cautious in taking each step so she would not obliterate any human tracks. She bent down and picked up a fallen branch, using it to carefully sweep aside the leaves.

"Here's what I'm looking for," Dean explained, as she pointed to the ground at a set of footprints she'd uncovered. They followed the prints in the dirt floor of the forest to a set of tire tracks at the side of the road, where they finally disappeared.

"Looks like a small car, probably a sports car of some type by the tire profile. I'd guess these were made sometime yesterday, maybe late afternoon." Touching the footprint, Dean shook her head slightly. "These footprints are small. Either came from a small man, or a woman."

"Why would someone be spying on us?"

"Why and who," Dean growled as she considered the evidence once more. "C'mon, let's get back to the house. There's nothing more to find out here."

When they got back, they found Tracy sitting in the kitchen

waiting for them. She had a furball planted in her lap, purring loudly, while two more were winding in and out around her feet. Looking up at her friends when they entered, Tracy shrugged and smiled. "I think they're trying to convince me to feed them," she commented as the cats ran to their food dishes looking up expectantly at the word "feed."

"Yeah, you look like a soft touch," Katie chuckled. "Is Col still asleep?"

Tracy nodded her head and explained that Colleen had just fallen asleep about an hour before, having had a restless night after the transmitters were found. "She's hoping you'll let her check out your security program. After all, she's a computer geek, so she was running possibilities through her head all night."

"Don't let her hear you call her a geek," Dean scolded in a friendly tone. "But I do appreciate her offer. Actually, I was going to ask her to check the program for me." Dean reached for a blank sticky note, wrote down her password for the computer system in the den, and gave the slip of paper to Tracy. "That'll get her into the computer so she can check it out."

Tracy nodded, accepting the paper and slipping it into her pocket. "So, what did you two find?"

"Not much, just some tracks on the forest floor. They eventually led to where a car had been parked," Dean replied. "I'll take the transmitters we found in to the lab. Maybe they can figure out exactly where they originated."

"Any ideas on who and why?" Tracy interjected.

"Not a clue. But in this business you make a lot of enemies, so who knows?"

* * * * *

At 0900, Dean was pulling into her parking spot at the Pentagon. Katie still had four days off remaining before she had to report for orientation at the DEA Training Center in Quantico, Virginia. She was planning on spending the time with Tracy and Colleen, giving them the real tour of Washington and the surrounding area. They were scheduled to meet Dean for lunch at 1200, at the Pentagon, where the food in the cafeteria was actually very good, since a large percentage of the users were Command

and General Staff personnel. Each branch sent the best of their best to prepare the meals at the facility, and the competition among them to put out excellent meals was fierce.

Entering her office, Dean placed her briefcase on the guest chair and hung her coat in the closet; then crossed to her desk and the large stack of mail sitting on top of her inbox, pacing her small area while sorting through it. Mumbling "keep" or "toss" as she scanned each item, she came at last to the bottom of the pile. The "keep" pile was placed on her desk blotter, while the "toss" pile quickly filled her wastebasket. She was about to go to her desk to check her computer for emails, when the intercom buzzed, followed by Sergeant Major Tibbits' voice requesting her presence with General Carlton. Reaching over the desk, she hit the talk button. "On my way, Sergeant." As a secondary thought, she reached over and turned on her computer, knowing that by the time she got back, it would be booted up and her programs ready for use. Dean reached into her briefcase, deciding to take the Ziplock bag of transmitters with her, along with her written report detailing the entire operation involving the Ares Array and Scott Gentry's mercenary crew. A separate report summarizing Sadaam's involvement in the situation was attached, with copies for the Joint Chiefs and the State Department. Armed with her reports and the Ziplock bag, Dean straightened her uniform, then left for the general's office.

Sergeant Major Tibbits stood as Lieutenant Colonel Peterson entered the office. "Welcome back, Colonel. Glad to see you made it back in one piece this time."

"Thank you, Sergeant Major. I'm glad we *all* made it back in one piece," Colonel Peterson corrected.

He beamed back at her. "Yes, Ma'am. Sorry to hear about Major Kidd, though. Please giver her my regards when you see her."

"I'll do that, Tibbits." Dean glanced towards the inner office. "Is the general ready to see me?"

"Yes, Ma'am," the sergeant replied, stepping over to the door and opening it for her to enter.

Dean strode to the front of the general's desk, stood at attention, and went through the formal reporting procedure.

General Carlton looked up from her papers as Dean finished.

"At ease, Colonel," she commanded, then indicated that Dean should move to the sitting area.

Brigadier General Mary Carlton had been temporarily appointed to her position as Chief of the Army's Intelligence Division nearly one year previously, replacing Major General John James shortly after his death. Although it was a temporary assignment, there had been a fairly smooth transition from her previous intelligence command with the Fifth Army Division stationed in San Antonio. Most of the intelligence gathering had been routine, until her friends Art and Gwen Lyons had come to visit her two months before.

As she stood and walked over to take a seat across from Colonel Peterson, she reflected that since then, her command had been anything but routine. She had been dressed down by the Joint Chiefs for her stance on the mercenary threat, initiated an unofficial operation on a gut feeling, allowed military equipment to pass through another country's embassy without authorization, and was finally justified for her insubordinate actions by the success of the woman now sitting across from her. The only reason she was not facing a court-martial was that the President himself had unknowingly intervened on her behalf by commending the Joint Chiefs for their astute understanding of the situation and their taking quick, decisive action. He further commended them on their selection of General Carlton as the replacement for General James, then requested her attendance at the White House, along with the operations team, on Wednesday of the current week. This meeting was to be a formal but unpublicized ceremony to recognize their actions, and especially the bravery of the team in the face of a terrorist attack. The Joint Chiefs were not happy about the turnabout, but remained tight-lipped for fear of exposing their opposition to the intelligence chief's recommendations. They were also resigned to the fact General Carlton would become a permanent replacement, and they would have to come to terms with having a woman in such a powerful position.

Dean waited patiently as General Carlton walked over to take a seat opposite her, mentally preparing to give her summary of the operation. The general smiled at Dean as she began to speak. "First of all, I want to commend you and your team for a job well done. You saved not only the joint exercises and the President and Vice President, but countless civilians from a horrible fate." General Carlton paused and smiled even more broadly for her next statement. "And, I want to personally thank you for keeping my butt from getting kicked out of the Army for insubordination. The Joint Chiefs have had to eat a lot of crow, and they're not too happy about it."

"Thank you, Ma'am, but we were just doing our job," Dean offered quietly. "If I may say so, General, I'm certainly glad you'll be around permanently. That is the scuttlebutt: that your duty assignment is now permanent?"

"That's correct, Dean. I received my permanent orders from the Joint Chief this morning." Sighing heavily, the general shrugged her shoulders before continuing. "Guess you won't have to break in a new CO." Dean grinned appreciatively, agreeing that this was definitely a good thing. "Do you have the written reports for me? I need to get them to the Joint Chiefs and State Department before this afternoon."

"Yes, Ma'am. They're right here." Dean offered the folders with the written reports. "Your copy is on top."

General Carlton stood and extracted her copy of the report, then went to her desk where she toggled the intercom. "Sergeant Major." Tibbits entered in response to her hail, and she handed him the documents. "Please deliver these reports to the Joint Chiefs and the State Department immediately." Tibbits saluted and left, and she returned to her seat opposite Dean.

Dean observed these seemingly simple actions with interest, surprised that the general had not reviewed the reports before sending them up the chain of command. It was a subtle, but very effective indication that General Carlton was placing total trust in Dean's abilities and judgment.

As General Carlton returned her attention to Dean, she noticed the Ziplock bag in her lap. "What do you have there?" she inquired as Dean held up the bag.

"Seems someone is very interested in me. I, that is, we found these last night in our home."

"Sure it's you and not Katie they're interested in?" the general questioned thoughtfully.

"Ah, never thought of that. I'm so used to being alone, I just assumed..." Dean felt the blush begin to rise and used all her biofeedback techniques to quell its ascent.

General Carlton took the proffered bag of transmitters and opened it, retrieving one of the bugs. Turning it over in her hand, she noted that it was European in design and definitely not standard issue. "Well, unless Agent O'Malley has enemies in Europe, you're probably right in your assumption." Returning the transmitter to the bag, she zipped it shut, handing it back to Dean. "Are you taking them to our lab?"

"Yes. I thought they would be able to pinpoint their origin more precisely. It might give us a place to start figuring out the who and why."

"Good point," the general agreed. "Now, are you ready for the White House visit on Wednesday?"

"Yes, Ma'am. Colleen is a bit nervous, but she and Tracy are both genuinely pleased about the invitation. I'm sure receiving a personal 'thank you' from the President of the United States is not something they expected for helping out."

"You're probably right on that one; however, it's going to entail a little bit more than just a thank you—there will be photographs, as well. As a field operative, I don't particularly want your picture splashed across the countries' newspapers, so I'll have to rain on the parade, so to speak. The White House photographer will be there, but at my request, the press won't be included."

"Well, I certainly will appreciate that. I much prefer a low profile myself," Dean confided.

General Carlton's voice assumed a more serious tone. "How is Tracy's recovery progressing?"

"Actually, she's doing quite well. She was discharged from Walter Reed yesterday. She and Colleen will be staying with us until Friday, when they return to New York. By the way, it was quite a surprise meeting her physician yesterday." Dean's eyes sparkled in combination with a beaming smile. "You certainly worked fast getting Pete on board. Thank you for doing that for him."

"Well, with his capabilities, I wasn't about to let someone else snap him up. I was able to get the paperwork rushed through, and the approval to move his residency went just as smoothly. He was sworn in just a couple of weeks ago, and his officer's training can be accomplished at the same time he works on his residency. The military needs good medical personnel, so it was easy for him to jump through the hoops." General Carlton stood, indicating that their session was over. "Thank you again, Colonel. I'm glad we will be able to continue working together." She extended her hand, not only in thanks but also in friendship. Dean stood also, accepted the proffered hand eagerly, sharing a firm handshake. Taking her bag of transmitters and her briefcase, she was officially dismissed from the general's office.

In the general's anteroom, Tibbits had just returned as Dean was closing the general's door behind her. "What have you got there, Colonel?" he asked, noticing the bag in her hand.

Dean told the sergeant major about the transmitters she'd found. "I'm taking them over to the lab for identification. I just can't imagine someone getting past my security without my entry code," she added with a shrug.

"Um, I can," Tibbits confided uncomfortably. "Oh, Ma'am, you are going to have my stripes for this."

Colonel Peterson looked at the sergeant, more than a bit confused. "What do you mean, Tibbits?"

"Last week, there was an awful ice storm here."

"Yeah, I remember seeing that on the TV. We were all laughing because you guys were freezing while we were basking in the sun. Go ahead, explain yourself." Dean began tensing unconsciously as the sergeant major began again.

"Well, I got a call from the utilities company office in Occoquan. They explained that they were going through your subdivision restoring power and gas to the homes, and insuring that each home was safe from possible gas explosions prior to the electric being turned back on. They wanted to know if you could be reached to meet them at your house to let them in." He paused, gulping a bit.

"Yesss, go on," the colonel hissed.

"Um, well, I told them you weren't available. Then they asked if anyone could meet them to open up the house, so I met them. I put in the code you'd given me, and... Well, they went in and did a safety check throughout the house to make sure the gas hadn't built up, then they left."

"I don't use gas in my house, not even in the fireplaces. It's all electric!" She ran her hand across her face in frustration. "Did you check their ID's?"

"Yes, Ma'am. They appeared to be in order."

"Did you call to verify them?"

"Um, no. I was in a bit of a hurry to get back. The general was expected back from a meeting directly, so I...I just didn't." Tibbits was visibly shaken at the jeopardy he had placed the colonel in. "I'm sorry, Ma'am. I thought, with the ice storm and all, that I was helping."

Dean exhaled sharply, then nodded her head in agreement. "Yes, I can see where you thought that. Well, whoever was involved didn't get much information. We'd only been home for twenty-four hours." She placed her hand on Tibbits' shoulder, "Do you think you would recognize them again? Can you give me a description to go on?"

"Well, they were pretty average looking, with the utility uniforms on and all," he responded.

"Male or female?"

"Both, actually. One man, one woman, both of average height, late twenties to early thirties, no distinguishing features I could see."

"Any discernable accents?" the colonel asked.

"Yeah, they did sound foreign. Poles, or maybe Russians? But that's not unusual with all the different nationalities living around here," Tibbits added as he shrugged his shoulders in defeat. "I'd recognize them again, though, if that's any help."

"Good. If we get any prospects, I'll run them by you."

"I'm really sorry, Ma'am. I was just trying to help," Tibbits apologized once more.

"I know, Sergeant. You were just doing a good deed." Dean clapped him gently on the shoulder. "Just check things out further in the future, okay?"

"Yes, Ma'am. I will."

Dean tossed the bag in her hand, and then turned to leave the office.

* * * * *

It was nearly 1130 hours when Colonel Peterson returned to

her office after taking the transmitters to the lab. She spent the time with the technicians as they analyzed them, coming up with inconclusive information as to their provenance; but the good news was they were short-range transmitters, and whomever planted them probably knew they were compromised.

Dean closed the door behind her and immediately went to her computer to check her email. Circling behind her desk, she sat in her large comfortable leather chair and swiveled around to her computer. When she gave the mouse a slight shake to bring the computer screen back to life, she brought up the mail program and noticed Katie had sent the first message listed. Eagerly, she opened it and found herself staring at a picture of Katie reclining on a lounge chair, wearing the lime green bikini she had purchased the day before they left the Bahamas. What startled and angered Dean, was that the picture had been altered to show Katie covered in blood, and her face removed and replaced with that of a skull. At the bottom of the screen was a message typed to her attention:

```
My Dearest Colonel:
How do you like the picture I took of your
little bitch lover... Don't you think
she looks good in red?
```

As Dean read the message, blood appeared to pour down from the top of the display, obscuring the picture as it flowed across the screen. Noticing the flow, Dean immediately hit the "print screen" button on her keyboard and quickly pasted it to her word processing program. When the flow stopped, her normal email format reappeared, however without this message listed. She furiously typed a series of commands on her keyboard, but was unable to retrieve or reproduce the message or the picture. Closing the mail program, Dean recovered the pasted page, and printed the captured message. Retrieving the printout, Dean looked at the paper, which showed the top half of the page covered in the flow, a partial image of Katie's blood covered body, and the message.

"What in Hades is going on?" she mumbled to herself as her hands began to shake, more with anger than with fear. "Just who the hell are you, and what do you want?"

She sat staring at the paper for a few minutes until her intercom buzzed. Dean toggled the talk button. "Colonel Peterson."

"Colonel, this is Sergeant Folks at Security. You have some visitors."

Dean looked at her watch, surprised to see that it was 1200 hours already. "Thank you, Sergeant. Please send them up. Agent O'Malley knows the way." She folded the sheet of paper, slipping it into her pocket. *Now, do I tell them about this, or play it close to my chest?* Dean considered the decision a bit longer before she made up her mind. *Not a good idea to start keeping secrets now, but let's get lunch over first.* As she waited for her friends to arrive, she placed a call to Dirk, Bill's partner, who worked in the computer center on sub-level three. She explained the situation, requesting he try and trace the source of the email, then prepared to meet her friends.

* * * * *

The four women were seated at a corner table in the cafeteria, enjoying their selections from the variety of food available. Everyone, that is, except Dean. She barely picked at her Moo Shoo dish, her mind seemingly off somewhere else.

This fact did not escape Katie, and the young woman nudged her elbow. "Are you all right?" the young blonde queried.

"Yes and no. But I can't discuss it here. We'll go to my office after we finish lunch," Dean answered as she pushed her plate away.

"So, Colonel, do we get a tour of the Pentagon today?" Tracy asked as she turned to face her old friend. Noticing the frown on Katie's face, and considering the quiet mood her old friend had been in during the meal, she changed her tack. "Or maybe, just a short chat in your office before we head out?"

Colleen picked up on the changes, too, and offered, "Or we could just head out now, and see you back at the house?"

"No. No, let's go up to my office." Dean pushed her chair back, picking up her tray as she stood. They disposed of their trays and trash, and soon the four women were headed to Dean's office in silence. Dean opened her office door, gesturing for her friends to enter in front of her. Entering last, she closed the door behind her before facing her worried friends.

"What's wrong, Dean?" Katie asked as she reached out to touch her friend's forearm.

Dean sighed. "Have a seat. I have some information on those bugs," she glanced at Katie, "and there's a new development." Once they were settled, she leaned against her desk, filling them in on Sergeant Major Tibbits' involvement with the transmitters, and then telling them about the email message.

"Oh my God, Dean. Isn't there any way to tell who sent it?" Katie asked, obviously shaken by the mental image of the described email.

"I've got Bill's friend, Dirk, working on that now. He'll call after he's had time to work on the problem, but I've got a feeling that the transmitters and the message are related." She pulled the paper out of her pocket and unfolded the printout, holding it out for their inspection. "This is all I could save of the message." She handed it to Katie, who sucked in a quick breath at the image displayed. Tracy and Colleen took the sheet from Katie, instantly comprehending the reason for the sudden pallor in their friend's face.

"Any ideas?" Tracy inquired as she returned the picture to Dean.

"Not a clue. I'm hoping Dirk will be able to pull off a trace for us." Just then, her phone rang. Dean picked up the receiver and listened as the caller began talking, leaving Dean to respond intermittently. Thanking Dirk, Dean apprised her friends of the results of his efforts.

"Seems, the email was bounced around a variety of civilian mail servers before landing on my computer. It was sent on 24 November at 1535 hours, EST, from a cyber café in Freeport, Grand Bahama Island. Dirk can't get much else at this point, but he feels the program used to create the self destructing email was pretty sophisticated, and if they're that clever, he doesn't hold out much hope of identifying the real user of the computer that sent the message."

"A lot of those mercenaries were computer geeks. Do you suppose we missed someone in the mop-up action, and they're responsible for it?" Colleen suggested as she shifted in her chair.

"A good thought, but I doubt that. If anyone got through the

Delta Force net, they probably high-tailed it out of the country. They wouldn't be stupid enough to hang around to take pictures and send emails." Dean sighed as she tossed the printout on her desk. "No, whoever is responsible for this, has a more personal agenda. The message makes that perfectly clear. Now, I just need to figure out who I pissed off that has these skills."

Tracy looked up at her old friend and smiled. "Well, is that a short list, or a long list?"

Appreciative of the attempt at levity, Dean smiled back before replying, "A long list, my friend. A very long list."

Chapter
3

General Carlton, Bill, Dean, Katie, Tracy, and Colleen were waiting outside the Oval Office in the White House. Tracy and Colleen appeared to be a bit more nervous than the others, but then, they had never before met the President of the United States. The outside door to the secretary's office opened, revealing two nattily attired men. Katie jumped up at the sight of the two ex-SEALs as they entered the office. She hurried over and gave each a warm smile and a fierce hug. Dean stood and introduced General Carlton to Tom Zedos and Tiny Freeman, before duplicating Katie's response.

"I'm so glad you guys decided to come up," Dean said, as Tom and Tiny grinned back at her.

"Well, Colonel, your call tipped the scales for us. If it had been anyone else calling, we would still be on the Lady Luck, sipping a Kalik and watching the clouds breeze by." They looked over at the general who seemed to be very amused by his statement. "Um, no offense, General."

"None taken, Mr. Zedos. I'm glad the colonel has expanded her powers of persuasion to include a verbal technique," she replied with a hint of humor, knowing that Lieutenant Colonel Peterson's powers of persuasion usually involved a more physical approach. The subtle humor was not lost on Tracy or Katie, as they tried to suppress a burst of giggles. Before the new arrivals were able to sit, the door to the Oval Office opened and the President's secretary invited them inside.

As the group entered, they were led to the sitting area, where the President stood waiting. General Carlton led the body of visitors, and was first to be greeted by the President. She then made the introductions of the rest of the assemblage. After the formal introductions were completed, the President indicated they should be seated, as he wanted to review the incident with his guests and have a chance to talk with each of them regarding their role in the operation. When the staff photographer arrived, the President nodded for his secretary to bring a box over from his desk. As the President stood, the rest of the group followed his lead. "As you know, my term of office will be over shortly, and it is with great personal satisfaction that I am able to formally thank you for your extraordinary accomplishments as one of my final official acts."

First, he thanked General Carlton for her astute grasp of the situation. He formally apprised her of her permanent appointment as the Chief of Army Intelligence and his hope that his successor would value her recommendations regarding intelligence situations.

Next, he asked Tom, Tiny, and Colleen to come forward. His secretary stood beside him, opened the box, and handed him three medals.

"Ms. Colleen Shore, Mr. Thomas Zedos, and Mr. Timothy Freeman, it is with my sincere gratitude that I award you the Presidential Citizenship Medal for your selfless acts of service and assistance at considerable personal sacrifice. I thank you, and America thanks you." He then placed the medals on each one, and shook their hands as the photographer's camera clicked away.

Next, he asked Tracy to come forward. "Major Tracy Kidd, United States Army, Retired. As of March 28, 1978, this award has been authorized for injuries incurred as a result of an international terrorist attack against the United States itself or any foreign nation that is friendly to the U.S. It is therefore with grateful thanks, that I award you the Purple Heart for your actions of heroism on November 17, 2000 that resulted in personal injury." He pinned the medal to her jacket and shook her hand as the photographer captured the moment on film.

Katie was summoned next. The President removed a medal

from the box and intoned, "Special Agent Katherine O'Malley, for your exemplary performance of service for the United States of America, and conduct to maintain our national security, I award you the Department of Defense Medal for Distinguished Public Service. Your patriotism and sense of public responsibility are appreciated by myself and Americans across this country." Again the photographer's camera whirred as the President placed the medal on Katie's jacket and shook her hand.

The last two to receive recognition were First Lieutenant William Jarvis and Lieutenant Colonel Deanna Peterson. At the President's beckoning, they stepped forward, saluting and standing at attention. The President moved in closer and whispered a few words to Dean, eliciting a smile from her. He then stood back and reached in the box one more time.

"First Lieutenant William Jarvis, in recognition of your exemplary performance of duty in service to the United States of America at significant personal danger, I am awarding you the Distinguished Service Medal. In addition, I am exercising my right as Commander-In-Chief, and promoting you to the rank of Captain." The President presented Bill with a box containing his new rank insignia, pinned the medal on his uniform and shook his hand. Dean, still standing at attention, couldn't help but sneak a sideways glance at her protégé and smile as the young man accepted the honors bestowed on him.

Finally, the President turned to address Dean. "Lieutenant Colonel Deanna Peterson, as your Commander-in-Chief, I am promoting you to the rank of Colonel, United States Army." He then reached up and removed the silver oak leafs from her epaulets and replaced them with the silver eagle indicating the rank of full colonel, before stepping back and reaching into the box one last time. "In recognition of your continued exceptional meritorious service to our country, and ability to perform your duty under extremely complex circumstances and against difficult odds, I award you the Distinguished Service Medal, Silver Oak Leaf Cluster." He pinned on the medal and shook her hand, grinning broadly as the photographer swooped in for the final shots. Dean was totally surprised at the two awards, thinking that she would be getting a pat on the back and a formal "thank you" for a second time. *Man, wait 'til the boys back at the Pentagon find out about this... This'll really tick them off!* She smiled at the thought, then a more somber reflection seeped in. *I wonder if this would have made my family proud. Sure, Thad would have been, and probably Mom, but Dad?* Her thoughts faded as she caught sight of Katie with tears in her eyes. *Well, at least I know someone who is.* Looking around the room, she could see Katie wasn't alone in her reaction. *Damn. I guess I have my own little family now.*

The group remained in the Oval Office while the photographer took a few more formal pictures and then some candid shots, and the President had the opportunity to talk with each participant in a more informal atmosphere. After a span of ten minutes, the President excused himself, and the group was led out of the Oval Office.

* * * * *

General Carlton's limousine was waiting for her as they exited the White House. As Captain Jarvis held the door for her, she suggested that Colonel Peterson and her friends take the rest of the day off to celebrate. "And, I think Major Kidd needs to sit down," she confided as they watched the group exit the White House.

Dean nodded in quiet acknowledgement. "Captain Jarvis, you're dismissed as soon as we get back to the Pentagon. You deserve to celebrate, too," she added, as the newly promoted captain slipped into the backseat with the general. Dean walked over to the limo's door and issued an invitation for Bill to join the group at her home after he picked up his vehicle from the parking lot. She also invited the general, who declined the offer citing another engagement. Dean thanked the general again, and then closed the limo door.

"Wow!" Katie enthused, as she and Dean walked toward their SUV. "I certainly wasn't expecting this. Were you?" She looked at Dean as she reached the passenger door. "And just what was that whispered exchange between you and the President?"

Dean chuckled, thinking of the President's comment about not being able to live down having his neck saved by women...once more. "No. It came as a complete surprise," Dean concurred. *Not bad old girl, a full colonel at thirty-four. Not bad at all.* "And the President was just thanking me for being in the right place at the right time...again. Said he was glad to be leaving office so I could save someone else's butt for a change."

"Hey! Could you just hurry and open that door?" Tracy cut in. "My knees are going to buckle right here and now if you don't snap to."

The group turned and looked over at Tracy, who was obviously still overwhelmed by the short ceremony. Colleen, in an attempt at levity, whacked Tracy on her good shoulder and said, "Oh, dress casual... It's not going to be a big deal... Yeah, right!" she grumped good naturedly as she slipped into the back seat. Tracy just shook her head and slipped in beside her, glad to be sitting down.

As Tom and Tiny reached the SUV, Dean asked if they had a ride. They were each carrying a small overnight bag, indicating that they had not yet had time to check into a hotel.

"No, but we can just walk down to the street and hail a cab. We came straight from the airport and didn't have time to rent a car or check into a hotel," Tom advised her.

"No way. Just pile in," Dean cajoled. "I know a nice place where we can sit back, relax, and have a few brews." It wasn't a decision that took much thought on the ex-SEALs' part, and after a little rearranging of passengers, Dean slid into the driver's seat, started up the vehicle, and headed toward Occoquan, Virginia.

* * * * *

The ride home was full of questions from Colleen and Katie about the awards that had been presented, especially the Purple Heart that Tracy had received.

"I thought that you could only get a Purple Heart if you were wounded in combat," Colleen stated as she read the certificate of award that had been given to each recipient.

"Well, until 1978, that was the case. But after March 23rd of that year, the Purple Heart was approved for wounds resulting from terrorist attacks against the United States or a friendly nation," Dean explained, smiling at Tracy. "Hell of a way to be recognized, though."

"Well, what about yours Dean? What does a 'silver oak leaf

cluster' mean?" Katie inquired as she reached over and stroked the medal on Dean's chest.

Tracy opted to answer this question, knowing that Dean would be too modest to relate the true significance of the award. "The silver oak leaf designation indicates the number of times Dean has received this particular recognition. In Dean's case, it means that this is the sixth time she has been awarded the Distinguished Service Medal."

"Wow. That's a lot of recognition," Colleen whispered.

"Yeah, you can say that again," Tracy concurred. "The best one though—that I think really floored our tall, dark, and bashful friend here—was the promotion to full colonel. Am I right?" Tracy peered at her friend and got a big grin and nod from Dean as she kept her eyes on the traffic. "Bet the boys at the Pentagon will be just tickled to see those eagles on your epaulets. You were the youngest Lieutenant Colonel in quite some time, and now a full bird! That'll set them on their butts."

"Oh, yeah," Dean agreed, smiling. "I know they were upset when I made Lieutenant Colonel ahead of them. I can hardly wait to see their reaction now."

Colleen chimed in asking, "So, you weren't the youngest Lieutenant Colonel the Army had?"

"Nope, the youngest Lieutenant Colonel in the history of the Army was Lieutenant Colonel Matt Urban. He was only twenty six when promoted to that rank," Dean explained.

"Wow, that's young! How'd he manage that?" Katie asked.

Tracy picked up the conversation. "Field promotion in World War II. He was also the most decorated soldier—seven purple hearts in twenty months of combat duty. It turns out he was more decorated than Audie Murphy, only his medals came thirty-five years later."

"Thirty-five years later?" Katie asked, astonished. "How'd that happen?"

"Army lost his records," Dean informed them. "Some of the men he'd commanded worked hard to have his bravery finally acknowledged, including the Congressional Medal of Honor."

"So, besides a field promotion, the President can promote you just like that?" Katie asked, already knowing the answer since he'd done just that.

"He's the Commander-in Chief," Tom exclaimed. "He can do that if he wants. Well, I'm sure he talked to the Secretary of the Army first, and probably the Secretary of Defense, too. I imagine that's why he did the Presidential awards for us, since they are totally up to his discretion. And with his term almost over, it was the most expedient way."

Before they knew it, they were pulling into the drive at Dean and Katie's. Dean pulled into the garage and exited the SUV, followed by her other passengers. As they stepped through the door in the back, the two men took one look and whistled softly at the sight of the house. "Nice digs, Colonel. Suits you two," Tiny drawled as they headed towards the front door.

* * * * *

Several hours—and beers—later, the group was still hashing over the latest events puzzling Dean and Katie. They all agreed that the computer message was a dead end, but Tom and Tiny had offered to check it out once they got back to Freeport. Dean had completed daily sweeps of the house without turning up any more of the transmitters, and no other emails had appeared on her computer, or on Katie's.

"Okay, guys, I'm gonna order some pizza before I get really buzzed," Katie advised, as she stood to make the call. "Anybody got a preference?"

"No anchovies!" came the resounding answer from the entire group.

"Got it," Katie chuckled, as she left for the kitchen to put in the order.

The pizzas arrived in forty-five minutes and disappeared in less than ten. Dean was pulling KP duty—gathering up the paper plates, napkins and pizza boxes—when the phone rang. Katie picked up the portable receiver, and after a short exchange, took the phone over to Dean.

"Dean, the caller says he's your father," Katie whispered as she passed the receiver to Dean, attempting to exchange it for the empty pizza boxes.

Dean hesitated at accepting the phone, raising both eyebrows in question. Katie took the pizza boxes from the tall woman with

one hand, while nudging the phone towards her once more with
the other. Dean finally reluctantly accepted the proffered instrument, slowly lifting it to her ear and softly answering, "Hello" as
she stepped into the privacy of the kitchen.

"Deanna, this is your father. Please don't hang up. I know
we haven't spoken, or even talked to each other since...well,
since—" His sentence was cut short by Dean's interruption.

"Since you killed Thad," Dean accused bitterly as the old
wound reopened. She had thought she had progressed beyond the
hate, but her father's voice brought it all flooding back with a ven-
geance.

"Yes, since my actions caused your brother's death." He hesitated for a few heartbeats before going on. "You don't know how
sorry I am about that, and I've paid dearly for my actions."

"Sorry doesn't cut it, Joshua!" she challenged, refusing to
refer to him as her father. "And you haven't paid dearly enough
for me."

"Deanna, please. I'm an old man now," he pleaded. "I just
want a chance to make it up to you. To try to be a family again."

"No way in hell! There's nothing you can do that will bring
Thad back, or bring back Mom and repair her broken heart. There
is no family anymore. You killed me too, that same night," Dean
spat angrily. "Goodbye, Mr. Peterson," she blurted as she terminated the phone call and sagged into a chair at the kitchen table.
Dean looked at the phone in her hand and it began to shake violently, until she finally lost her self-control and threw the instrument across the room. As the tears began to flow down her
cheeks, she cried, "Why now...why today?" then crossed her arms
on the table and laid her head down on them, sobbing uncontrollably.

The loud crash of the phone hitting the refrigerator alerted
the group in the living room that the call from Dean's father had
not been well received. Excusing herself, Katie quickly went to
the kitchen, while the others decided that this was a good time to
turn in for the night. Dirk and Bill said their goodbyes; then
before heading to the guest bedroom, Tracy and Colleen led the
way to the den, where Tom and Tiny would bunk down for the
night.

Katie stepped silently into the kitchen and saw her lover bent over the table with her head resting on her crossed arms. The heaving of her shoulders was a dead give-away of Dean's emotional state. She slipped quietly up to her partner and sat in the chair next to her, gently placing an arm around the sobbing woman. "Dean, is there anything I can do, love?"

Dean sighed heavily, barely shaking her head no. "I thought I had moved beyond the hate. Had started to forgive. But just hearing his voice...I, I lost it."

"C'mere, love. At least let me hold you," Katie persisted as she gently pulled Dean into her arms, all the while making soft cooing sounds in her ear. "Hey, it'll be okay. Go ahead and just let it out." The tears almost subsided as Katie stroked her lover's long dark hair.

After Dean regained control, she lifted her face to meet Katie's. Reddened eyes and a tear-streaked face looked up into the soft understanding smile on her lover's face. "Why did he have to call today?" she moaned. "It was such a perfect day. Why did he have to ruin it?" She shook her head as she buried her face against her lover's chest, sighing heavily once more.

"How about we get you to bed? Then I can hold you all night long," Katie suggested as she gave the top of Dean's head a soft kiss. Silently agreeing, Dean stood and allowed herself to be led to the bedroom. After washing up and stripping out of her clothes, Dean slipped into bed. Katie went out to the living room, making sure her guests were cared for before returning to the bedroom where she joined her lover. Convincing Dean to return to her embrace, she gently stroked the tall woman's hair and rubbed the tense neck muscles she felt under her fingers.

"Mmm, feels good," Dean mumbled as she relaxed into the warmth and loving safety of Katie's arms.

"Want to talk about it?" Katie offered as she kept up the soothing motions.

Dean sighed and hesitated for a moment, allowing her self-control to build up. "He wants to be a family again. He wants to become a part of my life."

"Umm, and I take it that the phone flying across the kitchen was a negative reaction to that request," Katie hazarded wryly as she gave her lover a crooked smile.

"Sorry. I guess I kinda lost it there for a minute," Dean confessed sadly. "I haven't had a reaction like that in a very long time. I thought I'd let go of all that anger." Looking up into Katie's emerald eyes, she smiled back saying, "Guess not, huh?"

"Well, let's just say you still have some issues," Katie offered sagely.

"Issues? I've got news for you. The Reverend Joshua Peterson would have some real issues about the two of us. No, I don't need that in my life, and I don't need him, either."

"Maybe there's more to it than it seems," Katie suggested. "Maybe it's the other way around, and he needs you."

"Well, he hasn't needed me for sixteen years. Why now?"

"I don't know, love...I don't know." The silence stretched out as the two women turned their thoughts inward to the possibilities, eventually succumbing to slumber.

Chapter
4

1 December, 0600 Hours

Thursday, Dean returned to work and as expected, received a very cold reception from some of her peers as they noticed her change in rank. Fortunately, there were many others who were genuinely pleased and gave their congratulations freely, especially Sergeant Major Tibbits. Captain Jarvis, too, received a few cold shoulders, but that was mostly due to his status as Dean's protégé. As Dean entered her office, she noted the lab report on the transmitters sitting on her desk. Reviewing the information quickly, the report indicated that they were most likely produced in one of the former communist bloc countries, and could have been bought by almost anyone since they were a hot item on the black market. *Well, back to square one*, Dean thought as she replaced the report in the file folder before tackling the stack of messages on her desk and reviewing her email.

Katie, Tracy, Colleen, Tom and Tiny spent the morning visiting Arlington Cemetery, with a stop at General James' gravesite. They visited the Women's Memorial, the Vietnam Memorial, watched the changing of the guard at the Tomb of the Unknown Soldier, and fit in a few other tourist stops, as well. Their afternoon ended with a trip to Ronald Reagan National Airport to drop off Tom and Tiny for their return flight to Freeport. When Dean arrived home, the foursome's evening was spent in quiet companionship as they enjoyed a surprisingly tasty meal prepared by Colleen and Tracy.

Friday morning, the house was bustling with activity as Dean prepared for her day at the Pentagon and Katie prepared for her first day of instructor's orientation at the DEA facility in Quantico. Tracy and Colleen were also busy packing to return to the Catskills of New York, after the required stop at Walter Reed to have Tracy's stitches removed.

"So, are you ready for the new assignment?" Dean asked as Katie put together her work clothes.

Katie was reading off a list as she placed items in her overnight bag. "Um, I think so. Let's see: sweats, tennis shoes, socks, toiletries, two ghi's for hand-to-hand practice, my Glock... I sure wish the DEA used the H & K Mark 23, I really like that weapon better." Then she continued going over her list: "Four ammo clips, holster, extra underwear, towel, ball cap, notebook, pens, PDA, orientation manual... Yep! I think I've got everything," Katie mumbled as she went over her list once more.

"You forgot something," Dean interjected.

"Hmm, no, I don't think so," the young agent answered as she triple checked her list.

"Oh, yes, you have," Dean insisted.

Shaking her head, Katie lifted her eyes to a smiling Dean. "What? I don't see anything missing."

Dean walked forward and bent her head. "This," she offered, gently placing a soft kiss on Katie's lips.

"Mmm," Katie replied around Dean's lips, "I wouldn't want to forget that. How about another, so I make sure I can remember it?"

"Gladly," her tall lover responded as she reached around the young woman before her, pulling her in for a full contact embrace, followed by a more passionate kiss.

"Oh, yeah. I've got that burned into my memory now," Katie chuckled, as she returned the hug enthusiastically. They remained holding each other close for a short moment longer, enjoying the love that flowed between them. "Umm, guess I'd better get on the road. I'd like to get there early," Katie explained.

"Yeah, I like to be early, too," Dean agreed. "Any idea what time you'll be home?"

"If all goes well, I should be back by 6:30 or so."

"Okay, 1830 hours it is! I'll be waiting." Dean's sapphire eyes pinned Katie's emerald ones. "If you think you'll be late, just page me."

Katie gave her a mock salute. "Yes, Ma'am! And the same goes for you."

Dean slipped on her uniform jacket, buttoning it as she walked to the hall closet for her trench coat before returning to the kitchen to pick up her briefcase. Tracy and Colleen were just finishing up a cup of tea in the kitchen when Dean walked in.

"Off to the Pentagon a bit early today," Colleen stated as Dean entered. "And off to Quantico, too, I see," she added as Katie entered the room. They both smiled and nodded. Dean reminded them of the procedure to set the security codes before they left. Goodbyes and hugs went around the room, then Dean picked up her briefcase and Katie picked up her overnight bag and headed to the door.

"Glad I'll be able to leave most of this at the facility," Katie commented, indicating the bag slung over her shoulder as they entered the garage and got into their separate vehicles. Dean's Durango SUV was spotless and shiny black, while Katie's turquoise classic '57 Chevy was as immaculate as the day it left the showroom. They drove in tandem to the Interstate 95 interchange, where Katie took the south ramp and Dean took the north ramp, each looking forward to a new day.

* * * * *

"Good morning, Colonel," came the salutation and salute from the Pentagon guard. This month the Marines were manning the checkpoint. "You had a delivery about fifteen minutes ago. I had Corporal Sterns take it up to your office for you. Nice flowers, Ma'am."

Dean returned the salute. "Thank you, Gunny. Was there any indication who sent them?"

"No, Ma'am. But I'm sure the card will explain them." He smiled shyly.

Colonel Peterson continued through the ID station and headed toward the stairs for a little extra exercise. *Never take the elevator when you can take the stairs,* she thought to herself as she remembered her physical education teacher's suggestion. Taking the stairs two at a time, she wondered who would be sending her flowers...at the Pentagon. She knew Katie would never do that, so she was eager to read the card. *Hmmm, maybe just a congratulations on my promotion.*

Opening the door to her office she set her briefcase down, removed her coat, and hung it in the closet. She spotted the bouquet on the windowsill behind her desk. Picking up her briefcase, she walked over to her desk and set it down before removing the card from the flowers. "Well, they certainly brighten up the office," she commented aloud. Removing the card from the envelope, she read it out loud:

> Congratulations on your promotion to Colonel. Too bad your new friend had an accident after he arrived home. Perhaps I should have sent the flowers to him instead?

"What the heck is that supposed to mean?" Dean mumbled to herself. Almost in answer to her question, the phone on her desk rang. She stepped over to her desk, sitting down in her leather chair before picking up the receiver. "Colonel Peterson," she answered crisply. "Yes, put him through." Waiting for the caller to be connected to her line, she looked at the card in her other hand and turned it around, looking for a clue as to who the sender might be.

"Hey, Tiny. How was the trip back?" the colonel questioned as the caller connected.

"Not good, Colonel. Tom's is in the hospital in Freeport. He's unconscious and in critical condition."

The card dropped from Dean's hand and she focused her thoughts on the caller. "What happened?"

"He was shot in the chest at the controls of the Lady Luck. We were just getting ready to take her out from the dock at the marina when I heard a loud thud above me, then some running steps. I came up from the engine room and found him bleeding on the deck," the ex-SEAL explained. "The locals are still investigating and are considering it a botched robbery attempt, but I think someone was out to kill him. I think he must have heard his attacker, 'cause he had time to pull out his Glock, but didn't get a round off in time."

"Any idea who?" Colonel Peterson questioned.

"No, Ma'am. You know Tom...everybody loves the guy." Dean could hear Tiny's voice start to crack. "I think they would have come down after me, too, if he hadn't surprised them by pulling out his pistol." He paused and excused himself as he blew his nose. "I just thought you might want to know, Ma'am," the ex-SEAL concluded.

"Thank you, Tiny. I'm glad you called." Dean picked up the card and began tapping it on the desk. "Let me know if I can do anything for you, or Tom. Hopefully, when he regains consciousness he'll be able to identify his attacker."

"Yes, Ma'am, that's what we're hoping for. But, right now, only time and prayer will help."

"Right," she answered, trying to think of the last time she'd prayed. "Keep us informed, okay? Call anytime, night or day. You have my home and cell numbers, right?"

"Yes, Ma'am, I do. I'll keep in touch," Tiny responded, before saying goodbye and disconnecting.

"Damn." Dean cursed as she looked at the card in her hand. "Just who the hell are you, and what are you after?" She picked up the phone, dialing the number for the florist listed on the card's envelope. When the phone was answered on the other end, she told them who she was and that she had received a bouquet of flowers from an unknown individual. She explained that the card must have come off in transport to her office, but the desk sergeant had remembered the company that had delivered them. She asked if they had a record of who sent them, so she could thank them. The florist explained that the order was received from an FTD website and repeated the message that was on the card and gave her a web address that had come with the order. Next, she called Dirk and gave him the web address, asking him if he could run down the sender. Replacing the phone on its cradle, she sat back in her chair and began rocking...and thinking.

* * * * *

At precisely 1830 hours, Katie pulled into the driveway, hitting the button on her visor to raise the garage door. Exiting her vehicle, she passed Dean's SUV, placing her hand on the hood. *Hmm, still warm. Guess she didn't get home much before me.* Wrestling with the armload of manuals she was carrying, she managed to close the garage door and headed up the path to their home. Dean greeted her at the door and relieved her of half of the manuals as she entered.

"Whoa. What have you got here?" the tall woman asked as she reviewed the stack.

"Just a bit of light reading," Katie groaned. "I never realized that being an instructor required four times the reading that the students have to do."

"Ah, well, I guess this means you'll be pretty occupied tonight?"

"Oh, I'd say that's pretty good deductive reasoning for an intelligence officer," the young agent chuckled. "Something smells good."

"Yeah, Chinese take-out. Right now, you need to get changed and have some dinner before you tackle these books." Taking the rest of the stack from her partner, Dean took the stairs down to the den where she deposited the stack of manuals on Katie's desk, while the young woman gratefully went to their bedroom to take a shower.

Over dinner, Katie excitedly filled Dean in on her first day of instructor orientation. A good portion of it was spent in checking out the new instructors' levels of fitness, knowing that they would be required to set an example for their future students. Katie was pleased with her performance, as she turned in the best times and scores of the entire group. "Guess your insistence on working out regularly has paid off," she explained, commending her partner for her persistence. "Some of my colleagues are going to be mighty sore for the next few days. Tomorrow, we'll be doing our weapons qualifications on the range. I'm going to see if they'll let me qualify with the H&K, too." Having finished the meal, the women took the dishes to the sink where they began the clean up.

Katie studied the quiet pools of her lover's sapphire eyes, knowing that something was bothering her. "So, how was your day?"

Dean sighed, not wanting to upset her partner with the events of the day, but realizing that she would have to know eventually. "Well, I was hoping to put this off until after you had a chance to hit the books, but I can see you'll persist until I tell you," the dark woman disclosed. Dean then filled her in on the assault on Tom, the flowers, and the message on the card. "Dirk ran into another dead end on the flower order. Whoever is responsible is pretty computer literate and knows how to get around the systems."

"Oh my God! Poor Tom." The blonde sagged onto a kitchen chair. "Why would someone want to hurt him?"

"It's all got to be connected—the email, the flowers, the message on the card. Why else would the sender have made reference to my new friend?" Dean sat next to Katie, looking for confirmation in her eyes.

"You're probably right on those, but do you think the person who hid the transmitters is involved, too?"

"I'm not one hundred percent sure on that one, but it is one of a string of strange happenings around here, so I guess I'd have to say he—or she—is connected somehow. I'm just not sure how, or why." Dean stood, pulling Katie up with her. "You'd better go hit the books. I'm going down to do a few miles on the treadmill. Next to rocking in my chair, I think best when I'm in motion."

It was 2230 when the two women finally collapsed into bed. Katie had made it through three manuals, while Dean had run five miles before settling in front of her computer to do some cyber sleuthing.

"Any luck with your computer search?" Katie inquired as she snuggled up to Dean.

The heavy sigh she received in response told her that Dean was not happy with the results of her endeavor. "I haven't turned up any files where the person used any of the computer methods we have encountered so far. Sooner or later, though, this person or persons will make a mistake, and then we'll have something concrete to go on. Right now, he's got to be getting pretty cocky about his success to date."

"Mistakes like the one where we found the transmitters so quickly, you mean."

"Yeah, that's the one thing he didn't count on. But so far, there's been no attempt to replace them, and I seriously doubt if that would happen anyway. Once compromised, you try not to expose yourself again." Dean unconsciously began stroking her partner's short, blonde hair. "Right now, those transmitters are the only things we have to go on. I've got some friends in Europe that are checking on them—where they're being sold on the black market, and trying to get a run down on who's buying them."

"Think it will help?"

"Not really. Too many hands could have been involved before they wound up here. But at least it's a place to start." Dean continued gently running her fingers through Katie's hair, and soon the young woman was sound asleep. Sleep did not come as easily for Dean, however, as she pondered the events of the last few days, trying to make sense of them. When she finally settled long enough to doze off, her sleep was restless—her mind running a continual loop of images and questions projected on the white screen of her mental theater.

Chapter
5

3 December, 1200 Hours

Katie was busily reading the holiday circulars included in the Sunday paper while Dean finished up the sports section. Looking up from her completed portion of the paper, the tall woman watched as Katie meticulously jotted notes on a pad of paper as she scanned the ads. *Oh boy, I can see where this is going, and I don't think I'm gonna like it one bit.* Hoping to do her own end run, Dean turned her sapphire blues onto the young blonde and put out her best "this is what I really, reaalllly, want to do today" smile. "Hey, wanna watch the Redskin's game this afternoon?"

Her partner looked up from her papers and smiled back, emerald eyes glinting from the sun shining through the windows. *Ah, trying to get me off track, eh?* Katie mused as she decided which tack she'd use. *Think I'll try the sweet approach this time.* Folding her ads and placing them on the footstool in front of her, Katie cocked her head towards Dean thoughtfully. "What time does the game start?"

Dean checked the television guide. "1330." *Do I have a nibble?* she thought hopefully.

"Oooo, good. That gives us just enough time to go out for that ice cream sundae you've been craving all weekend." Before Dean could reply, she stood quickly and walked briskly to the coat closet, retrieving both their leather jackets. "C'mon, I'll buy."

Dean wasn't sure if this was a trick, but the thought of a double hot fudge sundae with nuts, cherries, and whip cream was too enticing to pass up. After slipping on her Reeboks, Dean stood and joined the grinning young woman at the front foyer. "Okay, but you have to drive, too."

"Deal," the blonde replied as she grabbed the keys to her '57 Chevy and opened the front door, gesturing for Dean to go first. "After you, Ma'am."

Ten minutes later they were headed down the main highway towards the Baskin Robbins, which just happened to be located at the south entrance of the Galleria Mall at Riverside. There were few parking places left, and none near the ice cream shop, so Katie opted for the spots furthest from the stores. Finding an empty one next to a light pole, Katie pulled in, confident that at least one side of her precious antique was protected from inadvertent door damage. The two women set out for the confectionary treat after insuring that all the doors were locked and the VW bug parked next to the Chevy was not close enough to cause damage.

* * * * *

A solitary figure in a black Mazda Miata slowly crept up the row across from the walking duo. *Doing a little shopping, Colonel? Well, I hope you find a nice surprise today. I'd hate to see you disappointed. Maybe I can help?* The Mazda pulled in and parked in a spot that had just been vacated by a Cadillac. A gnarled right hand turned off the motor, leaving the keys to dangle from the ignition. Reaching into the jacket pocket, the driver pulled out a pair of leather gloves and slipped them on.

* * * * *

"Mmm, this is really good," Katie crooned as she licked her spoon. "Pralines and Cream with hot caramel sauce is my favorite feel-good food."

"This is mine," Dean confessed, as she dipped her spoon into the hot fudge sundae that was made with Chocolate Chunk ice cream and extra cherries. "Just like a chocolate covered cherry, but made with ice cream."

"Death by chocolate, eh?" the blonde giggled as she finished the last of her sundae.

"Can you think of a better way to go?" Dean bantered, as she reverently placed the last spoonful in her mouth, savoring the blend of sweet flavors.

Feeling a little feisty, Katie gave her partner a sultry look, raising an eyebrow seductively. "Well..."

Dean caught the gist of the gesture and felt a warm rush creep up her spine, causing her to nearly choke on the last of her ice cream. Katie quickly moved in and slapped her partner several times to keep her from gagging. Dean raised a hand indicating she could stop, and as their eyes met, they burst out laughing, knowing that this was not the "death" they wanted.

"How about we take a walk through the mall and burn off some of the thousands of calories we just consumed?" Green eyes twinkled as Katie waited for a response.

"Huh, something tells me this was your plan from the beginning," Dean teased, as the two women stood and left the ice cream shop, taking a right turn that would lead them into the thick of the holiday shoppers.

"Busted," Katie gulped as her partner pinned her with a piercing look. She removed the list she had been working on at the house and held it up for Dean to see. "I only have a few things to get. I promise we'll get back before the game is over." She smiled sheepishly at the taller woman, then added, "Maybe even before the first quarter is over?"

Dean just laughed and shook her head, then headed off towards the crowds, knowing that she would do anything this young woman wanted, no matter what it was.

Two and a half hours later, the women were walking out of the mall, carrying several shopping bags filled to capacity with Christmas presents. Dean had managed to catch glimpses of the game on the televisions in the appliance sections, and even snuck off to find a few things on her list for Katie. With any luck, they could get back to the house and catch the last couple of minutes of the game. Instinctively, Dean surveyed the parking lot, checking the exits for the fastest route home. Her gaze roved over the rooftops of the parked cars, unaware of the eyes watching them from the Mazda they had just walked past.

"Well, I guess we walked off the sundaes," Katie joked as she shifted the packages so she could reach for her car keys.

"Here, let me grab those." Stopping, Dean reached for the bags, freeing up Katie's right hand. Just as she turned towards the car, she caught sight of a quick flash from under the Chevy and instinctively reacted. She dropped her bags and grabbed Katie, throwing them both to the ground. The next thing they knew, they were lying on the blacktop, trying to shake the concussion of the explosives from their heads.

"Are you okay?" Dean quickly asked, as she checked out her partner lying beneath her. They heard muffled shouts from other shoppers, children crying, and the far off wail of a siren, as people began running toward them. Katie nodded her head, then looked up to the spot that had contained her prized possession. Tears began to well up in her eyes as she watched the flames lick at the charred frame. Dean put her arms around her, hugging her close. "Yeah, I know."

A black Mazda Miata pulled out of the chaotic parking lot, the driver smiling as the sight of the destruction came into the rear view mirror. A fire truck lumbered past, trying to make its way to the smoldering wreckage, all eyes of the firefighters focused ahead.

The mysterious driver spoke to the vision in the rear view mirror, "Hope you liked my surprise, Colonel," then cautiously headed away from the mall.

* * * * *

It took nearly four hours of giving statements to the police, fire department officials, and finally a check out by the emergency medical technicians before the two women were able to leave the scene. The first hour was the worst, until the police were able to confirm their IDs with the DEA and Pentagon; after that, things went much more smoothly. Bill and Dirk arrived at the scene to pick up the twosome and arrange for alternate transportation for Katie. As they left the scene, a police flatbed and tow truck was picking up the pieces of what was left of Katie's Chevy to transport it to the police impound lot. Samples would be sent to the State Police lab to determine what materials had been used in the incendiary device. They had already been able to determine that it was a remote detonator that had set it off.

"I can't believe this has happened," Katie murmured as she watched them load the wreckage. "Who would want to blow up my car?"

"I don't know, love, but trust me, we'll find out." Dean hugged the smaller woman before leading her over to Dirk's vehicle. Bill stowed their packages in the trunk before holding open the back door to the Ford Taurus. He waited for them to get situated in the back seat, then closed it and slid into the front passenger seat.

"Where to, ladies?" Dirk asked, looking over the backseat.

"There's a Hertz Rental off of US 1 in Woodbridge. We can pick up a car there for now," Dean looked over at Katie, who nodded her head in agreement.

"US 1, Woodbridge. Be there in a flash...um, sorry. Didn't mean for it to come out that way," Dirk's eyes apologetically met Katie's eyes in the rear view mirror.

"Don't worry about it, Dirk." She smiled weakly at his reflection. "I'm okay. I'm just glad we weren't in the car when it blew."

Dean reached out and found Katie's hand, pulling it into hers and giving it a gentle squeeze. "I don't think the bomb was meant to kill us. I think whoever planted it was somewhere in the parking lot, and detonated it before we got within range of being hurt."

Intrigued, Bill turned in his seat to face his CO, "Why do you think that?"

"Because, I saw a small flash just before it blew. I think whoever planted the device was in a hurry. There may have been a slightly loose connection that wasn't caught during the installation." Pausing, Dean considered a few more ideas before continuing. "With so many holiday shoppers in the area, I'm sure it was a rushed job. And I don't think our perp wanted to hurt anyone else, otherwise a different type of detonation device would have been used."

"Makes sense. But was he after you, or Katie?" Bill interjected.

"Good question. We both have made enemies through our work, but with the recent events, I'd have to say I'm the probable

target since I've received the messages. I think someone is trying
to get to me through my friends, so it would be a good idea if
everyone was a bit more cautious from here on out." Heads nodded in agreement as they silently considered the implications of
Dean's words. "The police took the surveillance films from the
mall security office. Maybe they'll be able to spot something on
them."

* * * * *

Dirk and Bill waited until they were sure there would be a car
available for Katie to rent. Knowing how unpredictable the holidays could be, it was interesting to see what kind of vehicles were
left. Pulling out of the Hertz lot, they couldn't help but grin at the
look on Katie's face as she stepped up to the sleek red Porsche
that was waiting for her.

"Wow, that's not what I'd call a modest upgrade, would you?"
She looked over at her partner and spotted the devilish grin on her
face. She immediately realized that something must have tran-
spired between her lover and the rental agent while she'd made
that quick trip to the restroom.

"Ah, well, that happens sometimes when they don't have the
car you want." Dean lied terribly, and was caught by the knowing
smirk on the blonde's face. "Um, want me to drive?" she added
eagerly.

"Oh, no. When we left the house, you said I had to drive, and
drive I will!" She tossed a smile at the dejected woman and slid
behind the steering wheel while Dean slipped into the passenger
seat. "Ohh, leather seats. Nice." Katie placed her hands on the
wheel and checked out the dash and set the mirrors. "Hmm, even
a CD player. I think I could get used to something like this."

"I think you'll find a button on the dash that will turn on the
heaters in these seats," Dean suggested as she felt the cold leather
through her jeans and shivered.

"Ah, there," Katie found the button, turning it on after she
started the ignition. The back seat, what there was of it, was
packed with their shopping bags—which had managed to escape
without much damage. "Thank you, Dean," Katie supplied as she
pulled out of the lot.

There was an innocent twinkle in Dean's sapphire eyes as she faced Katie. "For what?"

"For upgrading to this car," came the grateful response.

"Well, I just figured that a Chevy Cavalier was not going to lift your spirits, but this might—at least until you get a new car. Then the sticker shock is liable to put you into a tail spin."

"Oh, I don't know," Katie grinned back. "That Chevy wasn't the only thing my aunt left me."

"Really? You have another car stashed somewhere?" Dean asked, now curious.

"Nope. But I do have a sizable trust fund stashed away, and I just might buy me one of these with this year's interest dividend." *Ah, what the heck,* she thought, *she might as well know.* "I, um, could even get you one with the change...if you want one."

Dean was totally shocked by this little revelation. In the year she had known Katie, they had never really talked about her family. Dean figured that Katie would broach the subject whenever she was ready, so she'd never pushed for information—besides, it really didn't matter to Dean. She loved Katie for who she was, not who her family was. "Ah, so you're not only intelligent, talented, sexy, and beautiful...you're rich, too?"

"I guess you could say that; I'm just not into flaunting it. I much prefer a low profile."

"Well, in that case, next time you offer to buy me a sundae, I'm going to order a triple dip!" Dean teased, as the two women broke out in relaxed laughter.

Katie skillfully drove the shiny Porsche through the traffic and down the back roads to their home. As she approached the driveway, she realized that her garage door opener was still in the Chevy. "Oh, poop! The garage door opener was on the visor."

Dean reached into her pocket and produced a key chain version of the door opener, handing it to Katie. "Picked this up in Sears today. I was going to give it to you at Christmas, but I guess now's as good a time as any."

"Hey, cool. I thought about getting one after I saw yours. Thanks, love." Katie took the opener and pushed the button, waiting for the door to finish rising, then pulling in and cutting the engine. As they gathered their bags, they agreed that the sports car was not a vehicle to use for shopping trips, deciding that the SUV was much easier to load and unload.

When they opened the front door, they were greeted by a very insistent Spice, yowling at the top of her lungs, which brought the other two felines out from their hiding places. "Oh, so you think you've had a bad day just because your dinner is a little late? Well, I've got news for you." Katie removed her coat, hanging it in the closet before grabbing her shopping bags and heading for the kitchen with her three charges racing before her, tails held high. Dean watched the group leave, relieved that her lover was able to bounce back from the loss of her treasured vehicle. She hung up her jacket neatly, picking up her bags to follow Katie when she noticed the message light blinking on the answering machine. Stopping by the table, she set down her purchases and hit the play button. She wasn't completely surprised when she heard the mechanically disguised voice on the tape.

"Hello, Colonel. Glad to see you finally made it home. It was a real shame to have to destroy that beautiful old car, but better the car than Katie. Oh well, maybe next time."

"Damn it all to hell!" Dean bellowed. "I don't know who you are, but when I find you, you're gonna pay for this...for everything! Why don't you show your face, you little coward! Let's settle this now."

Having heard Dean's raised voice from the kitchen, Katie rushed into the room. She found her staring out the window, fists clenched in a tight ball. Katie carefully approached the angry woman, gently placing her hand on Dean's back. "What's wrong, Dean?" The warmth of Katie's touch helped unclench the fists, but the anger was still evident as Dean turned stiffly, nearly frightening Katie with the look of anger in the deep blue pools of her friend's eyes, and pointed at the answering machine. Katie hit the play button and listened to the message.

"Hon, don't let this person get to you. You're playing right into his hand. You're smarter than him." She gently rubbed Dean's arm, urging her to sit down in the love seat by the fireplace. "Let's hope he made a mistake today and is on that surveillance video." Katie reached up with her left hand, gently pulling Dean's chin toward her, smiling as she softly continued, "I know we'll find him, and I know you won't let any harm come to me. We'll get this sicko, Dean, just don't let him get to you."

Dean's expression softened and the tension in her shoulders and neck seemed to dissipate to a more tolerable level. She clenched and unclenched her fists, flexing her fingers a bit before taking hold of Katie's left hand, kissing it softly. "You're right, love. He, or she, is getting to me, and knows that my weakness is you. If anything happens to you, I won't rest until the SOB is torn apart by my own hands." Her eyes turned dark again and she looked out the window once more before commenting, "And that's a promise."

Chapter
6

6 December, 1057 Hours

Dean entered her office to the sound of a ringing phone. Walking quickly to her desk, she set down the cup of tea she had just purchased in the cafeteria and picked up the receiver, hoping she had made it in time. "Colonel Peterson."

"Hello, Colonel. This is Lieutenant Ted Green at the Woodbridge PD. I've been assigned your case...the bombing at the mall. I was told that I could contact you since Agent O'Malley is unavailable."

"Yes, Lieutenant. I was hoping to hear from someone soon."

"Well, I've got some good news and some bad news," he began, as he outlined the results of the security camera video review. "It seems that on one of the sweeps, we were able to pick out you and Agent O'Malley walking away from the Chevy and into the mall complex."

Dean walked around her desk and sat down as she focused her attention on the caller. "And were there any suspicious looking vehicles or persons in that scan?"

"No, nothing jumped out at us on the first look through. However, when we fast-forwarded to the time of the explosion, we picked up something unusual. After looking at the freeze frames from the before and after scenes, we noted that there was one car that had an occupant in it at both times."

"Well, that may not be too unusual, but go ahead." Dean picked up a pencil and started doodling.

"Yeah, well, that's what we thought, too, but we rechecked each sweep, and the occupant was in the car the entire time, except for one sweep. You see, the camera captures a 180 degree view of that portion of the parking lot every three minutes."

Dean was now listening carefully to what the Lieutenant was revealing. "Are you saying you caught this individual outside of the car?"

"Ah, no. Not really. At least we don't think we have. It just seemed strange that this car would be occupied for two plus hours, except for a three-minute interval. I mean, that's not even long enough to run inside to, uh, use the restroom."

"Okay. So, you think that this vehicle is perhaps suspicious, then?" Dean concluded correctly.

"Yes, ma'am, that's exactly what we thought. So we looked for it in the sweeps after the explosion, and found it slowly exiting when the fire trucks arrived. Now, what makes that interesting to me is that no one, and I mean no one else was exiting at that time. Human nature being what it is, everyone else in the vicinity was moving to see what was happening, not moving away from it. Anyway, we were able to get the plate number and run it." Dean suspected that this was where the bad news was coming in, and she was correct again. "Well, here's the bad news. The person in that vehicle was probably the one involved in the detonation, but when we ran the plates, they didn't match with the vehicle; and we found the vehicle abandoned yesterday by the riverfront. We ran a check on the Vehicle Identification Number from the engine, and found that it was reported stolen in New York City on November 20th. It was dusted for prints, but turned out to be cleaner than the day it left the showroom floor."

"Have there been any reports of vehicles stolen since yesterday?"

"Not in this area. He could have walked to a taxi, bus, or train station from there. But, we'll keep an eye on the reports."

Dean thought for a minute, and then decided to do a little sleuthing of her own. "Lieutenant, is there a possibility I can get a copy of the surveillance video? I'd like the lab here to take a look at it. We may be able to enhance the visuals better with our equipment, and maybe I'll be able to recognize someone."

"Sure thing, Colonel. I'll have a copy made right now. Do

you want me to drop it by?"

"No. I'll pick it up." Dean checked her watch. "Will you be there in about thirty minutes?"

"I will be now, ma'am. Just ask for me at the front desk. I'll tell them you'll be coming."

"Thank you, Lieutenant. I'll be there shortly." After disconnecting, Dean punched in the extension for the surveillance technology lab. The corporal who answered the phone confirmed that the equipment Dean wanted to use would be available that afternoon and slotted her in for its use. Next, she dialed Captain Jarvis, requesting his assistance at 1300 in the lab. Finally, Dean grabbed her trench coat and hat and headed for the parking lot.

She arrived at the precinct station in Woodbridge three minutes early, and headed to the front desk, fully conscious of the stares of the patrolmen she passed along the way. Obviously, it wasn't every day that an Army colonel entered their domain. Add to that that she was a strikingly beautiful woman, and she turned quite a few heads as she entered the main office. Upon reaching the front desk, the desk sergeant was so caught off guard, that he stood and nearly saluted before catching himself and inquiring as to her needs. Stifling a chuckle, Dean smiled graciously and asked to see Lieutenant Green. Sergeant Mills first started to give her directions, but then thought it would be better if he escorted her to Lieutenant Green's office. As they walked back, Dean removed her head cover and trench coat, swinging the latter over her arm while carrying her hat in the same hand.

Sergeant Mills knocked on the lieutenant's door, then opened it to usher Colonel Peterson into the small office. Lieutenant Green was a handsome man in his late forties, who obviously took very good care of himself. He was at least as tall as Dean, had a well-proportioned physique, wavy black hair that was graying at the temples, a trim mustache, and soulful brown eyes. As he stood and came around his desk to greet her, Dean noted his clothes were meticulous in appearance: neatly pressed slacks, and creases from the iron still prominent in his shirt. Even his shoes were well polished. His holster was attached to his belt rather than the usual shoulder holster rig many plain-clothes officers preferred. As she appraised him, he in turn was assessing her, taking in her appearance, command stature, and her surprisingly good looks.

She was definitely not what he had pictured in his mind from their earlier conversation; he decided he liked her.

As the desk sergeant left, Green reached over to shake her hand. "Colonel Peterson, it's good to meet you. Please have a seat." He indicated the wooden chair next to his desk and pulled up an identical chair to sit across from her.

"Thank you, Lieutenant," Dean replied as she sat in the chair, folding her coat into her lap. Her initial appraisal of this officer was positive.

"Excuse me," he began somewhat hesitantly, "but you certainly don't look like any of the command officers I knew when I was in the Army. That's quite a complement of ribbons you have, and you do look awfully young to be a full colonel." He blushed a bit, realizing that his comments may have been a bit too personal, but very impressed with the woman sitting before him.

"I'll take that as a compliment, Lieutenant, and I'm certain I'm *not* like most command officers." Dean smiled broadly at him before continuing. "I'd guess you were a career soldier in the military police?"

"Yes, ma'am. Twenty-five years. Last five at Fort McClellan's MP school. Came up through the ranks, retired as a major. Decided retirement wasn't for me, so I came into this job. Been here for five years now. Excuse me, ma'am. I'll go see if your tape is ready." He stood and left his office, leaving Dean to take in her surroundings. Everything was neat and orderly. Lieutenant Green's office was as squared away as he was. The police officer returned in five minutes carrying the tape. He handed it over to Dean and sat across from her once more. Reaching across his desk, he picked up a manila file folder and opened it.

"Mind if I ask you a few more questions before you leave? I wasn't present when the incident happened, and I'd like to get a first hand account of the event from you."

Dean agreed and reviewed the incident from the time they'd arrived until the time they'd left. As she recounted her story, Lieutenant Green jotted down a few notes and asked a few questions before closing the file folder.

"Ma'am, I realize that you're attached to the Intelligence section. Do you suppose this incident has anything to do with something you may be currently working on?"

"Not that I'm aware of, Lieutenant."

"How about Agent O'Malley. Could it be tied in with one of her cases?"

"It's always possible that it could be tied to one of us professionally, but we think it's more personal than that," Dean confided, deciding that having the help of this man might prove to be beneficial.

"What brings you to that conclusion, Colonel?"

Dean went into an explanation of the events that had occurred since returning from their vacation, including the probability that the attack on Tom may have been related in some way.

"May I ask why you didn't include this in the report on the bombing?" the Lieutenant inquired, somewhat offended.

Sensing the police officer's censure, Dean went on to explain that she had no real basis to connect the incidents; it was just her "gut" telling her there was a connection.

"Lieutenant, may I be frank?" Dean queried.

"By all means, please."

"I've been working intelligence for most of my career, and I have not had much opportunity to work with civilian authorities, therefore, I have a tendency to play things close to the chest. Especially since this seems to be a personal vendetta of some sort."

"So why disclose this to me?" The Lieutenant seemed genuinely interested in her answer.

"Let's just say it's another one of my gut feelings, and I've been batting a thousand on those to date."

Accepting her words for the compliment they were, the ex-MP commander smiled in return, as he was all too familiar with gut instinct himself. "Well, then, I guess I can deal with that. If anything new comes up, I'll be certain to inform you."

"And I will inform you of any developments, too," Dean echoed as she stood to leave. "Thank you for the copy of the tape. I'll dissect it frame by frame this afternoon."

"You're welcome, Colonel. Here's my card with my home number in case you need to reach me when I'm off duty." Dean pulled out one of her cards, exchanging it for the one proffered, shook the Lieutenant's hand, and left to return to the Pentagon.

* * * *

By the time Colonel Peterson returned to her office, she had just enough time to grab a sandwich and head to the surveillance technology lab to meet Captain Jarvis. When she walked into the lab, Bill was already there.

Bill pointed at the cassette in her hand. "That the video?"

"Yep." She tossed it over and took the seat next to him.

For the next three hours, they studied the video frame by frame. The equipment they were using was much more sophisticated than what the Woodbridge PD had available, and they were able to get crisp photos of the car, and a rough side view of the occupant. Unfortunately, the video was in black and white, so they were not able to distinguish hair color, but agreed that the individual was most likely female by the shape of the nose and petite chin. A large brimmed hat worn by the woman made a positive ID impossible, as it mostly obliterated the occupant's face. They were also able to freeze a blurred frame of this same individual slipping behind a group of shoppers as they passed Katie's Chevy, using them for cover as she made her way back to the car. They got the good side view, minus her face, as she re-entered the vehicle. Dean estimated that the woman was about five feet ten inches tall, approximately one hundred and fifty pounds, and seemed to be very fluid, almost cat-like in her movements. She was wearing a full-length leather trench coat and a matching large brimmed hat that continued to obscure her face from view.

"So," Bill began, "anyone you know?"

Dean studied the printed picture and shook her head. "Doesn't ring any bells at the moment. The profile is niggling at me, but I can't put a finger on it."

"Maybe it's someone Katie knows?" he commented as he studied his copy of the photo.

"Well, we'll find out tonight when she gets home from Quantico." Dean stood and held the photo in her right hand, gently tapping it on her open left palm. "Have a dozen of these made up for me and bring them up to my office. Oh, and put the photo out on our network. Maybe someone will spot her when she surfaces again."

"What about the tape?"

"Send that up, too, after it's rewound."

"Yes, Ma'am," the captain replied as he hit the rewind button.

Checking her watch, Dean was surprised to see that it was already 1745 hours. "I'll fax this photo over to Lieutenant Green in Woodbridge, then I'm heading home." As she exited the lab before heading back to her office, she thanked the corporal for setting up the equipment for her.

Chapter
7

Same day, Same time

Reverend Martha Lewistan was sitting at her small, green, metal desk which she had found at a surplus store, going over the bills for the month. *Good thing we've got that grant money coming, or I'm not sure where the money to pay for these bills would come from. God is certainly watching out for us.* A soft knock at the door interrupted her thoughts. Glad for the break, she gathered the bills, slipped them back into the folder, and placed them in the inbox before answering the knock.

"Come in," she called softly, folding her hands together on the neat desktop. Reverend Lewistan was in her early fifties, about five foot five, with dark graying hair that was neatly cut in a short, but soft style. Beneath large oval glasses, her hazel eyes sparkled with intelligence and compassion. Her warm smile and gentle ways had always been an asset to her stressful position at the Interfaith City Mission, where she ministered to the poor, the disheartened and frightened, the alcoholic and addict, the runaways, and lost souls. Like most big cities, Kansas City, Missouri had plenty of people in need of Reverend Martha's ministry, including the tall man that quietly entered her office and took the seat across from her.

"Good afternoon, Joshua. How are the sessions going?" she asked softly as Joshua Peterson took his seat.

"Pretty good, Martha. I can see a lot of improvement in Chester today. Tim's still not opening up, but Carolyn and Henry are doing much better." Joshua Peterson hesitated, swallowing hard before he began again. "I was wondering if you would be able to do me a favor when you go to DC tomorrow for your grant meeting?"

Martha smiled at Joshua, having a pretty good idea what that favor might be. Joshua Peterson had come to her mission at the request of Reverend Samuel Samms, from the state penitentiary in Wichita, Kansas. Joshua had been a Baptist minister prior to his fall, serving a total of twelve years of a twenty-year sentence. During his incarceration, Joshua Peterson had learned to cope with his actions and failings, completed certification programs in alcoholism counseling and anger control, and worked with Reverend Samms and the social work staff at the prison. His rehabilitation had been deemed a success, and the parole board offered an early release, hinging on his acceptance at the city mission in Kansas City. From her talks with the ex-minister prior to accepting him, Reverend Lewistan found a soul yearning to make amends for his past transgressions, and a desire to try and help others deal with their anger and alcoholism. His remorse over taking the life of his only son and the estrangement of his only daughter, along with the death of his dear wife, Sarah, led Martha to believe that his was a case she was willing to accept. In the eighteen months since he had come to the mission, she hadn't been disappointed with her decision. She attended to the spiritual needs of her charges, while he handled the alcohol abuse and anger control issues. Along with the HIV and addiction counselors, her city mission was doing a commendable job of turning around the lives of the individuals in their care. So much so, that the mission had received a sizeable grant from the Interfaith Community Services Office in Washington, DC.

"A favor? Certainly, Joshua, what can I do for you?" Martha leaned forward, encouraging the man to continue.

"I was wondering if you could stop by and visit my daughter," Joshua confided. "I..." he hung his head as he continued, "I haven't been able to reach her."

"The number I found for you was inaccurate?" Martha asked a bit surprised.

"No. It's the right number. I...she didn't want to speak to me," he acknowledged sadly.

"Oh. I see." Reverend Lewistan stood and circled around her desk and sat in the chair next to Joshua. "Now, Joshua," she spoke softly, "we talked about that possibility. That she would be hesitant to talk to you. It's quite understandable."

"Yes, I know. I just was hoping she'd see how much I've changed. I know I can't bring Thad back, or change what's happened over the years, but I need to try. I can sense the anger in her still." Looking up into Martha's face, he pleaded, "That anger will destroy her, just like it destroyed me. I want to help her before it's too late. Please, help me to reach her...please. I don't have much time left, and I'd like to know I did my best before I go."

Sighing, Martha reached over and took Joshua's hands in hers. As soon as she touched Joshua, she reeled with the images that assaulted her mind. Vivid scenes of the interior of a barn, a young boy huddled in a pile of hay that had turned red with the fluids oozing from his torn body, the sound of crying in the background. Then the scenes changed quickly to a young girl tied in her bed, empty alcohol bottles, dirty alleys and cardboard box homes, a cemetery plot, flashing red lights, and finally the bars of a jail cell. The sounds and smells were all there, too. The whimpering of the boy, the crashing of glass, the wails and sobs and the smells of the alleys, were all there in her mind. As she released Joshua's hands and opened her eyes, she saw Joshua staring at her with deep concern.

"Another vision?" he asked softly.

Reverend Martha nodded, then shut her eyes and inhaled deeply, cognizant of the glimpse she'd just had into Joshua's past.

"Is there anything I can do?"

"No, Joshua. But I'll do what I can for you." Martha was accustomed to these visions into the lives of the people she met. Some visions were worse than the one she just had seen and some were better, but each took a toll on the caring woman, leaving her exhausted, but determined to do what she could. She accepted them as the hand of God, helping her to see the pain in the people she tried to help. "God works in mysterious ways, Joshua. I can't make any promises, but I will try to get in to see her." Joshua's desire for forgiveness was complicated by the fact he had been diagnosed with a non-operable tumor, and was given six months to put his affairs in order.

"Thank you, Martha. That's all I ask." Joshua Peterson stood. Walking towards the door, he stopped and turned back to Reverend Lewistan, "Tell her I love her...and ask her to forgive me."

Watching the tall man leave, Martha whispered after him, "I will, Joshua. I will."

Chapter
8

Katie was seated in the first row of the small amphitheater, along with her fellow instructor trainees. On the dais in front of them were a long table and lectern, with three men and two women seated behind the table. She recognized the men and one of the women from her days as a DEA recruit, but the second woman must have been new to the organization. Special Agent Morley Smith stood and walked to the lectern. As he began to address the small group of new instructors, one of Katie's fellow classmates, Ken Devon, leaned toward her and whispered, "Hey, Katie, got any idea who the brunette is?"

"Nope. Must be someone new since we came through here." Agent Smith continued his address on the Agency's regulations regarding sexual harassment and the implications of such actions while an instructor at the school. *Yadda, yadda, yadda*, Katie thought, as she remembered a brief encounter with her hand-to-hand instructor when she was a recruit. *Guess Agent Deaver didn't pay attention to this class when he went through instructor training. Wonder what ever happened to him?* She was pulled out of her thoughts when Agent Smith began introducing the new female on the dais.

"...and along with those credentials, we were very lucky to have secured Dr. Meisha Prokov to head our Psychology classes for the next tour of incoming recruits. Dr. Prokov..."

Dr. Meisha Prokov stood and walked confidently to the lec-

tern, opened her notes, and began a presentation on criminal profiling.   Katie found herself totally focused on the doctor's
presentation, including new research on the criminal mind, on
which she took copious notes.   As the presentation continued,
Katie began wondering about the person that could possibly be
responsible for the latest series of events.   *What would the motive
be for her actions toward Dean and her friends...and why her
friends?   To hurt Dean even more?   Or were they somehow
involved with this person at one point, too?   But then, how did the
attack on Tom fit in?   Dean was certain that attack was part of this
madwoman's plot.   Was she acting alone?   Did she have co-con-
spirators, or was she taking orders from someone else?   Too bad
the surveillance pictures from the mall weren't more conclusive.
All they knew for sure was that the person in the Miata was
female.*   Katie jotted down her questions as she continued to listen
to the lecture.

By 1200 hours, all five of the presenters had finished their lec-
tures and the group broke for lunch.   Katie and Ken walked
through the cafeteria line together, adding their selections to their
trays.

"Katie, I just don't know how you do it," Ken commented and
shook his head.

"Do what?" Katie replied, as she picked up a piece of carrot
cake to add to the numerous selections already on her tray.

"Eat like you do and still manage to look so good."   Ken
shook his head again as he opted for Jell-O as his dessert.

Katie merely blushed as she accepted his roundabout compliment, and chose skim milk as her beverage.   "Hey, I work hard to
be able to eat all this stuff.   Besides, it's all healthy stuff.   Look,"
she teased as she held up the milk carton, "skim milk.   How
healthy can you get?"

"Um, so you want to explain how healthy that side of maca-
roni and cheese is?   Or that bowl of creamy potato soup?   Or the
cheeseburger and fries...and of course the carrot cake," he chuckled as they took their trays towards an empty table.   As they
walked, Ken asked what she thought of the new psychologist.

"I found her lecture very interesting.   Especially the new
research," Katie commented as she placed her tray on the table.
"What did you think of her?"

"I thought she was a bit spooky, but then most shrinks are a bit out there." Ken waved his hand off into the air to indicate outer space, then leaned in a bit closer and spoke a little softer. "How do you think she messed up her hand?"

Katie snapped her head up and looked at Ken. "What about her hand?"

"Didn't you notice how mangled her right hand was?" he asked incredulously.

"No, I guess I was just paying more attention to what she was saying and not studying her in detail." Katie was embarrassed that she could have missed something so obvious, but she had been listening intently to what the doctor was saying, and not trying to memorize her statistics as though she was a potential criminal.

"Look, she's sitting with Agent Smith by the window. Check out her right hand," Ken advised as he calmly ate his sandwich.

Katie took a discreet look in the direction Ken suggested, and gasped when she caught sight of the woman staring straight back at her. She blushed and smiled, then stood and walked over to their table.

"Excuse me, Doctor Prokov. My name is..."

"Special Agent Katherine O'Malley," the woman responded with a smile. "Please have a seat. Morley and I were just talking about you. You have quite a reputation for such a young agent." She winked at Katie as she noticed the blush creep up her neck.

"Thank you. I guess I've just been lucky with my assignments," Katie offered in a soft voice.

"Nonsense," Morley replied. "You are one of the best agents to have graduated from this training center. You're bright, inquisitive, pay attention to detail, and always get your man."

"Or...woman," Meisha interjected with a sly smile.

"Uh, well, I haven't had to bring in any female suspects yet," Katie offered, a bit surprised at the comment.

"Oh? I thought there was a woman involved in that New York case."

"Yes, I guess you're right. She wasn't our main target, but she was one of Kasimov's thugs."

"Well, even the 'thugs' count," Morley commented as he gave Katie a gentle clap on the shoulder. "The more of these guys, um, and gals, we can get off our streets, the better."

Katie nodded at Agent Smith in return before turning back to Doctor Prokov. "I just wanted to come over and tell you how much I enjoyed your lecture this morning. I find the criminal mind very interesting, and the current research you presented is very enlightening." She stood and turned to leave when the psychologist reached out with her good hand and gently touched Katie's arm.

"Perhaps we'll have an opportunity to chat again? Maybe you would like to drop by my office, and we could talk more about the new research." She offered her right hand to Katie, who shook it, consciously aware of the gnarled appendage in her hand.

"Yes, I'd like that." Katie smiled and turned to go back to her table, thinking, *Well, I guess she's not embarrassed about her hand. Maybe next time I'll ask her what happened to it. She does seem a bit strange, though. That comment about women took me by surprise. Maybe Ken's right, that was a little spooky.*

When she reached the table, Ken was eagerly waiting to hear about their conversation. Katie explained that the doctor seemed to be a very nice person, and did not seem to be at all inhibited about her deformed appendage. She added that the psychologist suggested that she drop by and discuss criminal profiling in more detail at another time.

"Yeah, right. Like that's what she's got in mind for you." Ken chuckled as he gave Katie a knowing look.

"You think she's interested in me?" Katie laughed at the thought. "No way, Ken!"

"Yeah, then why does she keep looking over here at you?"

That comment silenced Katie, and she quickly took a sip of her water to keep herself from looking back at Doctor Prokov's table. "Maybe she's interested in you?" Katie replied as she put her water glass down, but mentally she was hoping that Ken's instinct wasn't on target this time. *I sure don't need any more complications in my life right now. Just getting through the trainers' orientation and studies and, of course, the current investigation are going to tax me enough.* She didn't need anything else to divide her attention. *Doctor Prokov is a very attractive woman, even with her deformed hand. She's tall, well, taller than I am, with an athletic build, auburn hair, and brown eyes. She does have some tiny scars near her ears, perhaps an indication of a little facelift. And her speech is clearly indicative of an Oxford education. She didn't seem the type to be drawn to women, though. Surely, Ken is way off target this time.*

Chapter
9

Katie was flipping through her notes at the kitchen table
while Dean finished up the dishes from the evening meal. Over
dinner, they had compared their days and discussed the questions
that Katie had jotted down during the profiling lecture by Dr.
Prokov. They were in agreement that the woman was definitely
after Dean.

"She's just trying to get to you by these attacks on your
friends," Katie surmised.

"Yeah, I know. I sure wish I could get a handle on just who
this woman is. She's bound to make another mistake soon, and
I'll be there to jump on it." Dean was attacking the dishes in the
sink with as much vigor as if she had the woman in her hands.

"Easy, love. We only have one set of dishes right now," Katie
cautioned as she looked up to see her partner begin on the pans.
"What mistake has she made so far?"

"She got caught on the surveillance video. At least now we
know we're dealing with a woman."

"Ah. Not much of a mistake, but, hopefully, she'll make a
bigger one." Katie looked up from her studies once more. "What
if she's just a minion and not the brains? It could be a ploy to dis-
tract us from the real person behind the attacks."

"It could be...but my bet's on the woman."

Just as Dean finished the last pan, the phone rang. Katie
stood and walked over to the phone on the wall, picking it up to

answer, while Dean checked the caller ID and smiled when she saw it was coming from Freeport.

"Hello? Hey, Tiny. How's Tom doing?" Her face turned very solemn as she listened to Tiny's information about Tom having to be put on a respirator. "I'm really sorry to hear that. Keep us informed, okay?" As Dean wiped her hands and walked over to Katie's side, she motioned that she wanted to talk to Tiny. "Wait a minute, Dean wants to talk to you."

Taking the phone from her partner, Dean inquired about the investigation into the assault on Tom. "Have there been any developments in the investigation into finding his attacker?" Dean asked as she put the phone to her ear. "What kind of bullet was used in the attack? Yeah, a 9mm round is not unusual. Okay, well, if anything develops, let us know. Yeah, you too." She replaced the phone into the wall cradle and sighed. "Damn. I just know this is all tied in somehow." She threw the dishtowel she was still holding onto the kitchen counter, then leaned her tall frame against it.

"After listening to Dr. Prokov today, I'm sure this assailant is doing this to get at you. Tom, the email, the car bombing, even the house bugging. I'm just waiting for the next shoe to drop," Katie admitted as she wrapped her arms around Dean's neck.

"Don't forget the flowers she sent to the office," Dean added with a frown. As she looked down into the emerald eyes before her, she could read the questions in Katie's eyes, but was at a loss to answer them, so she did the next best thing...she kissed her. She put every fiber of her being into that kiss in an effort to convey her love, her concern, and her promise to protect the woman she loved, although she questioned whether she would be strong enough to defeat this unknown enemy and keep that promise.

As she pulled back from the kiss, Katie's eyes remained closed, but a small contented smile played on her lips. "Mmm, I do believe you," Katie disclosed without opening her eyes.

A bit confused, Dean asked, "Believe what?"

"That you love me, are concerned about something happening to me, and that you will do everything you can to protect me."

Dean's eyebrows rose in amazement. "You got all that from one kiss?"

"Umhm. And," she pulled her hands down across Dean's

chest, resting them lightly on her breasts, "if you follow me to the bedroom, I'll answer you."

Dean smiled in amazement at the connection they had, trailing her young lover toward the bedroom. "What about your studies?" she asked as they passed the pile of notes and books on the kitchen table.

"Piece of cake," came the response, as Katie gave the books a dismissive wave of her hand before resuming the walk to the bedroom, "I have something more interesting to study now."

Dean had already turned on the opaque mode for the windows in the house, but Katie didn't even bother to turn on the lights. As soon as they entered the bedroom, Katie turned towards her taller partner and allowed her hands to trail over the muscular frame. She gently tugged open the buttons on Dean's flannel shirt while she let her lips begin a sensual caress, starting at the collarbone and working south. With each button opened, she garnered soft moans from her partner as her lips touched newly exposed skin.

"Mmm, no bra tonight." Another kiss which elicited a moan from her lover. "Good plan." Then another kiss followed by a deeper, needier moan. "Makes my job that much easier." By now, she was at Dean's waist and had lowered herself to her knees, parting the buttons on Dean's 501 jeans. As she reached into the waistband of Dean's pants with both hands, she expertly slipped the jeans and the bikini underpants off in the same motion and helped her lover step out of the clothes now pooled at her feet. Still on her knees, she trailed her hands up the right leg, veering toward the center as she reached Dean's mound of curly black hair, then trailed her hand ever so slowly down the left leg. She reached up and circled her arms around Dean's legs as she looked up into her lover's eyes, caressing her buttocks with both hands before burying her face against her lover's abdomen.

Dean inhaled sharply at the heat rising from her center as Katie continued to caress and tease. As Dean's breaths became more rapid, she looked up to see if her ministrations were having the reaction she was seeking. "Umm, I think I've hit my mark," Katie cooed softly.

"Umhm," Dean growled as she reached down and pulled Katie up to her full five foot six inch height. This maneuver put

Katie's lips, with a slight dip of her head, right in contact with Dean's firm breasts. Taking advantage of her new position, Katie raised her right hand to cup the left breast while her lips paid homage to the right one. Dean moaned deeply once more and began pulling up Katie's t-shirt to expose a naked upper torso.

A raised eyebrow and smile noted that Katie had also removed her bra earlier. "Good," came the growled acknowledgement as she bent towards Katie's waist and broke contact long enough to pull the blonde's sweat pants off. "Ooo, no panties, either," she purred, helping Katie step out of the gray sweats with the large DEA initials down the right leg. Stooping, she lifted the lithe woman into her arms and carried her quickly to the bed, where they spent the next two hours in mutual pleasuring that left no patch of skin unattended and no desire unfulfilled. As their lovemaking peaked and finally ebbed, the two women fell into a comfortable embrace allowing their bodies time to return to within normal bounds.

Eyes closed, Katie murmured a need to go to the bathroom and felt a concurring nod from Dean. They rose and walked to the bathroom, deciding to shower while they were there. Not wanting to waste natural resources, they took their shower together, and never heard the phone ring, or the answering machine pick up. When they came out of the bathroom, Katie went to the kitchen to give Shug her seizure medication and turn off the lights, while Dean checked the security system, insuring all was well for the night. On her way back to the bedroom, she noticed the blinking light on the answering machine. Anticipating another message from the mystery woman, she called to Katie to join her before hitting the play button.

"Hello. This message is for Deanna Peterson. My name is Martha Lewistan. I was hoping to catch you at home, but I guess you must be out. I'll try you tomorrow at your office."

"Who is Martha Lewistan?" Katie's brows furrowed as she asked the question.

"Got me," Dean replied shrugging her shoulders. "Guess I'll find out tomorrow." She checked the caller ID, and noted that the call came at 2247 hours, and originated from the Hilton Towers in Arlington, Virginia.

Chapter
10

The morning began much as the night before had ended. Their dalliance between the sheets made for a hectic dash in the shower, a quick feeding of the felines, tea in their travel mugs, and a bagel to go. Katie envied Dean's limited choices of work attire as she finally opted for her field outfit of tan slacks, blue button down blouse and navy blazer. Having noticed a dusting of snow on the ground outside, she chose tan chukka boots instead of her normal loafers. As they exited the house and Dean set the security system, Katie tabbed the button to raise the garage door.

"Good thing the cars are garaged each night. I think we'd be late if we had to scrape the snow off."

"Nah, the way I drive, it'd get blown right off," Dean grinned at her partner as she closed the back door to the garage. "Be careful on the interstate. Some folks get real crazy when they see that white stuff on the ground."

Katie nodded her head in agreement as she slipped behind the wheel of her rented Porsche. "Yes, Mom." Her reply got her a faux evil look from her partner. "Don't forget we're going car shopping tonight, so be home on time," she called as she started her ignition.

* * * * *

The morning drive was uneventful, as the highway crews had

done a commendable job of sanding the roadways. Dean reached her parking slot right on time and was in her office at precisely 0700. She wasn't expected to be at her desk until 0730, but preferred the half hour of quiet time to get a lot of work done before the phone calls, meetings, operations reviews, and general intelligence operations took up her time. Today she was intent on reviewing the surveillance pictures one more time before her day began.

"There has got to be something in these pictures," she mumbled to herself as she pulled out the file and picked up her magnifying glass. She studied the photos one by one, inch by inch, several times over, until her neck was tense and a headache began to develop at her temples. She was just about to put away the photos when something in the last one caught her eye. It was a blow up of the Miata when it was unoccupied for that short three-minute interval. "Gotcha, you bitch!" Dean croaked savagely. She circled the area of the photo with a highlighter, then picked it up, grabbed the video, and walked purposefully to the door.

It took her ten minutes to get to the lab, having to wait for what seemed an eternity for the elevator to carry her from her floor to sub-level four where the technology lab was housed. Entering the lab, she asked the technician to roll the video to the selected frame, and to enlarge and focus it as best as possible. As the corporal followed her directions, Dean watched the video screen blur then focus several times, until she told the tech to stop.

"Print that and make five copies for me," she ordered as a feral smile crossed her face.

"Yes, Ma'am."

Two minutes later, Dean had the new photos in hand. She retrieved the video and original photo before thanking the tech. "Good work, Corporal."

"Thank you, Ma'am," replied the young media technician as he reset the equipment. "If you need anything else, Colonel, just let me know."

Dean nodded in response before heading out of the lab.

* * * * *

Once back in her office, Dean checked her watch, noting that

it was 0800 as she dialed the number for the Woodbridge Police
Department. When the operator picked up, she requested Lieutenant Green. The desk sergeant told her he was in his car on the
way to DC's 3rd Precinct to pick up a suspect, but he'd be able to
patch her through. She didn't have to wait long before he
answered on his end.

"Lieutenant, this is Colonel Peterson. I think I have something from the surveillance video that may be worth checking
out." Lieutenant Green informed her that he was just turning
onto the interstate and would be arriving in DC in approximately
twenty-five minutes. He suggested that he swing by the Pentagon
before he went to the 3rd Precinct. "Great. I'll leave word at the
security check-in to have a visitor's pass ready for you. One of the
MP's on duty will escort you up to my office." Hanging up with
Lieutenant Green, she placed a call to the security detail, giving
the sergeant on duty the information needed to have the police
officer escorted to her office. Next, she called Sergeant Major
Tibbits to make sure her appointment with General Carlton was
still on schedule. As it turned out, General Carlton was ahead of
schedule so Dean picked up her weekly report and headed to the
general's office. It was now 0805 hours, and she would have just
enough time to fill in the general before Lieutenant Green arrived.

Following her brief meeting with General Carlton, Colonel
Peterson was in the hall walking back to her office when the MP
escorted Lieutenant Green from the elevator. Recognizing the
men walking towards her, she waited at her door, observing them
as they conversed amiably while walking down the hall. Reaching
her office, the MP assumed attention and formally reported to the
colonel. She thanked him for the escort, and opened her office
door. Before he entered, Lieutenant Green paused to shake the
MP's hand, promising to get in touch.

"I take it you know Sergeant Riker?"

"Yes. He was in the last class I worked with at McClellan.
Glad to see he's done so well."

"I'm certain it's a tribute to the good leadership he had during his training. A soldier's success can often be traced back to
the initial training he received."

"I'll take that as a compliment, Colonel. I did pride myself
on the job I did, and was proud of each class that went through my

command." The ex-officer smiled as he took the seat Dean indicated.

She returned the smile as she picked up the photo from her desk. "Well, looking at your records jacket confirmed my original impression that you had been a top notch soldier."

The police lieutenant was not surprised that his military record had been reviewed. He had already checked out Dean's record with an old friend, and was quite impressed with the section of her record that was not classified. He had no doubt that he would have been even more impressed if he'd had access to that part of her record that was excluded from the sanitized version.

"So, what were you able to pull out of the video, Colonel? I'm assuming it's a lead of some sort."

Dean handed him a copy of the photo she had blown up that morning. She pointed to the set of keys dangling from the ignition in the Miata. "I was going over the photos we had made from the surveillance video and found this." The room key tag was only partially visible, but there was enough showing to piece together the name of the motel.

"Hmm, interesting. I know the place. As soon as I get the suspect I'm picking up at the 3rd into a cell, I'll go check it out."

"I was hoping you'd say that." She picked up one of the photos with the side views of the female suspect. "I know these aren't much to go on, but maybe someone at the motel will recognize her. It would be too much to expect her to still be there, but I figured it would be worth checking out. It's the best lead we have right now."

"Well, if she had the Miata with her at the motel, someone is bound to remember her. That's not the type of car usually driven by the clientele of that establishment. Most tourists use a higher class joint when they come to the area. It's not a flea bag, but it's not the Ritz, either." Looking up at Dean, he asked, "You want to join me?"

"I wish I could, but I have to go to a Joint Chiefs meeting this afternoon with my superior. I'd appreciate an update, though."

"You'll get it," he replied as he stood to leave. "Anything else show up in the video?"

"Nothing of any help. We missed this one on the first review, but I found it this morning and had our lab pull out the partial of the motel name on the room tag."

"Sometimes it pays to be persistent." He took the photo, smiling at Dean. "We'll get this woman, Colonel. Sooner or later, she'll make a mistake and we'll get her."

"The sooner the better, Lieutenant." She shook his hand as he turned towards the door.

"I'll be tied up all afternoon in meetings, but you can leave a message here or at my home."

Nodding, the police officer left her office, photo in hand.

* * * * *

It was nearly 1100 hours when Dean's phone rang. Hoping it was Lieutenant Green with good news, she picked up the receiver before the second ring. "Colonel Peterson," she said eagerly into the mouthpiece.

"Good morning, Colonel. I'm glad I was able to catch you in." Dean's mind raced, trying to place the voice on the other end of the line, finally assigning it to the mysterious Martha Lewistan.

"Good morning, Mrs., or is it Miss, Lewistan?" Dean obviously caught the caller a bit off guard as she heard a chuckle on the other end.

"My, you certainly have good recall," the woman acknowledged. "Actually, it's Reverend Lewistan, but please call me Martha."

Feeling the hairs prickle on the nape of her neck, Dean countered, "What can I do for you, Reverend?"

Not surprised by the formal use of her title, the woman began. "Well, I was hoping I could come by and talk to you." Before Dean could speak, Martha quickly continued. "I promise I won't take up much of your time, but you see, I promised a dear friend that I would look you up, and I do so hate to disappoint my friends. I will only be in town until tomorrow morning, when I have to catch my train back home."

"And, who is this friend that wants you to see me?" Dean inquired, knowing now that this woman must have a connection to her father.

"Ah, well, that would be your father, Colonel."

Mentally searching for options, Dean started to talk. "I'm

afraid that—" She was cut off by a persistent plea.

"Please, Colonel. All I ask is five minutes. Please allow me that much. If you still have objections after five minutes, I will leave immediately." The sincere tone in the woman's voice somehow managed to reach into Dean's sense of right and wrong and gently pull at her. She had no interest in her father, or what connection he had with this woman, but decided five minutes of her time could be spared if it meant an end to his desire to see her.

"All right, Reverend. But I am tied up all day today. What time does your train leave?"

"Oh, well...it leaves at 6:30 in the morning."

I guess we can go car shopping tomorrow, Dean thought before making her decision. "Okay. Would you be able to meet tonight?"

"Yes. Yes, that would be best. I have meetings myself this afternoon. Perhaps I could come to your home?" Martha knew that if she could just get her foot in the door, she would be able to extend that five minutes a bit longer. "I mean, if that would be all right with you? I'm sure I could find it."

Sighing, Dean capitulated. "Yes, that would be fine, but I would be happy to pick you up at your hotel. Or if you're tired, perhaps we could just meet in the lobby?" *Great, Dean, if she accepts, you'll have to listen to the woman all the way out to the house and all the way back into DC!*

"No, your house would be fine, and no need to pick me up. Really. I can get there on my own."

Relieved, Dean gave Reverend Lewistan directions to the house and set a time of 8:00 p.m. for the meeting. *At least Katie and I can have a quiet dinner before she shows up.* Dean's conscience stepped in and the words came out of her mouth before she thought about them. "Why don't you join us for dinner?" *Where the heck did that come from?* she thought, hoping the woman would refuse.

"Oh, that would be lovely. Thank you, I accept. I'll see you at 8:00, then." Martha quickly hung up before Colonel Peterson had a change of heart.

"Well, if it puts my father out of my life for good, then an hour or so of my time will be worth it." Dean was still mumbling to herself when she left her office to meet General Carlton for the

Joint Chiefs meeting.

Returning to her office at 1530, Dean checked her voice mail and was concerned that there was no message from Lieutenant Green. *Maybe he's staking the place out, waiting for her to return. Or following up on information he got from the staff there.* Dean kept running over possibilities in her head as she picked up the remaining photos and placed them in her briefcase before snapping it shut. As she walked over to the closet to get her coat, the phone rang. Crossing quickly to the desk, she picked up the receiver on the second ring, heart pounding as she recognized Lieutenant Green's voice on the other end.

"Any luck?" Dean queried.

"Sorry, Colonel. The lady was long gone. The staff did remember her, though, and their description matches the one of the woman in the video, only now we know she's a brunette with dark eyes, about 5'10", weighing about 130 or 140."

"Well that fits about thirty thousand or more women in this town," Dean sneered. "What about any distinguishing marks?"

"None that they saw. They mostly saw her going out or coming in, so she was covered up by her coat, hat, and gloves."

"Any peculiarities of speech?"

"The day clerk said she had a heavy Southern drawl." He paused. "That doesn't fit in with the woman that posed as a gas company rep to get in your house."

"No, it doesn't. But, she could have been faking the accent. I've used many voices during undercover operations. It wouldn't surprise me at all if she were doing the same. How did she pay for the room?"

"Cash in advance. She was there for six days. Checked out the day of the car bombing. No one saw anyone with her, either, but the day maid said there were used condoms in the trashcan, so she must have had company at some point. I'm sending some guys back to check with the evening and night shifts. Maybe they'll come up with something."

"Well, let's hope so. I'd like to nail her before someone else gets hurt."

"Me too, Colonel. I'll let you know what I find out from the other detectives. By the way, our homicide division found a body down by the river yesterday. It was listed as a John Doe until today. Seems the guy was an employee of the utility company. A guy by the name of Felix Waxmann."

"That's interesting. Too bad you don't have the condoms to run a DNA check."

"Yeah, that's what I thought, too. We're going to get pictures of him and have the guys take it with them when they visit the evening and late night shifts at the motel. The autopsy report should be ready tomorrow. If anything interesting turns up, I'll give you a call."

"Thank you, Lieutenant." Almost as an afterthought, Dean added, "Say, fax a picture of Waxmann to my office, would you? I'd like someone to take a look at it."

"You've got it, Colonel. It'll be waiting for you when you get back to the office on Monday."

"Thanks, Lieutenant. And don't forget, you can call any-time...day or night." Dean replaced the receiver, frowning as she went over the information Lieutenant Green had uncovered, thinking that maybe this Waxmann character was one of the utility people that had entered her house. *Maybe*, she thought, *we'll be able to get some additional information on our mystery woman by tracking this lead.* Out loud, Dean whispered, "Okay...you may have slipped through for now, but I'll find you." She slowly nodded with the solid resolve she felt coursing through her body.

Chapter
11

8 December, 1930 Hours

"I don't know what came over me, Katie. One minute, I'm backing out of even meeting the woman; the next, I'm asking her over for dinner." Shaking her head, Dean continued to put together the ingredients for one of her killer salads.

"Oh, don't be so hard on yourself, Dean. I'm sure eighteen years of being a preacher's daughter taught you to be respectful to the clergy." Katie hugged the tall woman as she continued chopping peppers and tomatoes. "Besides, maybe deep down inside, you really want to know what happened to your father over the years."

Dean stiffened and smacked the knife down on the cutting board. "Look, I may still show respect for a minister, but I *don't* give a flying rat's...behind...about my father! To me, he died over sixteen years ago, along with Thad. Nothing will change that for me now, nothing!" She hung her head and felt Katie's warmth seep through the tense muscles of her back, calming her. "How dare he think he can just waltz right back into my life?" She inhaled sharply to keep the tears she felt coming at bay.

Katie slipped her arms from around Dean's waist and moved them up to her shoulders, gently kneading the tense muscles until she felt Dean begin to relax.

Calmer, Dean suggested, "We'll just be courteous and listen to this woman, then send her on her way. Okay?"

"Mmhm. No problem, love. Now, just go relax, okay? I'll finish the salad." Dean turned to face her lover, eyes searching for understanding. Katie reached up behind Dean's neck, gently pulling her down into a loving kiss. As their lips separated, Katie whispered, "Everything will be okay."

Dean remained in Katie's embrace a few moments longer before taking her lover's advice and heading to the living room to put on some quiet music. Returning to the kitchen, she checked the lasagna in the oven, picked out a bottle of Cabernet, and peeled off the protective seal to uncork it. She placed the bottle in the proper position for the cork remover mounted on the side of the cabinet and worked the device, pulling out the cork neatly. Setting the bottle aside to breathe, she gathered the plates, glasses, and utensils to set the table. By the time she was finished, she felt more relaxed and even found herself humming along to the music. At exactly 8:00 p.m., the front doorbell chimed. Dean lifted her eyes to the clock in the kitchen, then found Katie's emerald eyes warmly focused on her. Her lover smiled and reached out for Dean's arm, giving it a gentle squeeze.

"I'll get it," Katie offered, releasing Dean's arm.

Nodding, Dean stayed in the kitchen with her thoughts, while Katie answered the front door. *What's wrong with me? Why am I dreading this so much?* Shaking her head, her mind raced on. *Could it be that Katie's right, and I really want to know what's happened to him over the years?* Her self-questioning ended as Katie brought their guest into the kitchen.

"Dean, meet Reverend Lewistan." Katie ushered the plain looking woman in, then left to hang her coat in the hall closet.

"Oh, please, just call me Martha," the minister replied with a soft voice. "I'm very glad you had time to see me." She walked over and extended her hand to the tall woman who was staring at her, obviously appraising her.

Pulling herself out of her visual evaluation of the woman approaching her, Dean reached for the hand towel on the cupboard and wiped her hands before accepting the proffered one.

"Uh, yeah. Nice to meet you." She spoke hesitantly as she shook the reverend's warm hand. "Can I offer you something to drink? Um, we have just about anything you'd like," Dean added as she waved around the kitchen feebly.

During that quick handshake, Martha could feel Dean's discomfort, so she looked around the kitchen and spotted the bottle of wine on the counter. "I suppose a small glass of wine would be just right."

Dean nodded and slipped three wine glasses off of the overhead rack, setting them on the counter. As she picked up the bottle to pour, Katie returned to the kitchen. Dean sighed inwardly, glad to have the silent support of her partner at her side.

"The dinner will take a little longer to bake. Let's take our wine into the living room," Katie offered smoothly, noticing Dean's hand shaking slightly as she poured. Taking the two glasses already filled, Katie winked at her partner before turning to offer one to Martha and leading the way to the living room. Dean remained in the kitchen for a moment longer, took a healthy gulp of her wine, refilled the glass, then joined the women in the other room.

"You have a beautiful home, Colonel."

"Thank you. We like it very much."

"Dean worked very hard to capture the spirit of Frank Lloyd Wright's Falling Water house on this piece of property," Katie offered, smiling proudly at her lover.

"I'm a great fan of Frank Lloyd Wright. I've actually been to Falling Water," the minister admitted as she looked around the room. "I see you did away with the boulder," she chuckled softly.

Dean couldn't help but smile at the comment. That boulder was one of the first things she'd eliminated in her attempt to duplicate the home. "Yeah, wouldn't do to be tripping over a boulder in the middle of the night." Feeling a little warmth rush up her neck from the gulp of wine in the kitchen, Dean relaxed a little. "I tried to fit as much of his style as possible from that home into this one. I don't have a natural waterfall running beneath, but the design fit the land very well."

"Well, just from what I can see, I think you captured it quite nicely."

Dean smiled proudly at the compliment. "It's going to be a few more minutes before the lasagna is ready. Would you care to see the rest of the house?"

Martha nodded vigorously as she set her wine glass down on the coffee table. *Good move, Martha,* the reverend thought, mentally giving herself a pat on the back, *you picked the right topic to get her to relax. She obviously takes great pride in her home.* "Please, I'd love to see it all."

Dean stood and began describing her search for the right contractors, the huge amount of time she'd spent researching Wright's various homes, and the months she'd spent looking for the perfect lot. By this time, they were headed for the stairs leading to the lower two levels. Dean cast a glance back at Katie, who was still seated on the couch. "Aren't you coming?" she asked cautiously.

"Um, no. You go ahead. I'll keep an eye on dinner." Katie winked at her lover and shooed her off with a flick of her hand. Dean smiled and returned the wink before joining Martha on the next level. Katie sat watching her partner descend the stairs, marveling at how quickly the minister was able to identify Dean's soft spot for her house. "I think everything is going to work out just fine," she whispered softly to herself.

Dean led the interested woman through a complete tour of the house. Every room's design and function was discussed in detail, receiving appreciative "oooh's and ahh's" at the appropriate times. When the tour reached the master bedroom, the petite minister stopped and gasped at the open-air feeling of the room. The expansive curtain-less windows raised questions, but the demonstration of how they turned from clear to opaque answered the lack of curtains question. Dean explained that the skylights were not part of Wright's plan, but added much to the ambiance of the final product.

"Katie and I enjoy our bedroom immensely." Dean put a slight emphasis on the word "our" to see what kind of a reaction she would get from the minister.

Not one to miss a beat, Martha raised an eyebrow at her tour guide and smiled sweetly.

"Very nice indeed, I'm sure you both do," she replied, and quickly followed with, "How long have you and Katie been lovers?"

Touché, Dean thought to herself before replying, "A little over a year, but we just moved in together shortly after the house was completed this October. Katie was on assignment in the Midwest for most of that time, though."

"Well, from what I can see, you two seem to be made for each other." She took Dean's hand and gently squeezed it. "I could feel the love between the two of you the minute I entered the kitchen."

Somehow, that gentle touch and simple statement lifted a weight off Dean's shoulders that she hadn't even noticed until just then. "Thank you, Martha. We do love each other very much. Now, how about some dinner, and then we can talk about my father." On the way back to the kitchen, Dean couldn't help but feel that this woman was more than she seemed, and she liked what she was feeling. *Maybe her coming here will resolve the conflict I've had all these years and help me to forgive Dad. Katie started the process last year; maybe now it's time to finish it.* In a much better mood, Dean entered the kitchen and found a knowing Katie waiting there.

The meal was accompanied by conversation about Katie's job, how they'd met, and some minor disclosures about Dean's life during the past seventeen years. When she shied away from speaking about her past, the reverend sensed Dean's hesitation and did not try to pry for any details. She was just glad to see the woman before her talking openly about her love for Katie. Realizing that she had the capability to love after all that had happened in her life, gave Martha hope that she would be able to convince Dean to see her father. By the time dinner was over, they were all on a first name basis and were genuinely enjoying the evening. The three women made short work of the clean up, and soon found themselves in the living room once more, enjoying rich espressos.

"Dean, I think it's time to talk about your father," Martha suggested as she set her coffee cup down. Dean nodded as she sipped her espresso. Katie stood to leave, when Martha shook her head and asked her to please stay. "I think Dean will want you here," she offered sagely.

"Yes," Dean agreed, pleading with her eyes for her lover to stay by her side. "Please, stay with me?"

Katie took one look at the beseeching face and smiled gently, returning to her seat. She could sense Dean's apprehension, so she took hold of the tall woman's hand and slipped it into her lap, softly stroking it with her thumb.

Martha began her well-rehearsed speech, starting with her

first interview of Joshua Peterson during visiting hours at the penitentiary. Martha omitted any mention of her "visions" of Joshua's pain, not wanting to upset the delicate balance established between her and Dean. She talked about the many hours of counseling she had spent on Joshua, and how she had decided he was a soul in need of saving, and that just maybe, his coming to the city mission would be a means to continue his journey toward healing and salvation. The small woman painted a picture of Joshua that Dean had never envisioned before: a picture of a man traveling through hell on earth for the wrongs he had committed. The loneliness endured by a man who had destroyed everything he cared for. His time spent in alcoholic oblivion, the stabbing pain delivered by the death of his wife, and the ultimate loss of his soul for the taking of his son's life. Last but not least, the toll on his tattered existence by the estrangement of his daughter. She sketched his first steps toward forgiveness: turning himself in for his son's death, his life in prison, the healing process of dealing with his anger and alcoholism, the eventual counseling certifications he'd earned, and his work for the past eighteen months at the city mission.

"Dean, I'm not condoning what he did. It was an act of raw anger...where his pride overruled reason. In the eyes of the law, he's paid for his crime, but in the eyes of the Lord, he is still paying and paying. But, he is a man. A mortal being that makes mistakes, just like we all make mistakes. And he's slowly returning to productivity as a humble man who is able to help others because of what he has gone through." She stopped, trying to read Dean's thoughts about how she was now feeling about her father. "We've all done things we regret. Taking another human being's life is not an easy thing to live with. Taking the life of your own flesh and blood is a soul-crippling deed."

Dean closed her eyes and let Martha's words soak into her soul. She was all too familiar with the taking of someone's life. In all honesty, she admitted that she herself had acted in anger and rage as she terminated a life. And, she knew that she, too, had taken the life...lives...of innocents, even though there might have been no way to determine guilt or innocence at the moment she'd executed her orders. She knew Martha was right: he deserved forgiveness, and so did she...but could he forgive her?

How can my actions be judged different from my father's? I've done things that were more horrible; and I was fully aware of my actions, not blinded by emotion. Dean thought of her life and her father's life, then wept for his soul and for hers. When the tears began to streak Dean's cheeks, Katie moved closer, pulling her lover into a tight embrace, all the while whispering soft words of comfort into her ear.

Martha sat back, confused by Dean's emotional reaction. Her words were meant to pull at Dean's conscience, but she was taken totally by surprise by the depth of her sorrow. She looked questioningly at Katie. "I'm sorry..."

Katie held her lover, gently rocking her. "Dean has her own demons to deal with," she said softly. "Would you mind making some tea? The pot is on the stove, and the tea is in the cupboard next to it." Martha quickly agreed and went to the kitchen, glad to give them the time alone together they obviously needed. When the teapot started to whistle, Katie entered the kitchen carrying the espresso cups from the living room. Dean had regained her control and left for the bedroom to wash her face.

"Katie...what did I say? I knew I planned a powerful speech, but..." The minister looked at Katie, still quite concerned over Dean's reaction.

"You just brought up a past that Dean had pushed out of her mind."

"I'm sorry. I had no idea," the concerned woman offered.

"No, don't be sorry. It's actually a very good thing—a healing process that she needs too." She began assembling the teacups and tea bags on a tray while Martha poured the hot water into the cups.

Starting to fit the pieces together, Martha asked, "And forgiveness?"

"Yes. She needs to forgive herself as much as she needs to forgive her father." The two women smiled at each other and returned to the living room to find a quiet, but very composed Dean waiting for them. Sipping their tea in silence, the three women sat in the living room, each with a cat looking for attention in their lap and, in their own way, providing the women with an outlet for the stress of the past half hour. Dean was the first to break the silence.

"I'll put in a request for leave on Monday morning. I should be able to catch a flight to Kansas City by Wednesday at the latest."

"That would be wonderful, Dean. I know your father is anxious to see you." She looked over at Katie. "Will you be able to come, too?"

"No. I'm afraid I can't leave my training program right now." She looked over at Dean, placing her hand in Dean's larger one. "Besides, I think you need time alone with your father."

"One thing, Martha. Why now? Why has he waited so long?" Dean cocked her head to the side with the question.

"That's mostly my doing," she conceded. "There's never a right time to reconcile, but the sooner the better. He's been wanting to do this for so long, but was afraid, and now he's running out of time."

"Running out of time?" Dean echoed. "I don't understand."

"I hadn't intended to divulge this, but since you have agreed to see him, perhaps it's best if you know what to expect." She paused, seemingly searching for the right words. "There's really no way to say it, except to just say it." Dean and Katie both looked at her questioningly. "The man you will be meeting will not resemble anything you can conjure up from your memories. Prison is a hard life. Add to that the physical failings of the body, and you have further complications. In your father's case, his health has been further compromised by what has been diagnosed as an inoperable tumor. The doctors have given him six to eight months. The last month will be the worst. The doctors fear seizures will begin toward the end and he won't know anyone by then, so time really is of the essence."

"A tumor? They're sure?" Katie asked, sensing Dean's turmoil at this new piece of information. Martha nodded. "When...how much time is left?"

"Two, maybe three months." She paused again. "It took me a bit to get him to work up his courage to call you. When you refused to talk to him, he was extremely depressed. He finally came to see me the other day, when he found out I was coming to DC. That's when he asked if I would try to contact you. He desperately wants to make peace with you before his time is up."

Dean sat there speechless, reeling from the emotions dredged up from her past, her conflicting feelings about her father, and now, the fact that he was dying. Finally finding her voice, she thanked Martha for her persistence in making contact. The three women rose from their seats and walked toward the front entrance.

"Will you be able to find your way back to your hotel?" Katie asked as she helped Martha put on her winter coat.

"Yes, I have a very good map in the car and the route isn't very complicated." Reverend Lewistan turned and looked at her hostesses. "Thank you for inviting me into your home." She reached up and hugged Katie, and felt a warm glow of love emanating from the woman. Then she turned to Dean and cautiously wrapped her arms around the tall woman. The graphic visions that assaulted her mind nearly caused her knees to buckle. The smell of death and the cries of sorrow overwhelmed her senses and would have caused her to collapse had it not been for Dean's strong grasp.

Dean sensed the small woman's near collapse in her arms and turned concerned eyes toward Martha. In that brief moment when their eyes locked, Martha's vision changed to one of light. A light that was very bright and golden and full of goodness. It was a beautiful ray of light, piercing through a blackness that surrounded it.

"Are you all right?" Dean asked as she helped hold Martha up.

Concerned that her body's reaction to Dean's embrace would give her away, Reverend Lewistan shook her head and mumbled some comment that was barely audible about new shoes and a long day. She convinced the two women that she was perfectly fine, just a little clumsy and quite a bit tired, then quickly left to compose herself in the quiet of her rental car. She now had a better understanding of the demons that Dean had to deal with on her own, but was comforted by the light breaking through the darkness of her soul, a light she was sure began in the connection between Katie and Dean.

As the two women watched Martha pull out, they both hoped that she would be okay for the thirty-minute drive back to her hotel.

* * * * *

After Reverend Lewistan left, they finished cleaning up in silence before heading to the bedroom for the night. Katie slipped into the living room to retrieve a book first, and Dean opted to boot up her computer and check on air travel to Kansas City. After preparing for bed, Katie propped up her pillows and situated herself to read a textbook she had been given by Dr. Prokov. Earlier in the day, Katie had stopped by the psychologist's office to discuss some questions she'd had regarding profiling criminals. She did not go into details with the DEA psychologist, but she was trying to profile the person who was currently plaguing their lives. Meisha recommended she start with the textbook, *Murder, Mayhem, and Madness: Getting Into The Criminal Mind*, that she had written, and eagerly gave Katie a copy to take home with her. She was starting on the second chapter when Dean finally came to bed.

"Studying?" the tall woman asked as she slipped under the covers.

"No, not really. Just doing some reading on criminal profiling. Maybe I can pick up some clues about our mystery woman. Dr. Prokov loaned me this textbook." She held up the book so Dean could read the title.

"Hmmm. *Murder, Mayhem and Madness*...sounds like a fun read." She raised an eyebrow, smirking at her lover.

"Well, I'm certainly glad to see your sense of humor returning." She gently poked Dean with the book before opening it to where she'd left off.

"What can I say? You bring out the best in me." Dean returned the poke and added a soft kiss on Katie's cheek before lying on her back to study the night sky through the perfectly positioned skylights.

Katie marked her place in the book, turning her head to face her lover, examining her strong profile before speaking. "Dean?"

"Hmm?"

"Are you going to be okay going to Kansas City?" Her voice conveyed the concern that was in her mind.

Dean thought about that for a few seconds before replying. Sighing heavily, she answered, "Yeah, I think so. It's time my dad and I get everything out in the open."

Katie closed the book and set it on her nightstand. Rolling over to face her partner, she reached out to gently stroke Dean's face and brush aside a few wayward strands of hair. "I'm glad you have decided to go. I just wish I could be there with you." She rolled over on her back once more and stared out the skylights along with Dean. "But," she sighed, "since I can't, I'm glad that Martha will be there."

Dean pondered that statement for a bit before replying. "Yes, I am too. I've got to admit that I like the woman. She just seems to have this way about her. I felt very comfortable in her presence."

"I know what you mean. I'm amazed at how much information I gave up about myself tonight without realizing it." Katie turned her head to face Dean. "I noticed that you didn't say much, but then, your life has been—and needs to be—on a...a..."

"Need to know basis," Dean added, helping Katie find the words.

"Yeah, I guess you could put it that way," the blonde agreed.

"We've never spoken much about your family," Dean considered as she reached over to pull the young woman into her arms. "I didn't realize that you lost your parents at such an early age."

"It's been nearly fifteen years, and I can still picture their faces. Dad was always smiling, and Mom...well, I think Mom and I had some kind of a cosmic connection or something. We always seemed to tune into each other's thoughts, especially when it came to caring about Dad. It used to drive Dad crazy the way we would both dote on him. We both adored him, and he us." Katie snuggled deeper into Dean's embrace, exhaling deeply. "I often wondered how my life would have turned out if that avalanche hadn't buried them. I mean, my aunt did a great job raising me, but, I just question where I would be now, if Mom and Dad had lived."

"Well, we most likely wouldn't be in each other's arms right now."

"Yeah, and that's one of the things that makes me feel more at ease about the way things turned out. You, and of course, Aunt Lois." A silence permeated the room while the two women held each other, tuning in to each other's heartbeats and body rhythms.

Thinking about Martha's near collapse as she hugged Dean

good-bye, Katie said, "I sure hope Martha gets back to the hotel okay."

"Yeah, I wonder what brought on that little episode?" Dean hesitated then asked, "You don't buy the tripping-in-new-shoes thing, do you?" It was more a statement than a question.

"Nope. If those were new shoes, then our cats are really panthers in disguise."

"That's what I thought, too."

They each thought about the incident as their bodies slipped into sync, matching heartbeats and respirations. Soon, they were both sound asleep, unaware of a third party that had been tuned in to their conversations during the course of the evening, compliments of a miniature transmitter sealed into the spine of *Murder, Mayhem, and Madness.*

* * * * *

"Oh, how touching. And if it hadn't been for you...well, I could be ruling my own little country by now. Oh well, sleep my little pretties," the listener cackled with a fairly good imitation of the Wicked Witch of the West. "Now, let's see, what shall I deliver tomorrow? Murder?" Answering herself, she said, "No, not yet. Madness, then?" Tapping the index finger of her gnarled hand against her temple, she thought out loud, "Oh, that will come in time." Smiling broadly, she finished with, "I guess it'll have to be Mayhem then!" Chuckling at her own cleverness, the woman removed the headset and flipped off the receiver, then started up her car and headed quietly down the lane.

Chapter
12

9 December, 0800 Hours

The ringing phone woke the duo from their heavy slumber. Extricating herself from her lover's arms and legs, Dean reached for the phone on her nightstand.

"Peterson," she croaked groggily into the mouthpiece as she tried to wake her senses.

"Morning, Colonel. Hope I didn't wake you." When the caller didn't get a quick response, he added, "This is Lieutenant Green."

"Ah, Lieutenant. No, I'm awake." *At least, I am now,* she thought as she swung her legs out from the covers and sat on the side of the bed. "Any news from the night staff?"

"Yes...and no. We did find out that the woman who was on night desk duty may be able to provide a description of our mysterious woman, but unfortunately, she's on vacation and won't be back until Wednesday. We'll be able to contact her on Thursday and get back to you with a sketch, if all goes well."

"Okay, that sounds good." Then, remembering she'd be catching the 9:00 a.m. flight to KCI on Wednesday, she informed the lieutenant that she would be out of town, but he could send the sketch to Katie. She gave him her cell phone number so he could contact her if anything more definite came up.

"Roger that. Well, I'll be in touch then. Have a safe trip."

"Thank you, Lieutenant. Good bye." She replaced the

receiver and shook her head once more in an effort to wake more fully. Turning to see if her lover had been wakened by the phone call, Dean found Katie fully awake and smiling.

"I take it Lieutenant Green wasn't able to get a description?" Katie inquired as the tall woman slid back under the covers and scooped the blonde into her arms.

"Not yet. The night clerk is on vacation and won't be back until Wednesday. They'll catch up to her on Thursday and have her work with the police artist to try and create a sketch of the suspect. He'll get it over to you as fast as he can." Dean gently ran her fingers through her lover's sleep mussed hair. "Maybe I should put off the trip to Kansas City until this is all over," she said somberly as she searched Katie's face for an excuse to stay there.

"Nonsense. You need to go see your father. That wacko will still be here when you get back," Katie replied forcefully. "Besides, I'll be fine. In fact, I could even stay at the training center until you come back. No one in their right mind would try to penetrate that place to get at me."

"What about the cats?"

"No problem. The veterinarian at the center gave me a new medication for Shug that will last a week. And, as long as they have food and water, they'll be good for at least three days." Katie looked up at Dean, seeking approval for her quickly thought out plan.

Peering into the sparkling green eyes, Dean considered that Katie would certainly be safer at the center than alone in the house. She didn't doubt Katie's ability to take care of herself, but agreed that her lover would be safer in the company of hundreds of DEA agents, FBI agents, Marines, and all the others at Quantico, than alone. "Okay, that sounds like a plan. I'll try to be home on the first flight Sunday. Maybe by then, we'll have more information on our mysterious woman and will be able to flush her out."

"Good. Now that we've got that settled..." Katie reached up and pulled Dean down until their lips were a breath apart, "I think we have some time before the car dealers open for business."

A seductive purr rumbled from Dean's throat, "Mmmhmm. And what would you like to do with it?"

In response, Katie sensually licked her lips and smiled as she pulled herself on top of the taller woman, straddling her. Sliding her hands up Dean's arms then back down across her breasts, she could feel the sexual tension building in her lover. Slowly, she lowered herself until she met soft lips with her own, gently coaxing them to part to allow her tongue entrance into the warm, sweetness of her lover. Each kiss deepening and lengthening until the bonds of restraint could no longer hold, allowing the love they held for each other to flow from one to the other, consuming them with their passion.

* * * * *

"I really like the red one," Katie crooned, letting her fingers trace the line of the spoiler as she walked around the rear of the vehicle.

"But," Dean offered seriously, "statistics show that the police stop red cars more than any other color. I think the black one would be much better."

"Maybe that's because there are more red cars on the road than any other color?" Katie countered as she walked up to the driver's side door, checking her reflection in the window. She noted the look of dejection on her friend's face and bit her lip. She had already decided to get the arctic silver metallic one, but couldn't help taunting Dean, knowing that black was her favorite color. Deciding that she had teased her lover long enough, she turned to face Dean. "How about a compromise? Let's go talk to the salesman and see how long it will take to get the arctic silver one ready." Eyes twinkled as she caught Dean's approving nod as she checked her watch.

Two hours later, they were winding their way along the back roads, enjoying the power of the new Porsche Boxster S, as Katie expertly drove through the countryside. Dean slid a k.d. lang CD into the player and cranked up the sound, crooning along with the powerful singer as they belted out *Big Boned Gal*. After the first hour at the wheel had passed, Katie pulled over and turned the car over to Dean.

"Are you sure?" Dean asked hesitantly. "I mean, you just laid out over eighty thousand dollars for this baby. I wouldn't want anything to happen to it while I'm driving."

"Oh come on, Dean! You and I both know you're a better driver than I am." Katie winked. "Besides, that's what insurance is for."

Grinning, Dean quickly slid out of her seat and walked around to the driver's door, holding it open for Katie. By the time Katie snapped her seat belt on, Dean had all the mirrors adjusted, the seat moved to accommodate her longer legs, and was checking for traffic. Not seeing anything in sight, she gave Katie a feral grin, a waggle of her eyebrows, and then slipped the car into first gear. Before Katie blinked, the car was smoothly accelerating to ninety miles an hour, whipping past barren pastures, scenic horse farms, and an occasional stream. It was too cold to put the top down, but the two women thoroughly enjoyed the feel of the powerful sports car.

"Did you know that the top track speed of this car is 161 mph?" Dean marveled as they neatly threaded their way through a gentle S-curve in the road. "That's a lot of power you have under the hood."

"Umhm," Katie responded as she reached over and gently placed her hand on Dean's thigh, giving it an affectionate squeeze. "Thought you'd like it." *I wonder what she'll say once she sees the black one in the garage on Christmas Eve.* Katie had ordered that Porsche on-line, and it was going to be delivered in time for Christmas. She had already worked out a plan with Bill to get Dean out of the house long enough to have the Boxster delivered. *Good thing it's a three-car garage,* she mused as they headed back toward home. *I certainly hope she won't balk at accepting it. After all, if you can't use your inheritance to make someone happy...* Katie adjusted her seat back so she could recline a bit, giving her a better view of the rear view mirror and the glee in her partner's eyes as she maneuvered the sports car towards home.

* * * * *

"That, love, is one awesome automobile," Dean commented as she hit the button to raise the garage door. She looked at her watch and noted that it was almost 1700 hours.

"Glad you approve. I really like the color. It'll be a lot cooler in the summer than a darker color."

"Yeah, that's true, but a black one looks really sharp when it's clean," Dean persisted.

"Unhuh," Katie agreed as they exited the car, "but I don't want to spend all my spare time cleaning and waxing it."

"I could have gotten you one of those duster thingies. As small as this car is, it wouldn't take long to dust it off each night." Dean pretended to dust off the Boxster as she quickly stepped around the car. "Voila!" she said, bowing to Katie.

Oooo, good idea. I'll look for one of those while she's gone. Katie bit her lip trying to maintain a neutral expression during this discussion so she wouldn't arouse any suspicion about her Christmas gift. She chuckled at Dean's antics, reaching out for her lover's hand. "Oh, Dean, you certainly are in a playful mood today. Maybe we should go out and buy a new car every day."

"Not at that price, love. No way, no how. But, I guess you're right. The drive did pick up my spirits a bit." She entwined her fingers with Katie's as they left the garage and headed up the path to the house.

Dean was first inside and noticed the red light blinking on the answering machine. After hanging her coat up on the coat rack by the door, she walked over to the machine and hit the play button, surprised to hear Dirk's voice.

"Hey gals...are you there? Listen, it's almost three o'clock. Please call my cell phone as soon as you get in."

Dean frowned as she recognized the sounds in the background of Dirk's call. She quickly picked up the phone and dialed. The other end was answered almost immediately and Dean identified herself. After a brief conversation, she replaced the phone and went looking for Katie in the kitchen, finding her feeding the cats.

"What did Dirk want?" Katie inquired as she finished dividing the food between the three felines. When she didn't get a response, she turned to look at her partner and was shocked to see tears spilling from concerned blue eyes. Tossing the spoon and empty can into the sink, she quickly closed the gap between them, reaching up to wipe tears from Dean's cheeks. "What happened?" she asked as she pulled her lover into an embrace.

"It's Bill. He and Dirk were out jogging in Rock Creek

Park...a car...hit and run. Bill's in GW Hospital," she said in gasps, regaining control of her emotions. "He's stable right now, so they're going to transport him to Walter Reed. Dirk said they'd be there in about an hour. I told him we'd meet him there."

"Oh, Dean, you don't think this is related to our mystery woman do you?"

"I'm not ruling it out, but I'll have to wait until I can talk to Dirk and Bill." Dean searched her lover's eyes, finding the support and calm she needed. "We have got to find this woman, Katie. Before she does any more damage."

Katie nodded, knowing that the circle was getting smaller, and sooner or later, they would be the targets of this madwoman. They needed some kind of break. Maybe the night clerk would be the key.

* * * * *

When the ambulance pulled in, Katie was sitting and Dean was pacing the floor in the emergency waiting room. As the doors opened, Dirk exited the ambulance to allow the EMTs access to the gurney. He followed the gurney into the ER, then was directed to the waiting area.

"Hey," Dean called as Dirk entered the room. "You okay?"

Nodding, he replied, "Yeah, just a bit tired. I hate all this waiting."

"Yeah, I know what you mean," came the identical response from the two women. Katie stood, putting her arms around Dirk in a fierce hug, while Dean put her hand on his shoulder.

"So, is he going to be okay? I mean, do they know how badly he's hurt, yet?" Katie asked softly as the three friends sat in the chairs by the door.

"Yeah. He's got a fractured pelvis and femur, sprained right wrist, and a concussion. Plus some scrapes and bruises. They're not sure if his spleen or kidneys are damaged. They'll do more testing here." He sighed heavily before continuing. "He's conscious, but in quite a bit of pain. They couldn't give him anything for it yet because they're shipping him off to surgery as soon as the doc arrives."

Dean nodded as she flashed back to one of her trips to the

hospital after an op turned nasty. It was just supposed to be a quick insertion to pick up a field agent who was about to be compromised. All the intel reports came back clear for the pick up, but somewhere along the line, someone had dropped the ball...badly. The insertion went smoothly, but the extraction became complicated when thirty uniforms showed up with guns blazing. Her team took cover in an abandoned warehouse as bullets streamed in through the broken windows. They had almost made it out the back when the floor gave way, sending her and the field agent they came to rescue into the basement, along with several floor beams and discarded machinery. When the soldiers carefully crept into the building and looked down into the gaping hole, they assumed that no one could have survived the fall. After waiting for nearly thirty minutes to see if they heard any moans from the rubble, they finally cleared out, thinking Dean and her team were dead. They didn't realize that most of Dean's team had made it to cover in the nearby jungle and were waiting for the soldiers to leave. As soon as the area was clear, the team returned to the warehouse and began the laborious process of digging out Dean and the field agent. They found them protected by some of the flooring that had formed a shelter by falling against the back wall of the basement. Dean's leg, though, was pinned under a heavy beam, and just by looking at its position in relation to the rest of her body, they knew it was badly broken and would require surgery. By the time they got them out and back into the jungle, the pain was excruciating. Dean endured the pain all the way back to the States, where she finally found relief in the anesthesia administered as she went into surgery.

Coming out of that memory, Dean nodded her head and commented, "Yeah, the pain's a bitch, but he'll be okay once the surgery is over." She looked up at a worried Dirk. "He's as tough as they come. He'll be okay."

Dirk and Katie smiled and nodded in agreement, before Katie spoke next. "Tell us what happened."

"Well, we were out for our regular Saturday run. We drove over to the park, did our stretches, and then started out on the jogging path. We were jogging in place at the crossroad waiting for the traffic to clear, when a beat up Chevy came barreling up the shoulder of the road."

"The car came down the shoulder?" Dean asked for verification.

"Yeah, it just veered off the roadway as it came to the crosswalk. Bill saw it first and pushed me out of the way. Next thing I knew, I saw his body bounce off the front fender and land about thirty feet from me."

"Did you get the plate number?"

"No, it all happened too fast."

"Okay, how about a description of the car?"

"Yeah, I already gave that to the police. It was a two door Chevy Malibu, about a '69 model, cream colored, but it had a lot of rust. The roof was one of those fake leather look jobs, but the cover was flapping on the right front."

"That's a pretty good description," Dean drawled. "What about the driver? Did you get a look?"

"Nope. Didn't have time to look."

"Okay," she said, patting Dirk's shoulder. "The police have a good description. Hopefully they'll be able to find the car."

The threesome looked up as a familiar face came into the waiting room. A grim faced Captain approached the group.

"Hello, Colonel, Katie." They nodded at Captain O'Brien as he took a chair across from them and pulled it up closer. He looked over at Dirk, "You must be Captain Jarvis' friend, Dirk."

"Yes," Dirk nodded. "Have they taken him up to surgery yet?"

"He's on his way now. I thought I'd fill you in before you go up to the surgery waiting room." He cleared his throat before continuing. "He's a very lucky guy. He could have been in a lot worse shape, but he's in excellent physical condition, and he must have had time to react some, because the damage should have been more severe. Right now we're looking at some pins for his femur and a few more for his pelvis. The abrasions will heal with very little scarring, and the concussion is mild." Peter maintained a serious look as Dean waited for the "bad" news. "Unfortunately, he landed very forcefully on a concrete park bench before he hit the ground. His left kidney took the brunt of the blow, and it looks like it will have to be removed."

Dirk paled at the news. "Oh..." he stammered, "but...he'll be okay, won't he?"

"Yes, he will. But, he'll only have one functioning kidney from here out. If he loses that..."

"I understand, Doctor. How long will the surgery take?" Dirk inquired.

"About three hours, give or take. Then, he'll be in recovery for about another two hours. The Colonel," he nodded in Dean's direction, "arranged for a private room. I'm going to observe the surgery and when it's over, I'll come out with Colonel Adams to speak to you."

Captain O'Brien stood, leading the group to the surgical waiting room before he left to scrub for the observation. Dean, Katie, and Dirk sat at a table by the window, ready for the long wait. Conversation was minimal as they waited, but each felt the comforting support of the others as the clock slowly ticked off the minutes. After three hours and forty-five minutes had passed, Captain O'Brien and Colonel Adams entered the waiting room. They informed the group that the surgery had gone well and Captain Jarvis should be out of the recovery room in about two more hours. After the doctors left, the three friends headed to the cafeteria.

* * * * *

Dean and Katie waited with Dirk until Bill was out of the recovery room and settled in his private room. Bill was too groggy from the anesthesia to be able to give them any more details, but they hung around for moral support for Dirk until the night nurse finally kicked them out. It was nearly midnight by the time Dean and Katie crawled back into their bed. Exhausted from the long wait for surgery to be completed and Bill to be transported to his room from the recovery area, the duo was quite content to hit the sack without pursuing any ideas of play to sidetrack them from getting some needed sleep. Katie was already in dreamland and Dean was just about there herself when the phone rang. Both bodies jumped at the sound, frightening two slumbering cats from the bed in the process. Katie was the first to reach the phone, picking it up quickly. As she spoke her name into the receiver, she heard an electronically disguised voice laughing. She immediately hit the speaker button so Dean could hear the caller too. Once the forced laughter subsided, the caller spoke in quick concise sentences.

"Oh, Katie...good to hear your voice for a change. Nice to see the colonel allows you to answer the phone once in a while...or is she indisposed? Hmmm? Have a little late night tête-à-tête? So sorry to interrupt..." Laughter again. "And here I thought you'd be too tired to play after sitting at the hospital all night!"

"You bitch!" Katie shouted. "You did that, didn't you?" Dean reached over to hold Katie and try to get her to calm down, but managed to get smacked in the face as Katie's anger became more...expressive.

"Of course I did! Silly question!"

"And Tom, too?" Katie bellowed at the phone's speaker.

"...And your car...and the email...and the flowers..."

Maniacal laughter could be heard on the other end as Dean finally managed to put her arms around Katie.

"Why? Why are you doing this?" Katie croaked, as Dean's embrace brought her calmness.

"Why? Oh, that's simple...to get the colonel's attention."

Dean bristled at the comment. "You've got my attention."

"I'd thought so... Now, dear Colonel, are you up for a bit of a challenge?"

"I'd love to face you, bitch! You name the place and I'll be there!" came her forceful reply.

"Ah, ah, ah...not yet dear Colonel. But don't worry, I'll be...in touch."

The phone line went dead, leaving Dean and Katie staring at each other in disbelief.

"That bitch 'touches' another one of my friends, and I'll do some 'touching' of my own when I find her," Dean growled.

Chapter
13

10 December, 1300 Hours

Sunday morning began with a flurry of activity as the two women completed their household chores and spent a little extra time on their exercise routines, having missed their Saturday session. After a light lunch of Caesar salad and grilled chicken breasts, the women were now catching up on some reading. Katie was in her favorite chair with her feet propped up on the ottoman, totally engrossed in Dr. Prokov's book. Dean was in the den surfing the net, trying to gather as much information on cancer as she could before her trip to Kansas City. The three cats, as usual, were on the floor in a pool of sunshine, and sound asleep.

Dean dropped her head to her chin, and then began slowly rolling it in a clockwise direction as she tried to work the kinks out of her neck from her hour at the computer. "Don't think I can handle much more of this sitting," she mumbled softly. She logged off her computer, swiveled the chair out from the desk, and headed to the living room and Katie. Taking the stairs two at a time, she entered the living room and slipped behind Katie's chair, reading over her partner's shoulder. Whispering, Dean questioned, "So, you find anything interesting that can help us find our woman?"

Katie marked her page, closed the book, and looked up into Dean's clear blue eyes. "Nope, not yet. But I do find this field very interesting."

Dean shifted from her position to a seat in the recliner next to Katie. "Well, what have we got so far?"

Katie reached over and picked up her notebook from the end table next to her chair. She had been taking notes as she read and now went back to read the ones she had circled. "Okay. First we know we are dealing with a female, and I'd guess she's probably in her thirties."

A raised eyebrow asked the question.

"That's my guess from the reports by the motel staff so far, and just a feeling I have."

Dean nodded in understanding. "What else?"

"She's intelligent, organized, competent, highly skilled, and...arrogant. She seems to have a variety of skills that include an advanced knowledge and competence in computers, bomb making, disguise, information gathering, and she is very motivated. She also seems to be a bit over the edge psychologically." Katie looked up from her notes and found Dean nodding in agreement. "Her vocal tone, even though it's disguised, and her laughter are without doubt a bit maniacal. Then there's the hurting of others just to hurt you..."

"Yeah, I think you've pegged her," Dean drawled. "What about motive?"

"The only motive that I can figure is revenge for something you did to her, or something she thinks you did." Katie looked over at Dean. "Remember that last phone call?" Dean nodded. "She said she was trying to get your attention. Can you think of anyone who would want to do these things to hurt you?"

Dean shook her head, thinking back to the last call. "You know, I've been trying to come up with someone since that call, Katie. It's just that I...I don't know where to start." She dropped her head and looked at her hands. "I've been at this so long, I can hardly remember the 'whys' let alone the 'whos' I've dealt with."

Katie reached into Dean's lap and gently took Dean's hands into hers, surprised at the unusual coldness of them. She covered both with her hands, allowing them to absorb the heat radiating from hers.

"Mmm, your hands are very warm," Dean commented as she looked up smiling into Katie's eyes. "That's unusual for you."

"Yeah." Katie returned the smile. "I was just thinking the

same about the coldness of your hands. Are you feeling okay?"

"Mmhm. Just restless, I guess." Dean looked at her watch. "Let's take a run into town and check on Bill."

That brought a big smile to Katie's face and she asked, "Do you suppose he can eat regular food yet? I know how he loves truffles."

"He sure does, but I don't think they'll let him have any just yet. But we could take him some for later." Dean rose, taking Katie with her. They went to the closet, donned their winter gear, and headed out.

* * * * *

Dean poked her head around the door and was relieved to see a wide-awake Bill propped on his good side, conversing quietly with Dirk. "Hey, you guys want some company?" She swung the door open to allow her and Katie to enter the room.

Bill flashed a valiant smile as he saw his commander. Katie looked around, noticing several vases of flowers, balloons, and...a stuffed teddy bear? "Hey, check out the big tough Army captain... He has a stuffed teddy bear!" Katie giggled as she picked up the aforementioned item, wiggling her eyebrows as she walked it through the air over to Bill's bed. "Awww, isn't this a cute picture?" She turned to face a grinning Dean as she placed the bear next to Bill.

"A real Kodak moment," Dean responded as she watched Bill and Dirk blush.

"Hey, just because I'm a big tough Army captain doesn't mean I can't have a soft side, too."

"Yeah, besides...I'm the one who gave him that bear," Dirk added confidently.

"Hey, you don't have to explain anything to me." Dean held up her hands waving off the verbal assault before changing her expression to a more serious one. "So, Pooh...how are you feeling?" She neatly ducked the empty water cup that was tossed at her and took a seat in the other empty chair by the bed. Katie was laughing so hard she excused herself to the bathroom before she wet her pants, while Bill tried to control his laughter so as not to pull on his incision and cause himself unnecessary pain. Dean set the box of truffles on the bedside table, informing Dirk that Bill wasn't supposed to have any until the nurses okayed it. This got a quick pout from the big man. "Well, you still look a little green around the gills, but not bad for a day after surgery." Her tone took on a more serious quality. "Did you remember anything else from the accident yesterday?"

"Not much to tell, Colonel. I heard the car before I saw it, grabbed Dirk and pushed him out of the way, then got hit. Next thing I remember clearly is waking up here after the surgery and seeing all your cheery faces."

"How about the driver? Did you get a good look at the driver," Katie asked as she returned to the foot of the bed.

"Only thing I remember is that she was laughing. I thought that was pretty strange, and I remember thinking that it would be just my luck to meet my end getting hit by a crazy civilian." He thought a minute longer. "Nope, not much else to give you. I guess her laughter was what I focused on."

"No hair color, eye color, or approximate height?" This time the question came from Dean.

"Short hair...or it could have been in a pony tail. She had a baseball cap on. At first I thought it was a young kid, but then I saw the red lipstick and hoop earrings." He smiled, "Of course, it still could have been a guy... Kids these days..."

"Can you remember anything written on the baseball cap?" Katie asked.

"Nope. Sorry." He sighed deeply. "Like I said, I just focused on her laughing at me."

"Well, it definitely was a female that hit you. I'm sorry to say that she's the same one that has been causing all the havoc in our lives lately and you just happened to be one more of her targets to get at me." Dean reached over and gently placed a hand on Bill's shoulder. "I'm sorry you had to get involved in this. If there is anything I can do..."

"Don't worry, Colonel. I'm not blaming you, so don't feel guilty over this." Bill flashed a tight smile at his commander. "I just hope the loss of my kidney won't interfere with continued service in the Army."

Dean nodded, knowing full well that it probably wouldn't interfere with his performance of duty, but he would have to be very conscious of exposure to infections, especially right after surgery. "We won't worry about that now, Bill. Let's just concentrate on you getting better."

The three visitors stayed until the duty nurse came in to give Bill his pain medication. Shortly after that, Bill started to drift off. Dean and Katie said their good-byes and were walked to the lobby by Dirk before he returned to his partner's bedside.

* * * * *

"Will Bill be able to stay in the service?" Katie inquired as they rode back to Occoquan.

"Probably shouldn't affect his performance once he's recuperated, so I don't see a problem. He'll just have to be a bit more careful and he'll never be assigned to field duty."

"That's good," Katie replied with a sigh of relief. "I know you'd miss him if he had to leave the service."

"Yes, he would be a hard man to replace." Dean smiled as she thought of the young, brash second lieutenant she'd met six years earlier. She could still hear his challenge that he could take on anyone in the obstacle course and beat them by at least five seconds.

Dean had been observing the field training exercises in hopes of finding a young officer that would be able to measure up to the high standards she set for her assistant. His boasting drew her attention, so she'd challenged him, eager to see what he was made of. He'd eagerly accepted the challenge, grinning with self-confidence. Dean had taken off her field jacket and done a few stretches to warm up.

"So, care to make a wager on the outcome?" the young second lieutenant queried. He had heard the rumors about Major Peterson being a hard core field operative, but had no doubt he could beat any man in the training squad, let alone this female officer.

"What did you have in mind?" Major Peterson asked.

"Loser has to buy a round for all the trainees at the Officer's Club tonight," he stated loudly to the hoots and cheers of his fellow trainees.   •

"*Done. But let's give you a little personal incentive,*" *Dean offered as she strode up to the starting line.* "*If you win, you can pick any assignment you want after finishing your training.*"

Second Lieutenant Jarvis nodded his head in agreement, thinking of all the choice assignments he would have to select from.

"*But...if you lose,*" *Dean drawled,* "*you get to work for me.*"

Bill's fellow trainees became very silent at hearing the last part of the wager, and a few shook their heads and began to shout encouragement to Bill, hoping he hadn't bitten off more that he could chew.

The two challengers stepped to the starting line, sizing each other up as they waited for the training officer to begin the race. "*Ready?*" *Two heads nodded in affirmation as the officer raised his hand, knowing in advance that the young lieutenant was probably going to be serving the devil when he lost this bet. The major and the lieutenant assumed the ready position, waiting for the arm to drop. When it did, both were off to a very fast start, taking the dash to the first obstacle neck and neck, then diving to crawl under the rows of barbwire. Dean had the advantage here with her smaller frame and agile moves, but out of the corner of her eye, she noted that the big man was moving extremely well for his bulk and was only a half body length behind her.*

The next obstacle was the mud pit. Dean was up and leaping for the rope just a fraction of a second in front of the young lieutenant. She flew over the pit easily and landed on the firm ground. Bill's weight carried him to the other side, but not quite onto firm footing. Slipping on the edge of the pit, he quickly recovered and sprinted to the climbing wall. His muscular strength had him back in the running as he caught up to the major at the top of the wall, giving her a broad smile as he started climbing up the netting to the drop line platform. His mistake came with that smile. He lost contact with the webbing and slipped sideways towards the edge of the rope net. They were about twenty feet in the air; and though a fall from this height might not be deadly, it would surely result in some damage. Dean caught his slip with her peripheral vision and adjusted her direction in time to reach out and grab the lieutenant's belt from behind, stopping his fall over the edge. Once he regained his balance, Dean released her hold, made sure he had recovered and, grinning, returned to the race.

Reaching the drop line platform, Dean grabbed the rig and swung off into space, lifting her legs straight out in front of her so her body descended through the air in a perfect "L" position. Glancing to her left, she noted that the young lieutenant was almost even with her descent. They both stretched the ride to the maximum, releasing the rig only three feet above the water. Surfacing, the two officers swam the short distance to the shore and headed to the last set of hurdles, easily clearing them for the final sprint to the finish line. When they were twenty-five yards from the finish, they could hear the trainee's cheers of encouragement for their comrade. Bill was inches behind the major, but the cheers were just enough to give him the incentive to push harder. As they crossed the line, they were virtually tied. Slowing down and finally coming to a stop, the two competitors bent at the waist with hands on knees, sucking air greedily into their oxygen-starved bodies. When their breathing and heart rates returned to normal, Bill looked over at the major, grinning.

"So, Major...do we go at it again, or settle for a draw?" Bill stated as he stood, extending his hand to Dean.

"Think a draw will be just fine," Dean replied as she accepted the proffered hand.

"Guess we could both buy the drinks tonight," they agreed, as they walked back to the group of trainees who were still hooting and clapping.

"That was a good run you gave me, Lieutenant. At least I can still say I've never been beaten." Dean looked over at the young man, making up her mind. "I'd still like to offer you an assignment of your choosing. Just let me know after you've had time to think about your choice."

"Thanks, Major. I appreciate that." Nodding as he thought about the opportunities that were now available, he turned and faced her. "I have something in mind already."

Surprised, Dean lifted an eyebrow waiting for him to continue.

"I'd like to be assigned to you, Ma'am, if that meets with your approval." Bill had made up his mind on the rope net, win or lose—he wanted to be assigned to the major, no matter what

the rumor mill said about her. He knew that she was more than she appeared.

This request had both Dean's eyebrows into her hairline. Dean had heard the rumors: how she was referred to as the bitch from hell that had ice in her veins, how she would rather work alone than with a team, and how ruthless she was in the field. Shaking her head in disbelief, she asked him why he would choose her when he could have any assignment he wanted.

His reply was simple and honest. "Well, Ma'am, I've heard that you're a hardcore loner, and that you demand perfection when you work with others, and that's just fine with me. But, when you stopped to keep me from falling off the net up there, well, that tells me something a lot more important about the real you. I know that if anything happened to me in the field, you wouldn't leave me hanging, or leave me behind." His eyes searched the ice blue ones across from him. "Besides, how else could I get the chance to challenge you again?" He broke into a wide grin as he watched the ice in her eyes warm and a sliver of a smile appear on her face.

"Consider it done, Lieutenant," Dean said softly. "But you'd better finish at the top of your class, or I'll retrain you myself."

"Yes, Ma'am," Lieutenant Jarvis replied sharply.

"Now, how about those drinks at the Officer's Club?" Dean said as they returned to the waiting group of trainees.

"Earth to Dean," Katie called as she waved a hand in front of Dean's face, glad that she was driving and not Dean.

"Huh? Oh, sorry. I was just thinking about how Bill and I first met," she offered, as she returned her focus to Katie.

"I bet that was quite a meeting."

"It certainly was," Dean agreed, and began to tell Katie the story.

Chapter
14

Dean and Katie stopped at the Golden Swan in Occoquan for dinner on their way back from Walter Reed. As they entered their favorite restaurant, Ling Soo, the elderly owner, greeted the couple, her wizened old face melting into a smile of genuine warmth as she watched the two women enter. Stepping from behind the cashier's counter, she slowly moved toward the door.

"Ah, Missy Dean and Missy Katie. You want usual table?" the elderly Chinese woman asked as she bowed with her greeting.

"Sure thing, Ling Soo." Dean was truly fond of the old woman, and she placed her hands on the elder's stooped shoulders. "How's business?" The concern on Dean's face captured the old woman's attention.

"Ah, it go good since you chase bad man way. You look." She turned toward the crowded room and waved her hand around. Dean followed the motion with her eyes while her mind went back to the day she'd stopped a two-bit punk from collecting "protection" money from the newly established immigrants. For five months now, she had been coming back regularly, just to make sure he didn't try to return. "Been busy all day. Chang have to call in number two son to help in kitchen," she said in her clipped Oriental accent. Looking back at the women, she added, "You go now. Table ready. I have Chang make you special dinner." Ling Soo called instructions to her daughter in Chinese, quickly clapping her hands twice as she finished. Smiling, she added, "Number one daughter bring you nice plum wine, okay?" Both women nodded their approval, smiling as they made their way through the crowded establishment toward their usual table.

Dean's favorite table was in the rear of the establishment. There, she could put her back to the wall and watch everything that went on. At first, Katie thought this precaution was a bit over the top for their now-friendly neighborhood, but she soon began to appreciate the advantages of being able to watch the clientele as they came and went. As avid people watchers, Katie and Dean often made a little game of trying to guess the backgrounds of the people they observed.

"Okay, the lady in the navy sweater by the window," Katie began, as they focused on the partial profile the woman presented. "Looks like a teacher to me. The back of her head reminds me of Ms. Lumpetti, my seventh grade math teacher."

"Nah." Dean looked more closely at the woman in question, catching the target's reflection in the window for more clues. "I'll bet she's a minister. Just look at the dowdy outfit, and the old fashioned shoes."

"Yeah, right," Katie chortled and looked the woman over one more time, trying to picture her in front of a math class, then in front of a congregation. "Nope, still looks like a math teacher to me."

Within seconds, the woman in question removed the napkin from her lap, picked up her check and pocketbook, and stood. As she turned towards them to head to the cashier, the clerical collar she was wearing stood out clearly.

"Holy cow!" the blonde groaned as she turned to face Dean. "You're good!"

"Not really." Her partner grinned back at her, eyes twinkling mischievously. "I caught the reflection of her clerical collar in the window. Just pays to use everything at your disposal to supplement your powers of observation."

Katie just shook her head and filed that information away for retrieval the next time she found herself on a stakeout. They continued with their little game as they waded through each course of their excellent meal. As the owner brought the fortune cookies and the check, Katie caught a movement in her peripheral vision. When Ling Soo left the table with Dean's credit card, Katie was surprised to see a familiar figure standing at the cash register.

"Hey, that's Dr. Prokov by the register," Katie whispered as Dean looked up for a view of the forensic psychologist. "I sure didn't see her when we came in, did you?"

"Well, considering I didn't know what she looked like, I'd have to say no to that one, love." They watched as Ling Soo's daughter brought a bag of carry out to the register and handed it to Dr. Prokov. Dean looked over at Katie and winked. "Guess that answers that question, doesn't it?"

"Would you like to meet her? I can catch her before she leaves."

"No, not tonight, I have more important things to do tonight." Dean lowered her gaze and spoke in a sultry voice. "I was thinking that maybe we could find something better for dessert than these fortune cookies."

Just listening to Dean's voice sent shivers up Katie's spine, and she felt the heat rise in her cheeks as she caught the passion in her lover's sparkling eyes. Finding her voice temporarily absent, Katie grabbed the fortune cookies and stuffed them into her pockets, slipped her right hand into Dean's left, and pulled her partner to her feet. Dean grinned at the eager response to her suggestion, picking up their coats from the backs of the chairs with her free hand. They stopped at the cashier's counter long enough for Dean to sign the credit card slip, then put on their coats and exit for the parking lot, leaving a grinning Ling Soo behind. In ten minutes, they were pulling into their garage, eager to explore dessert possibilities. By the time they reached their bedroom, neither woman had a stitch of clothing left on her body.

Dean stopped by the bed and pulled Katie into her warm embrace. "I'll never tire of loving you, Katherine O'Malley," Dean whispered as she drank in her lover's beauty.

Katie's arms wrapped around Dean's back and began a slow dance up and down, finally settling on her buttocks and giving them a gentle squeeze. "Mmmm, and I'll never tire of receiving your love," Katie answered seductively as she nuzzled her head between Dean's breasts, inhaling the welcome scent of her partner. "I don't know what I did to deserve your love."

"I think that should be the other way around, sweetheart. I certainly don't deserve to have someone as wonderful as you."

Dean bent her head and sought the comfort and confirmation of mutual love in Katie's soft lips. Finding what she was seeking, she deepened the kiss, her tongue requesting permission to explore further. Katie moaned as she parted her lips to allow complete access, beginning an exploration of her own as she dueled with Dean's thrusting tongue, intent on matching the passion she felt from her partner. Soon, hands began to move, exploring every inch of skin, kneading breasts and teasing nipples until they were taut and begging for attention from lips and tongues. As their passion rose with each stroke of their hands, press of lips and lick of tongues, Dean slowly backed toward the bed, falling in a controlled motion, bringing Katie down on top of her. During the entire descent, she never lost contact with the breast she was attending to.

Katie moaned again in pure joy as she felt her body react to her lover's touch. "Oh, Dean," she whispered, "please...don't ever stop loving me."

The reply came in a deep timbre as Dean barely removed her mouth from Katie's nipple. "I'm yours for as long as you'll have me, my love."

"Then you're mine for eternity," Katie breathed into Dean's ear as she was gently turned onto her back. Dean moved over Katie's body, where she resumed her efforts to bring her lover to a complete, satiated, climax.

* * * * *

Two hours later, Dean was picking up articles of clothing that were scattered from the front entrance to the hall outside the bedroom, while Katie fed her three felines, praising them for being so patient and giving them an extra spoonful of their favorite food for their trouble. When Dean entered the kitchen, arms full of clothing, Katie couldn't help but chuckle at the sight of her naked lover bearing their discarded clothes.

"What?" Dean asked, both eyebrows raised.

"You just look adorable, love, standing there with your arms full of clothes and not a stitch on your body."

"Well, you look pretty adorable yourself, sweetheart." Dean gave both eyebrows a quick Groucho motion and grinned. "And, either you're cold, or you're glad to see me."

That comment earned her a quickly wadded and tossed kitchen towel, which she snatched out of the air and added to her pile without dropping a single item.

"You...are...incorrigible," Katie admonished as she walked over and gave Dean a quick kiss. "But," she kissed her again, "that's one of the things I love about you."

"Just one?" Dean questioned, as she bent her head for another kiss.

"Mmmm, one of many things," Katie offered, as she placed her arms around Dean's neck and fell into her lover's gaze.

"Ah, that's good, 'cause I have many skills." Dean grinned at Katie as she balanced the clothing between them, then moved one hand behind her lover's back while stooping and tucking the other under Katie's knees. She stood, carrying Katie and the clothes towards the bedroom, stopping at the kitchen light switch long enough for Katie to flip it off. A short time later, both women were snug under the bed covers, nestled in each other's arms and slipping gently into the welcome state of deep REM sleep.

* * * * *

The woman in the car slipped off her headphones and smiled evilly while picking up the fortune cookie she had saved from her dinner. Unwrapping it, she pulled out the thin strip of paper and read her fortune aloud. "The battle between good and evil is as continuous as a whirlpool seeking its center." Tossing the paper on the floor of the car, she popped the pieces of the cookie into her mouth, mumbling around the bits as she chewed, "Well, isn't that special." Swallowing her cookie, she began laughing as she started the vehicle and began the drive back to Quantico.

* * * * *

Katie felt the bonds release, and her body began to fall forward into the blackness of the abyss, her screams lost in the deafening roar that surrounded her as she tumbled through icy cold space. Her last view before blackness overcame her was of Dean's sapphire eyes as she fell away from her lover... Katie awoke when her body jolted upright, arms reaching out into the darkness of the bedroom, her scream still echoing in the room.

Dean sat up with Katie's scream, assessing the room around them. "What's wrong?" were the first words out of her mouth, as she determined there was no threat existing in the room. "Are you all right?" she added as she quickly pulled Katie into her arms.

Katie eagerly welcomed the safety and warmth of her lover's embrace. Shaking from the images still vividly emblazoned in her mind, she began to cry.

"Sweetheart, are you okay?" Dean asked again as she cupped Katie's chin and lifted it to peer into her face.

Heaving raggedly, Katie nodded slightly. Dean wiped away the tears, pulled Katie's head to her chest, and started to gently rock her. "Shhh. It was just a bad dream. You're safe, love."

"Oh, Dean...it was so real. I...I tried to call out to you, but you couldn't hear me." She stopped and shakily sucked in a breath. "Then whatever was holding me, let go; and I began to fall." Looking up at Dean, tears still falling, she added, "And all I could see were your beautiful eyes." Katie put her head back against Dean's chest and tightened her arms around her.

Still rocking and cooing softly, Dean stroked Katie's hair, placing several soft kisses on the short blonde tresses until she felt Katie settling down. "Hmmm, no more Kung Pao for you so close to bedtime, sweetheart," she chuckled, and felt Katie grin at the comment.

"Yeah, that third helping was probably the culprit," Katie considered, as her sense of security returned. Both women giggled as they remembered Ling Soo's expression as she came to the table to see how they'd liked Chang's special dinner. *Ling Soo could not believe that the two women had eaten the entire meal and had no leftovers to take home. The old woman even looked under the table for the telltale carryout containers, questioning them when she couldn't find any. "How you eat all food? Chang not make enough? I go get more! So sorry...be right back." They'd had a hard time stopping the old woman from fetching more food and reprimanding Chang, but she finally conceded, although not completely convinced, that Chang had made enough food for them.*

"Mmmm, and the glasses of plum wine didn't help either,"

Dean added. "Think you can go back to sleep now?"

Katie nodded, and they eased back onto the pillows. Dean positioned herself to cradle Katie in her arms, supplying the young woman with the sanctuary she needed to fall back to sleep.

Chapter
15

11 December, 0600 Hours

"What time will you be home?" Katie called from the bathroom as she stepped out of the shower.

"Probably about the same time you pull in. I have a late meeting with Mary before I can leave." Dean stepped out of the walk-in closet, already dressed in her uniform, but still shoeless. "I'll feed the cats and give Shug her medicine."

"Thanks, love. That extra fifteen minutes in bed put me off track this morning." Katie exited the bathroom, still wrapped in her bath towel. She glanced at her lover and smiled appreciatively, taking in the striking beauty that was accentuated by the uniform with all of its accoutrements. Sighing, she said, "I guess I'll always be a sucker for a woman in uniform."

Dean smiled in return, stepping in close to Katie so she could caress her face with a gentle touch. "Mmhmm," Dean replied in a husky voice, "and I'm a sucker for you wrapped in a towel." The lovers leaned into each other's lips for a heated kiss, which would have led to them both being very late had not the ringing of the phone interrupted them. Dean backed away reluctantly and headed for the phone, picking it up on the third ring.

"Peterson," she spoke into the receiver with authority.

"Colonel, this is Lieutenant Green. Sorry if I woke you."

"Not at all, Lieutenant. I've been awake for quite a while now. What can I do for you?"

"Well, I was hoping I would catch you before you left for the

Pentagon. I read the report about Captain Jarvis' accident, and I was wondering if it would be okay for me to drop by to see him." The police officer paused before continuing. "I know it's not in our jurisdiction, but with the information you've provided about the incidents you've been experiencing, I couldn't help thinking it's related."

"Oh, it's related all right. The bitch called here and took complete responsibility for it," Dean scoffed bitterly.

"Ah, I see." Pausing, Lieutenant Green then added, "Do you think the captain would mind if I stopped by to see him?"

"No, I'm certain he wouldn't. He wants to see this woman caught as much as we do. By the way, any luck with getting a sketch drawn yet?"

"No, not 'til the night clerk comes back from vacation. She'll be back on duty Thursday night."

"That's right," Dean sighed. "With everything that's been happening, I forgot about that."

"Well, I'll give Captain Jarvis a call later this morning. Maybe he'll remember something new by the time I get there."

"He might; but he was pretty lucid when we talked to him yesterday, and he didn't have anything to add. But keep me informed, will you?"

"Absolutely, Colonel. Have a good day." Lieutenant Green hung up, and Dean replaced the receiver in its cradle then slipped on her shoes.

Katie was nearly dressed and was working on drying her hair as Dean left the bedroom to feed the cats. She had just finished setting their bowls on the floor when Katie came in and hugged her as she stood. "Hey, maybe we'll get a break soon," Katie offered as she gave Dean a gentle squeeze.

"Yeah, maybe." Dean returned the hug before releasing her partner. She took two travel mugs out of the cupboard and set a tea bag in each. "Want some cereal this morning? I bought some Frosted Mini Wheats."

Katie gave Dean an affectionate poke. "You and your sweet tooth."

"What's wrong with Mini Wheats? They're good for you," Dean responded, a mock look of hurt on her face.

"You are sooo bad," Katie teased as she wrapped her arms

around her partner. Looking at her watch, she said, "I think I have time to sit and eat a quick bowl of cereal with you before I have to head out. I guess you can pour me a bowl, too."

The two women ate their cereal and discussed the day they had ahead of them. Dean was following up on reports from the field that might expose a threat to one of their installations in Europe, and Katie was going to be at Quantico, spending the day back in the classroom for more orientation sessions.

"I really hate sitting in a classroom all day," she commented as she picked up the cereal bowls, taking them to the sink.

"Are you sure you want to do this?" Dean questioned as she put the box of cereal back into the cupboard.

"Oh, yeah! Teaching a class is a lot better than taking a class. I'm actually looking forward to that part." She finished washing the breakfast dishes, opting to let them air dry in the dish rack. "By Friday, we'll be finished with our orientation classes. Next week, we'll be able to concentrate on putting together our class outlines and lesson plans. I'm really looking forward to making my classes as interesting and challenging as possible."

"Well, I've got to hand it to you sweetheart. I don't think I would have the patience to deal with new recruits." They exited the kitchen, picking up their briefcases as they headed to the coat closet by the front door.

"They won't all be rookies, Dean. Some of the recruits have already been through a police academy and are just making a change in their careers."

Setting their briefcases down on the bench by the front door, they removed their coats from the closet. Dean slipped on her coat, before helping Katie into hers. "Mark my words, love, those will be the toughest ones to teach."

Katie tilted her head in thought. "You really think so?"

"Oh, yeah." Dean nodded knowingly. "While some injuries healed, one of my temporary postings was as an instructor for the Intelligence Section. I was never so glad that I heal quickly." Dean snickered as she reflected on the assignment. "I think the class was even happier than I was."

Katie reached over, placing a hand on her lover's arm. "But, Dean, what about the terrific job you did with the ROTC group up in the Catskills?"

"Hey, they were kids, very teachable, and not seasoned officers who thought they knew everything. That's what I'm getting at. A little knowledge can be a dangerous thing." Dean bent down and placed a soft kiss on Katie's lips, not wanting to part as the kiss was eagerly returned. Unfortunately, Dean was aware that they were getting off a bit later than usual, so she forced herself to break off. "Mmm, love you," she whispered softly.

"Love you, too," Katie replied, eyes still closed from the kiss, the corners of her mouth raised in a slight smile. "See you tonight," she added, opening her eyes to meet Dean's deep sapphires still locked on her face. After another quick kiss, the women ruefully grabbed their briefcases, set the security alarm, and headed their separate ways.

*   *   *   *   *

Wow, the morning sure flew by; and boy, am I hungry! Katie's thoughts swirled in her head as she gazed across the cafeteria looking for a quiet spot to have her lunch and do a little reading. She managed to find a lone table in the corner and walked quickly toward it. Intent on reading more of Dr. Prokov's book, she settled in, propping the book up in front of her. Holding her BLT carefully so it wouldn't drip on the borrowed volume, she managed to eat her sandwich and read. She was so focused on the chapter she was reading, she did not see Dr. Prokov approach.

"You really should give it a rest, Katie," the psychologist commented in her Oxford accent as she stood next to the table, lunch tray in her hand. A surprised Katie looked up to find the woman smiling down on her. "May I join you?" Meisha asked, indicating the empty chair in front of her.

"Oh, um, yes...of course, Dr. Prokov. Please do." Katie quickly marked her place and closed the book, putting it on the other empty chair.

"You know, you really don't have to read that thing to try to impress me," the doctor commented as she sat in her chair, waving at the book Katie was setting down. "After all, you're not one of my students," she said with a wink and a chuckle.

Blushing, Katie lowered her head in embarrassment, but quickly regained her composure. Looking up at the psychologist, she smiled back and nodded. "I just really find your book quite fascinating, Dr. Prokov."

"Well, evil is my forte," she chuckled lightly. "And, please, call me Meisha. We are colleagues after all."

"Okay, Meisha." Katie grinned back at the woman. "Mind if I ask you a personal question?" Dr. Prokov raised both eyebrows in surprise, indicating her permission with a slight nod. "You look too young to be able to have acquired the experience needed to be an expert in this field. I'm just amazed at all the information that you have access to." Blushing again, Katie realized that she hadn't phrased her question the way she should have. "I'm sorry. That didn't quite come out the way I wanted. It's just that you don't seem much older than I am."

Meisha smiled at the question. *Well, dearie...if you only knew the truth,* she thought. *The real Dr. Prokov was a bit of a recluse and a good bit older and is now quite a bit dead... And thankfully, she hated having her picture on her book jackets.* "Oh, I guess you could say I'm a prodigy of sorts. Always had an inquisitive mind as a child, and was especially good at mind games. Guess I just come by it naturally."

The two women ate while engaging in companionable conversation, Katie doing most of the questioning and Meisha deftly providing the answers. By the time their lunches were consumed and it was time to return to class, Katie felt much more relaxed around the intimidating psychologist. Picking up their refuse and walking over to the tray drop off, Katie thanked Dr. Prokov for having lunch with her. Meisha suggested that they have lunch again the next day to continue their conversation. Katie agreed enthusiastically before heading off to her next session.

Well, that went quite well, the imposter thought to herself as she walked back to the office she had been assigned. *Come to me little fly... Come rest in my web. I promise not to hurt you...much!*

* * * * *

Colonel Peterson was pacing the conference room as several officers from the European Intelligence Section filled her in on the situation in Germany. Their reports verified that the threat to the

Command and General Staff Symposium to be held in Heidelberg during the upcoming weekend had some substance. Since a lot of Europe's top brass were going to be in attendance, General Carlton wanted Dean to evaluate the reports and make a recommendation by 1700 Thursday.

Dean stopped her pacing in front of a young captain. "Captain Jaynes, are you sure this isn't a false report?"

"Yes, Ma'am. We've been watching this group for a while now. They're really hard core, Ma'am...way off the zealot's scale."

"That's right, Colonel," added another officer. "They've been up to some real nasty crap lately, and are tied in with some neo-Nazi factions here in the US. With ATF cracking down on some of their US factions, they're figuring to do some damage to our command staff as a retaliatory action, in hopes that it will cause us to back off."

Dean nodded at the comments and paced back over to her seat at the table. She sat down and pored through the reports and pictures one more time. Selecting a picture of one of the suspected agitators, she studied his face as it rekindled memories of a happier time. "Okay, tell me about this guy again."

Captain Jaynes picked up a file and flipped it open. "That's Gunter Krieg. He's the new leader of this faction: born in Frankfurt, educated at Columbia University in the U.S., graduated magna cum laude, received a Chemical Engineering degree with a Political Science minor. Some say he's the mix-master for the recent bombings that have been taking place. Both parents are dead. He lost his only brother in an ATF raid here in the States, and his sister was supposedly raped by a group of drunken U.S. soldiers." He closed the file and looked up at Colonel Peterson who was still staring at the picture. "His followers will do whatever he tells them. He's quite a charismatic leader and can really whip them into a frenzy when he wants. Some think he could have given Hitler a run for his money."

Dean looked up at this comment. "That good, huh?"

"Yes, Ma'am, he certainly is. He's kept a very low profile; no one knew anything about him until just recently. We think his sister's rape sent him over the edge. She's been in a psychiatric ward since the attack and is uncommunicative. He joined the group shortly after the assault on her."

"Has he been linked to any of the recent neo-Nazi actions?"

"We haven't been able to pin anything on him...yet. But he's definitely up to his eyeballs in this one."

Dean nodded at the information presented by the captain. She set the picture down, raised her arms, and folded her hands behind her head. "Well, gentlemen, what do you propose?"

"A black op to take him out," the captain replied immediately, hoping to get quick approval and set his men in motion.

Dean pursed her lips as she considered the pros and cons. The cons were overbalancing the scales for the moment, so she shook her head in a negative response. "I don't think that would be wise, Captain. At least, not at this time." The six officers around the table sat in silence, waiting for the colonel to continue. "I'm going to fly to Germany on the first available transport. I want to check out a few things before I make my recommendation to the general." Heads nodded around the table. "That will be all, gentlemen. Dismissed." Seats pushed back, folders were collected, and the six officers filed quietly out of the room, leaving Dean alone with her thoughts.

Gunter, what are you up to? Last I knew, you were happily teaching in the university, Dean thought as she removed her hands from behind her head. She picked up her copy of the files and looked at Gunter's picture once more. *It's been a long time since our undergraduate days. You've gotten older my friend...and your boyish look has turned very hard. Will you listen to me? Will you trust me to help you? I've got to try to reach you before you do something very stupid.* With determination, Dean stood and collected her paperwork, slipped it into the olive drab file folder, and headed back to her office.

* * * * *

Katie flipped open her cell phone as she walked to her car. "Agent O'Malley," she answered, as she pulled out her car keys.

"Hey." Dean's deep tones needed no identification.

"Hi, love. What's up? I'm just getting into my car."

"Mmm, good. You'll get here before I have to leave, then."

"Leave? Did something happen to your dad?" Katie threw

her backpack onto the passenger side, slipped into the driver's
seat, and closed the door.

"No, not Dad. I have to catch a transport to Heidelberg at
1900."

"Oh, that situation is worse, huh?" She started up the Boxster and checked her rear view mirror before backing out of her
parking slot.

"Yes, and no. I'll fill you in when you get here. Drive carefully, love."

"I will. See you in a bit." Katie closed her cell phone and
slipped it back into the pouch on her backpack as she slowed to a
stop at the exit from the DEA training campus. *Good thing our
session was over early, love. I'd hate to miss seeing you before
you left.* The Boxster pulled out into the light traffic, quickly
heading north. Katie managed to cut the twenty-five minute commute down to nineteen as she pulled into the garage. She hurriedly grabbed her bag, exited the sports car, and jogged to the
house. The door opened before she reached it, and she dropped
her backpack just inside the door and fell into her lover's embrace.
Still holding on tightly, Katie whispered, "Glad I was able to leave
early."

"Mmm, me too. I don't have much time before I have to leave
for the base." Dean checked her watch. "It's nearly 1800 now,
and it will take twenty minutes to get there. C'mon, you can help
me finish packing, then you can drive me to the airfield."

Katie released her hold on Dean and slipped off her coat,
hanging it on the doorknob before picking up her backpack and
following Dean to the bedroom. "So, how long will you be gone?"

"Not long. I have to give Mary my recommendations by 1700
Thursday. I figure I can catch another transport back to Fort
Leavenworth from Heidelberg, then rent a car from there to Kansas City." Dean selected another uniform and folded it neatly into
her suitcase. "I already called Martha and told her I wouldn't be
in until Thursday or maybe Friday."

"I'm glad you're still planning on going to KC," the blonde
commented as she folded a pair of Dean's jeans. "Will you be able
to extend your visit?"

"That will depend on how things are going back here. I hate
leaving you alone too long with that nut case still on the loose."

Dean stopped her packing and turned to face her lover, placing both hands on Katie's shoulders. "Katie, you have to promise me you won't put yourself at risk. Keep a low profile while I'm gone, okay?"

"Don't worry, love. I'll probably stay at Quantico until you're back."

"What about the cats?" As if on cue, Spice jumped up on the bed and began examining the suitcase lying there. Deciding it looked like a nice place to nap, she jumped in and curled up into a ball on top of Dean's leather jacket.

"Dirk's going to pick them up tonight on his way home from the hospital," Katie replied as she slipped out of Dean's hands to scoop Spice out of the suitcase. "I called him on the way home. He said he'd be glad to take care of them for a few days."

"Good. I'll feel much better knowing you're safe at the center." Dean reached over to pet the purring cat. "That woman would have to be crazy to try to get to you there."

* * * * *

A half-mile from the house, Meisha smiled as she listened in on the conversation. "Perfect! My little fly will be staying close to my web. Now I just have to lure her into my little trap, and then, Colonel...we'll get to play again. Only this time, I'll win."

* * * * *

By 1730, Dean was removing her suitcase from the backseat of the SUV. The women had said their more personal goodbyes at the house, knowing that they would have to maintain their distance at the military installation. Dean slipped her head back through the still open passenger door and winked at her lover. "I'll call you when I get there. Promise to stay out of trouble?"

"Me stay out of trouble? How about you? You're the one that's going to try to talk to a neo-Nazi fanatic," Katie challenged, "while I'm going to be safe and sound at Quantico."

"Yeah, well, make sure you stay that way," Dean countered. "I'll be fine. I'll find Gunter and get this mess straightened out without any bloodshed. Keep your cell phone on. I don't know when I'll be able to call once I start looking for him, but I'll contact you as soon as I can." With that said, Dean left the SUV and headed off at an easy jog to the tarmac and the waiting transport. Even in BDU's, Katie could sense her lover's power and strength hidden beneath them. She continued watching Dean's athletic body maneuvering toward the plane, leaving her parking spot only after her lover had disappeared into the bowels of the huge aircraft.

Chapter
16

The insistent chirp of a cell phone finally broke through Katie's deep slumber. One eyelid slowly opened, allowing Katie to make out the shape of the offending instrument on the night-stand. "Okay, okay...I'm coming!" she grumbled, as she slipped her arm out from under the bed covers and grabbed at the phone, fumbling it and almost dropping it. Finally flipping the phone open, she mumbled into the receiver, "This had better be good."

"Mmm, well, how good do you want it to be?" Her lover's sultry tones reverberated in her ear. "I could tell you how much I miss you already, and what I plan on doing to you when I get back... Will that do?"

Katie closed her eyes and smiled as her mind easily pulled up the image of her lover. "Hey. So you're there already?"

"Yep. Just touched down," Dean replied. "Had to refuel over England, but we're here now."

Katie opened her eyes and looked at the clock. "Did you get any sleep on the way over?"

"Mmhm. Slept like a baby. I'm going to change into my civvies and see if I can find my friend quickly." She paused, smiling into her phone as she walked down the tarmac toward a waiting jeep. "I just wanted to say good morning, and remind you to be safe."

"No problem on this end. I left for the Training Center at 9:30 last night. Got a nice cozy room and a comfy bed. All I'm missing is my personal bed warmer. You have such a way of warming me up."

"Well, hold that thought. I'll be back as soon as I can. Gotta go now. Keep your phone on, and I'll call later."

"Okay, I will. You be careful, too." Katie yawned as she flipped the phone closed and replaced it on the nightstand. "Ugh. I'm glad my classes won't be starting this early."

She stretched, yawning again, then rolled over to catch another thirty minutes of shut-eye until her alarm went off.

* * * * *

Dean closed her cell phone and slipped it into the breast pocket of her BDU jacket, buttoning it closed to keep it from falling out. As she neared the jeep, a young corporal jumped out from behind the steering wheel and saluted before taking her luggage and placing it in the back of the jeep.

"Where to, Colonel?" the young man asked as they slid into the front seats.

"VOQ first, then motor pool," Dean replied as she snapped the canvas door shut against a brisk winter wind. "Nice weather."

"You could call it that, Colonel. Today is actually pretty mild compared to yesterday, but this isn't normal weather for Heidelberg." The soldier put the jeep into gear and drove quickly through the gate separating the airstrip from the rest of the base. Winding between drab buildings and blowing snow, he expertly threaded his way to the Visiting Officers' Quarters, skidding to a stop next to the main walkway. "Can I take your bag in for you, Colonel?" the corporal asked as he moved to open the door.

"No thanks, Corporal. Just wait here and keep the engine running," Dean replied as she turned in her seat and grabbed the handle to her small bag. "I'll be out in less than five minutes if they have my room assigned."

"Yes, Ma'am. Everything should be in order. I checked before I left to pick you up."

Checking the nameplate on his uniform, Dean said, "Good work, Corporal Jenkins. I'll be right out."

She opened the jeep door and stepped out into the blustery wind, hanging on to her headgear and her bag as she trotted up the short walk to the main entrance. True to her word, she was back in the jeep in under five minutes, dressed totally in black: jeans, turtleneck, V-neck sweater, and leather jacket. She'd replaced her combat boots with a pair of well-worn hiking boots. Her hair was down and pulled back into a ponytail, and a black knit ski cap covered the top of her head. Slipping back into the passenger seat, she directed the soldier to take her to the motor pool. Corporal Jenkins immediately put the jeep in gear and headed out once again. Catching a few glimpses of her with his peripheral vision as he drove through the base, he couldn't help but wonder about his passenger. Within fifteen minutes, they were inside the motor pool office, grateful to be inside a warm building. Another fifteen minutes, and Dean was pulling out of the garage in an old VW van, with Corporal Jenkins in the passenger seat.

"You really don't have to take me to my barracks, Ma'am," the young man offered sincerely.

"No problem, Corporal. It's on the way off post, and I wouldn't want you to freeze your tail off on the way home." She turned to the soldier and smiled. "Besides, I may need you again, and it wouldn't do to have you in the infirmary suffering from exposure." Her smile alone warmed the corporal as he blushed at her genuine concern. He'd never had a "full bird" treat him like a real person before; and he wondered again about this curious officer—who seemed way too young to be a full colonel—and just what she was doing in Heidelberg. She certainly didn't seem like the rest of the brass that was coming in for the symposium.

* * * * *

Checking her watch, Dean parked the car along the Neckar River and walked across the old stone arch bridge. Passing through the old Gate Arch, she turned left and headed to the Vetter Bar to meet with her intelligence contact. The Vetter Bar was a popular place any time of year, but especially around Christmas when they had their special Christmas beer on tap. Dean opened the door to the bar and was greeted by a mixture of aromas: cigarette smoke, food, beer, and of course, humanity. Slipping easily through the packed lunch hour crowd, she scanned the room and estimated it to be a balance of tourists, students, and townsfolk. As she approached, the woman behind the large oak bar asked for her order.

"Ein Glas Ihres Weihnachtsbier, bitte." Dean waved at the sign advertising their special holiday brew. The bartender nodded and drew a large stein of the beer and, placing it in front of Dean, asked if she wanted to order anything to eat. Dean shook her head and gave the woman a Deutschmark for the drink. Hefting the mug in hand, she turned and leaned back against the bar, surveying the crowd once more. As she sipped the potent brew, a young man dressed like many of the town folk took a position next to her at the bar.

"Afternoon, Colonel," he whispered as he put his beer stein to his lips. Dean nodded and took another sip of her beer. "I've got a table in the back by the kitchen. It's a little quieter there."

"Lead the way," Dean said, pulling away from the bar.

They made their way through the crowd and around the left corner of the bar, heading toward the table. Dean took the seat that placed her back to the corner so she had a full view of the throng.

"So, Captain, any leads on where Gunter is holed up?"

"Our best guess is that he's somewhere in the Black Forest area to the south. We have a man in his camp, but he's not scheduled to contact us until tonight." The captain paused to smile at a young blonde server as she came out of the kitchen.

"Good." Dean slipped a plain white envelope out of her pocket and gave it to her contact. "When he checks in, give him this message for Gunter."

The captain was surprised by this move, but calmly placed the envelope in his breast pocket, curious as to the message it contained, but not wanting to open it in this public place. "Will do, Colonel. Anything else?"

"Yes. Find out what you can about the rape of Gunter's sister. Her name is Elsa." Dean paused, shaking her head slightly as she remembered the time she'd first met Elsa. At fourteen, she was already turning heads with her youthful beauty; Dean could just imagine what adulthood had done to enhance it. "And, make sure your man gets the message to give to Gunter. With any luck, we'll be able to end this without any bloodshed." As the captain left the table, Dean realized that it had been twelve hours since she'd had anything to eat. She spied the blonde server heading toward her table and figured she'd better eat now while she had the chance.

* * * * *

Katie hit the snooze button on her alarm three times before she finally rolled out of bed. After hurrying through her shower, she blew her hair dry and dressed in a set of DEA warm ups and a light brown Gore-Tex anorak. She grabbed her backpack, shut the door to her room, and headed off to the cafeteria for a badly needed cup of caffeine. She was jogging down the path through the woods when she noted a figure stepping out of a Yellow Cab. If the trees had been full with leaves, she never would have been able to see the road, but with their cover gone, she was able to see down to the roadway fairly easily. As the automobile headed off toward the gate, the figure turned and started up an intersecting path. As she neared the junction of their paths, Katie was surprised to recognize the figure as Dr. Prokov.

Hmm, wonder where she's coming from? I thought she was housed in the staff dormitory on the other side of the complex, Katie thought as she slowed her approach. *Well, maybe she stays with a friend off-site.* She slowed her pace a bit more to arrive at the juncture at the same time as Dr. Prokov. Obviously lost in thought, Dr. Prokov was not aware of the figure watching her approach.

"Good Morning, Doctor," Katie called as the psychologist entered her line of sight.

Quickly looking up, Meisha scanned the area where the voice came from with a predator's fierce glare, and just as quickly softened her visage as she recognized Katie. The initial gaze directed at Katie unnerved the young agent, sending a chill down her spine as it seemed to slice right through to her soul.

"Oh, Katie," Meisha responded, pasting on a smile. "You surprised me. I was running late, and didn't expect to find anyone on the path."

Recovering, Katie smiled. "I was a bit late myself. Guess I hit the snooze button one too many times!" Both women forced a laugh as they walked toward the cafeteria together. Katie raised a hand to rub her neck in an effort to subdue the prickling feeling she was experiencing at the nape. The savageness she'd seen in Doctor Prokov's eyes stirred memories and began to fire synapses in her subconscious brain. Her conscious mind, on the other hand, continued to wonder just where the profiler was coming back from, but after the glimpse into those fierce eyes, she decided not to ask...at least not just yet.

They continued up the path in relative silence until they reached a cluster of buildings. Katie asked if Meisha wanted to join her for a quick bite. The psychologist declined, indicating that she had already eaten, but suggested that they might share a table at lunch. Katie smiled and waved goodbye, then hurriedly headed into the cafeteria for a quick, light breakfast, wondering just where the psychologist had had her breakfast.

* * * * *

Dean finished her meal and sat back, observing the crowded room from her vantage point. *Looks like the students are getting ready for the holiday season early,* she surmised, as she noted the youthful faces in the early afternoon crowd. *Hmm, a number of tourists, too.* She continued scanning until she caught the gaze of a young man at the bar staring at her. They locked eyes for a brief second before he managed to avert his gaze. He looked to be in his late twenties, perhaps early thirties, and dressed in a hunter green ski sweater, blue jeans, and hiking boots. His face was clean-shaven, topped by short, curly blonde hair; and from what she could tell from where she sat, he had very dark blue eyes. Dean's gut reaction told her he just didn't fit in with the people around him, so she carefully watched his actions, waiting to see if her instincts had been affected by jet lag, or if they were on target.

Five minutes passed and the young man was joined by another man, similarly attired, who looked to be his twin but was a few years older. She watched as they spoke to one another, lips barely moving. When she picked up the minute nod in her direction, her mind affirmed her gut feeling with a solitary—*Bingo. Well, boys, let's see what has you so interested, shall we?* Dean finished her beer and motioned to the waitress for her bill. The perky, blonde server immediately came to her table and presented the check. Scanning the total, Dean mentally calculated the amount in American dollars, reached into her jeans and gave the bills to the waitress, along with a healthy tip. Dean told the young girl, *"Danke. (Es) stimmt so,"* earning a big smile when the server realized the size of her tip.

"Danke, auf Wiedersehen," the girl replied as she began cleaning up the dishes from the table.

Dean nodded as she stood and donned her jacket, stealthily slipping the cloth table napkin into her pocket. As she approached the bar, she turned her head to focus directly at the two men who had been watching her. As they met her stare, she gave them a crooked smile and winked at them, then headed directly for the door. Once outside, she turned left and jogged up the sidewalk to the first alley she could find. Turning the corner into the passageway, she looked over her shoulder and saw the two men leave the establishment. Their heads swiveled to the right and left, trying to determine which way to go. Finally, the older of the two men directed his friend to the right, while he took off in her direction. Dean slid back into the shadows and waited for him to get within reach. As soon as the man's head showed past the brick wall, Dean reached out with lightning speed and grabbed the man's jacket collar with one hand, pulling him into the shadows. Before he could call for help, she released the collar and slid her hand around his throat, while the other hand stuffed the wadded napkin into his mouth. She was glad she had on thick leather gloves, because the man tried to bite her as she gagged him. Then she grabbed his flailing hand and yanked it up high behind his back, effectively putting him on his toes.

"Ah, ah, it's not nice to bite," she whispered into his ear. "Let's move a little further back into this alley, shall we?" She herded him back behind several stacks of boxes, placing his chest against the wall as she increased the pressure on the arm behind his back.

"Now, I'm gonna ask you some simple questions, and all I want you to do is nod your head yes, or shake your head no. Okay?" The man stood still as though he did not understand her. Giving him a little encouragement, she pulled his arm up higher, almost to the point of dislocating his shoulder. This move brought a muffled cry and an affirmative nod. "That's better," Dean told him in a low growl. "Now, I know you were following me, so let's just get to the point." The man nodded vigorously. "My guess is, you and your pal know exactly who my earlier tablemate is, right?" Again, a series of nods. "Do you know who I am?" His head shook in the negative. "Okay. So you want to know more about me, then?" Nodding. "Well, before we go there, let me take a guess about you." She looked the man over, appraising him. "My guess is that you aren't from around here." She noted the crisp look of his jeans, the spit shine of his black boots, and the cleanliness of his heavy black parka. The man's eyes widened as she spoke. "So, just a wild guess here, I'll bet you're part of Gunter's little troop." Her captive closed his eyes and made no motion. "Hmm, is that a yes, or a no?" She increased the pressure on his arm, noting the beads of sweat now forming on his brow. "Okay, no matter. We both know you are." She gave him her best feral smile before continuing, "I want you to give Gunter a message for me. Tell him his old friend Deanna Peterson wants to meet with him. If he's interested, tell him to meet me in the middle of the old Arch Bridge at midnight...and to come alone." She paused, adding, "Give him this." She took out a small package and slipped it into the parka pocket. Looking around the passage, she heard the sound of laughter coming from the main street. "Now, I'm sorry I have to do this," the colonel whispered as she raised her free hand and executed a quick chop to his neck, sending the guy to the pavement for a brief respite. She moved him into a more comfortable position, walked quickly up to the passageway entrance, and checked for his partner. Not finding him in the immediate vicinity, she strolled out of the alley, and headed back to her vehicle and her quarters at the post. She felt that Gunter would get her message more quickly from this man than from the captain's infiltrator. *Always hedge your bets,* she thought as she got into the van.

* * * * *

"What do you mean, you were attacked by a woman!" Gunter shouted at his two men.

The one that Dean had collared began to protest. "Not *a*

woman! That American pig had the strength of a man...two men...and she had a gun stuffed in my mouth."

"So, you told her everything?" Gunter approached the now shaking man, and got nose to nose with him, which caused him to stoop down to the man's level. Gunter was six foot four and looked more like a handsome, mythical god than a neo-Nazi. The lines around his eyes and a peppering of gray hair were the only outward signs of age or the strain of his command. His physical presence was one of command and power.

"I told her nothing," he answered weakly.

"Ah, yes. It would be hard to speak with a gun in your mouth." Gunter's face softened into gentle repose as he delivered the sarcastic remark.

"I did not have to tell her anything. She already knew." He lowered his head to avoid his commander's stare, finding his boots a much friendlier sight. "She gave me a message for you."

"A message? What was her message?" Gunter, now intrigued, stepped away from his comrade and turned slightly to the right.

"She said she wants to talk to you, and for you to meet her on the old Arch Bridge tonight at midnight...alone."

"Alone? After she's turned one of my fiercest men into a quivering, spineless mass, she wants me to meet her alone?" He laughed as he turned once again to face the man.

"Yes, but I don't think that's a good idea, Gunter." The man looked up, hoping to win absolution but receiving a harsh look instead.

"Did she say anything else, Fritz?" he asked as he began pacing around the twosome.

"Yes. She said her name is Deanna Peterson." Fritz stumbled through the name. "And she said to give you this." He pulled the small package out of his pocket and handed it to Gunter who was now standing at his side.

Upon hearing Deanna's name, Gunter stopped abruptly and turned towards the men. Slowly, he reached out for the package, fingering it gently as he gazed at the small bundle. The mention of her name brought a rush of feelings that nearly overwhelmed him, and he quickly turned away from the two men. He continued his pacing until he was behind the men, slipping the package into his pocket and his feelings back into his heart, before he came back around to face them.

"I suggest you two learn to better defend yourselves against women," he said as he gave them a stern look. "Go. I have work to do." Fritz and his brother Hans quickly turned and exited the small room, leaving Gunter alone with his thoughts as he opened the small package he removed from his pocket. It contained a framed picture of Deanna and a youthful Gunter on a ski slope. His thoughts went back to the holiday ski trip they had taken with a group of undergrads from Columbia. He and Deanna had spent a lot of time together on that short trip, but it was long enough for him to know he was falling in love. A love he would never be able to acknowledge because of his family obligations. His parents had recently died and so he was the family patriarch; and with that came responsibility. So he finished his semester and returned to Heidelberg...but he never forgot about Deanna, and never gave his heart to anyone else.

* * * * *

Having returned to the Army post, Dean began interrogating Captain Kern. "So, the sergeant was acquitted of the rape?"

"Yes, Ma'am. There was absolutely no proof that any U.S. soldier, sailor, airman, or citizen committed the rape," the captain concluded.

"So why does Gunter think the U.S. is responsible?" Dean raised an eyebrow in question.

"That's what this group has been telling him...whipping him into a frenzy to get him on board." The captain shook his head, "Evidently it worked. The Military Police, hell, even the Base Commander tried to reason with him. He's just not buying our proof."

Dean turned to the captain and pinned him with a cold stare. "Then, Captain, I suggest we do everything we can to find the real rapist. I hope to meet with Gunter tonight, and I'm going to see if I can reason with him. If not, we'd better hope we can find this rapist, and fast!"

Chapter
17

12 December, 1300 Hours

"Katie!" Dr. Prokov called over the din in the cafeteria. Hearing her name, Katie looked around, searching for the caller. When her eyes met Meisha's, she hoped that her innermost thoughts would not be revealed to the profiler. Ever since her morning encounter with the doctor, she'd had the most eerie sensations when she thought about the violent expression she'd seen on Dr. Prokov's face. Although she'd agreed to meet her for lunch, Katie was hoping to avoid another get-together until she could get a better understanding of why she was reacting this way. *It's probably just all the reading I've been doing on the criminal mind,* Katie thought as Meisha pulled up a chair at her table.

"Hi," Katie offered with a forced smile, then lowered her head to stare at her barely touched meal.

"Hello, Katie," the psychologist replied. "Is something wrong?" *Ah, my little fly is nervous. Maybe she saw more than I thought. Hmm, maybe I can get her to open up to me. If she suspects anything, I might have to move up my timetable.* Meisha put on her best concerned, caring expression.

Still lost in thought, Katie raised her head and was taken in by the doctor's façade. "Mmm, nothing's wrong. I guess I was just lost in thought when you came up," Katie answered as she took in the soft lines of the psychologist's countenance. *Maybe I'm just projecting my worry about Dean and the neo-Nazi's into this morning's meeting on the path.*

"Well, if there's anything you want to talk about..." Meisha smiled sweetly while she let the sentence trail off, hoping that Katie would take the bait.

"No, no. Nothing. Guess I'm just realizing that the new class of recruits will be here after the holidays, and I'm wondering if I'll be ready for them." *Yes, there's a lot bothering me, but I'm not feeling like I should trust you. Why is that? Damn! This is not a good time for Dean to be gone. I need to bounce these feelings I'm having off of her. She'd know what to do.*

"Oh, I'm sure you'll be ready. I've read your file, and I can tell that you're very competent." Meisha reached over and laid a hand on Katie's arm, noticing the subtle stiffening of the muscles as she made contact. "You've always been a stern taskmaster, following up on all the little details, so I don't see you failing now." She removed her hand and picked up her fork, stabbing gently at her salad.

Katie wasn't sure of her feelings towards the psychologist at the moment. She was even beginning to wonder if the morning glimpse into another side of the woman had really happened. Glancing across the table at the psychologist as she ate her salad, she saw only a soft, caring person. *Maybe I just misread her this morning. I'm sure if I had been startled on a secluded path when I was not expecting anyone else to be around, I might have reacted the same way. This mystery woman plaguing our life right now really has me on edge. I'm seeing potential threats everywhere, and I'm losing my focus.* Meisha looked up at that moment and smiled sweetly at Katie, looking as innocent as a lamb. *Now, how could that woman be a monster? I'm really losing it.* She shook her head and returned the smile, then began a more aggressive attack on her tuna salad sandwich.

"So, I see you've moved into the dormitory," Meisha commented between bites. "I thought you lived somewhere north of here."

"Mmm, I do," Katie replied as she set her glass of milk down. "My, um, housemate is out of town for a few days, and I thought I'd just save some commute time and stay here for a bit." Sensing the woman's reluctance to divulge information, the psychologist offered no response and just kept eating. Katie relaxed a bit, while realizing that Meisha was putting on her psychologist's hat by allowing Katie to make the next move. *Aw, what the heck! It might do some good to bounce some of this off of her,* she thought, and decided to plunge in just a bit.

"You know all those questions I've been asking about the criminal mind...well, we're working on a bit of a problem right now."

"You and...your housemate? She's the Army officer, right?" the psychologist queried.

"Yes. It seems that someone from one of our pasts is playing a game with all of our friends. A very deadly game." Faking intrigue, Meisha motioned for Katie to continue, which she did— from the very beginning. She started with the email and continued right up to the recent incident with Bill and the hit-and-run. "So, I guess I've been a bit out of sorts lately. Please forgive me if I seem a bit detached."

During the recitation, Dr. Prokov had set her fork down and devoted her complete attention to Katie. She was surprised to learn of the possible ID by the night clerk at the motel, and decided that she needed to clean up that loose end as soon as possible. She also hadn't counted on them finding Felix so soon, but that didn't bother her as much because dead men couldn't tell tales. The night clerk, on the other hand, was a definite liability that had to be attended to. *Ah, a villain's work is never done,* she giggled internally, *or is it 'no rest for the wicked'? No matter, I have plenty of time to get to her before the police go knocking on her door.*

Katie finisher her narration of the events and looked expectantly at Dr. Prokov. "So, what do you think?"

Meisha folded her hands and placed them in her lap as she struck a suitable, thoughtful pose. "Hmm, I can see why you're a bit distracted. Your evil-doer hasn't given you much to go on, other than that you're dealing with a female." The psychologist shook her head and sighed. "I'm afraid you really have your work cut out for you. She sounds like a highly intelligent and cunning adversary. I think you did the wise thing by coming here to stay while your friend is out of the country. I'll put some thought into this and see if I can help you out." She looked at Katie, a solicitous expression on her face. "I'll give you a call if I come up with anything."

"Thanks, Meisha. We just keep running into brick walls. It's nice to be able to bounce things off someone else."

"I just hope I can help you find her before she does something else." She reached out and patted Katie's arm with her gnarled hand. Katie subconsciously tightened her arm muscles at Meisha's touch, blushing a bit in embarrassment at her reaction. They sat there staring at each other for another second or two. Katie broke off first and picked up the last of her sandwich, popping the final bite into her mouth with a flourish.

"Well," Meisha smirked, "at least this hasn't affected your appetite."

* * * * *

Dean opened her eyes for the tenth time in as many minutes and sighed heavily. She had been attempting to try and catch some shut-eye before her midnight meet, but was not successful. Staring at the tan colored ceiling, her mind conjured up an image of Katie, sitting in her favorite lounge chair and surrounded by her feline crew. The vision brought a smile to her face, and a warm feeling spread through her body. "Sure wish I was home with you, love," Dean whispered to the shimmering vision. "I'd slip right up behind you, lean down, and give you the most passionate kiss...maybe even two or three of them." Her mind played out the scene on the pale ceiling above her. Dean could see herself standing behind her fair-haired lover, feel her hands slide down the back of the chair and onto Katie's shoulders before they traveled further and came to rest on the full breasts. She could almost smell the herbal scent of Katie's shampoo as she bent down to meet Katie's upturned head. When their lips touched, she could sense the softness of her lover's lips, feel the heat of Katie's exhaled breath and the wetness of her tongue as she opened her mouth onto hers. She felt her breath catch as her mind vividly continued the scenario, her heart rate quickening while a warm sensation began to course through her body, wakening her desires. She felt herself begin to move on her cot. A low growl escaped her lips as her body began to rock with the physical need that was growing within and desperately seeking release. The longer the image of her lover played on in her mind, the more her need grew, eventually leading her over the edge and into the ecstasy beyond. The next time Dean opened her eyes, it was 2300 and she felt completely rested, albeit a bit disheveled. Quickly sitting up on the side of the bed, Dean checked her watch. Deciding she had time, she picked up the phone and dialed Katie's number. Katie answered on the first ring.

"Hey," Dean said in a sultry voice.

"Hi, love. I was hoping it was you." Katie walked over to her bed and sat down. "I miss you."

"Miss you, too. How was your day?"

"Different," she replied with a slight hesitation.

Dean's eyebrows rose as she picked up on the hesitation. "Something happen?"

"No, nothing new. It was just a bit strange today." Katie went on to tell of the chance meeting with Dr. Prokov on the path, and the conversation they had at lunch. "I just can't seem to shake this weird feeling I had when I saw Meisha on the path...but then, lunch seemed better."

"Katie, you have good instincts, so pay attention to them. You really don't know Dr. Prokov very well to begin with." Dean paused, formulating her next comment. "Go with your gut, Katie. Be cautious around her."

"I will, I just miss you. This wacko has me really on edge. I'm just waiting for the next shoe to drop."

"I know, love. Believe me, when I get back, we're going to get to the bottom of this. Lieutenant Green should have an ID for us by tomorrow night. Then maybe we can get somewhere."

"I sure hope so, Dean. Just hurry back, okay?"

"As soon as I get this situation under control, I promise." Dean sighed as she looked at her watch. "Gotta go love. I'll call you when this is over."

Okay, hon. Be careful."

"I will." Dean flipped the phone closed, caressing it softly with her hand. Standing, she straightened disheveled clothes, then walked over to the small bathroom. She stripped out of her clothes and took a quick shower, then dressed in a fresh outfit before she slipped her black jacket back on, grabbed her knit cap and gloves, and left for the rendezvous.

* * * * *

Dean parked in almost the same spot as she had earlier in the day. She looked at her watch and noted that it was 2350 hours. Picking up the night vision scope she had borrowed, she scanned the bridge and both sides of the river. Next, she focused on the rooftops and the windows of the buildings across from the bridge entrance on the far side. She saw a man pushing a wheelchair onto the bridge. The woman in it had her head resting on the back of the chair, but skewed off to one side, as though she couldn't hold her head up straight. They were both bundled in winter parkas with hoods, so she couldn't see their faces. Checking her watch once more, she put the scope back under the seat, zipped up her leather jacket, and exited the car. She was thankful that the wind had died down to nothing, making the night air crisp but comfortable. Slowly making her way to the middle of the bridge, she passed the couple as they came closer to her, still unable to discern their features due to their hoods. Maintaining her pace, she arrived at the mid-point and stopped. Turning toward the water, with her peripheral vision she caught the watery reversal of the couple she'd passed as they came back toward her. As she continued looking out into the darkness, her mind began to consider her options. *What do we have here, friend or foe?* Readying herself for action, she relaxed and waited for the couple to come within six feet, slowly turning to meet them. What she saw startled her. It was Gunter and a very gaunt, vacant-eyed Elsa.

"Deanna," Gunter called softly.

"Yes," she said, barely audible as she stared at the sad visage in front of her. The once vibrant, spontaneous, intelligent preteen that had been Elsa was now just an empty shell, staring into the night with listless eyes. The beauty was still beneath the gaunt surface, but the life was ebbing from her soul. "Oh, Gunter, I'm so sorry," she exhaled as she lifted a gloved hand and caressed the unresponsive face.

"This is what your soldiers did to my beautiful Elsa!" he spat out with a hiss. "I brought her to you so you could see why I want your soldiers out of my country...so they won't be able to do this to someone else's sister! And, I'll do it any way I can."

"You know why I'm here?" Dean asked the tall German,

unable to take her eyes off his sister.

"Yes, I know. I know a lot about you, Deanna. More than you would want me to." His eyes saddened as he looked at her. "I know the pain you carry inside you. That's why I'm here. I trust you, Deanna, but I don't trust your government. They are cowards—hiding behind their military courts, afraid to publicly punish my sister's rapist!"

"That's not true, Gunter." Dean turned to face him. "You say you trust me, then let me find Elsa's rapist. I promise I will hand him over to your government for punishment, no matter who it is. Just don't interfere with the symposium."

"It's been three months, Deanna. You can't find him now. Too much time has passed, and he's probably been redeployed." Gunter looked down at his sister, tears welling in his eyes. "They will pay for this, I promise you. Those cowards will pay." The tears freely fell as he raised his head and stared at Dean. "I suggest you leave Heidelberg as soon as you can," he said in a gruffer voice.

"I can't do that, Gunter. I have a responsibility here, and I can't leave until I know it's over...one way or another." Dean looked into her old friend's eyes, pleading with him to reconsider. His eyes seemed to soften as they held hers; he was falling in love all over again.

Nodding, he said softly, "The symposium starts in 40 hours. You have 36 hours to find her rapist." Then he bundled Elsa's parka tighter and pushed the wheelchair back toward the city.

Dean watched them leave for a few heartbeats before heading back to her car at a dead run.

* * * * *

The vehicle slid to a stop in front of a low, non-descript building. A solitary light was on over the doorway. Dean had the door open before the vehicle came to a stop, and was running up the desolate walkway as soon as her foot hit the pavement. Yanking open the door, she quickly entered, continuing to run until she came to the last office on the right. A dim light shone through the opaque glass in the door, verifying that someone was still on duty. Entering the office, she noted a sleepy corporal at the duty desk.

As he roused himself to attention, Dean shouted, "Corporal, get Captain Kern here on the double!"

"Yes, Ma'am!" The corporal rushed to get out of his chair, grabbing his BDU jacket as he ran toward the door.

"Wait! Did Captain Kern leave any files for me tonight?"

Skidding to a halt, the young soldier returned to his desk and sifted through the in-box, removing a stack of files. He handed them to the colonel, waiting to see if there was anything else this officer wanted. "Um, Ma'am? Do you need anything else before I go?" the corporal added a bit hesitantly.

Looking at the clueless expression on the corporal's face, Dean replied, "No, just go get Captain Kern. Tell him to hurry."

Dean picked up the files and headed into the adjoining office. She flipped on the overhead light, squinting at the brightness of the fluorescents. Walking over to the desk, she tossed the files on top of the green blotter, turned on the desk lamp, then walked back to the doorway and snapped off the overhead lights. Next, she unzipped her leather jacket and hung it on the coat rack by the door before walking behind the desk and taking a seat on the worn wooden chair. By the time Captain Kern arrived, she had skimmed through the top two files that held the initial crime report and interviews, as well as the court transcripts.

"What's up, Colonel?" Captain Kern questioned as he slipped off his BDU jacket and hung it on the coat rack.

"Are you always this easygoing with a superior officer?" she asked with a definite frost in her tone of voice.

Snapping to attention, Captain Kern quickly exchanged his relaxed attitude with a more appropriate bearing and replied, "Ma'am, no Ma'am."

She made him stand there allowing beads of sweat to trickle down his forehead before she commanded him to be at ease. "Sit," she commanded once more. "We've got 36 hours to find Elsa's rapist. If we can't find the perp in that time, we'll have to rely on other means to defuse the situation." She looked up at the captain with an icy stare. He fully understood the unspoken implications. She nodded at the two files she'd already read. "Solid work by the MP's and the JAG. Sergeant Dover is definitely innocent." Captain Kern looked pleased at his superior's comments, but soon wiped the smile off his face when she lifted her eyes to meet his. "The only thing I don't understand is why no one bothered to pursue the case to find the real rapist."

The captain stammered a bit before speaking, "Well, um, Colonel, we knew our man was innocent, so, we...ah..."

"Decided that it wasn't your problem?" she finished for him.

"Yes, Ma'am. That's exactly what we decided." He swallowed hard as he watched her eyes turn to ice, with an expression to match.

"So...you decided that it was okay to ignore Section 36A of the SOP for Complaints Filed on Bases Housed on Foreign Soil?"

Turning a deep red, the captain knew that they should have pursued the matter, but never realized that failure to do so would have such devastating repercussions. He hung his head and nodded. "Ma'am, we just ran out of leads and figured that there was nothing left to do."

"You realize I could bring you up on charges?" Dean inquired.

"Yes, Ma'am."

"Well, I'm not going to do that. You've got a second chance here, Captain. You need to pull your investigative team together and go over every detail and every lead again and again, until we find the person responsible." She looked straight into his eyes, imprinting the strength of her conviction on him. "Now," she said, picking up the third file, "is this what you've collected since this afternoon?"

"Yes, Ma'am. We were able to run down a couple of the supposed witnesses this afternoon and evening." Hoping to regain some stature with this powerful woman, he continued eagerly. "These two guys, Fritz and Hans Krantz," he said, pointing at the first two sheets of paper, "were nowhere to be found after they gave their initial testimony. They were supposedly out of the country when the trial came up, so they didn't show for the trial. Without the ability to cross-examine them on the stand, their statements didn't carry any weight. They aren't exactly models of respectability around here, so the JAG was disappointed when he couldn't examine them on the stand."

Dean looked at the reports, starting to sort out pieces of the puzzle. "Where are they now?"

"They were seen at a bar on Dorfmund late this afternoon.

I've got two guys out looking to bring them in."

Dean read their descriptions again and thought they fit the two guys she'd seen in the Vetter Bar that afternoon; but then, their descriptions fit half the population in Heidelberg.

"Do you have pictures of these two?"

"Yes, we do." He stood and went to the computer behind Dean and turned it on. "We take pictures of everyone who comes in to place a complaint or even give us a compliment. It's SOP by the Intelligence Section. Never know when you might need it."

Dean nodded at the information. *Yeah, that's exactly why I wrote that SOP.* They waited in silence as the computer booted up and Captain Kern entered the log request. In less than two minutes, Dean and Captain Kern were staring at the pictures of Heinrich and Friedrich Wertz, alias Hans and Fritz Krantz.

"I'll be damned," Dean muttered, as she recognized the two men from the bar. "These guys have any connection with the neo-Nazi group?"

"Not that we've discovered. Why?"

"They're the same guys that tried to follow me this afternoon." She stared at the photos, slotting more pieces into place. "As soon as your men find these guys, I want to talk to them." Captain Kern nodded, glad to see the thin smile appear on the colonel's face.

"Make me a copy of these pictures, then you can go back to your billet. I'll check with you back here at 0700 hours."

"Yes, Ma'am," the captain replied as he hit the print button.

Dean stood and walked over to the door, retrieving her jacket. She put it on as the printer spat out the completed prints. Captain Kern picked up the photos and reached across the desk to hand them to Dean. "Thanks," she said as she took the photos in hand, contemplating them once more before folding them and putting them in an inside jacket pocket. Zipping her jacket, she stepped through the doorway, nodding at the now fully awake corporal who had returned to his desk. She walked briskly down the hallway and readied herself for the cold air of the night as she opened the door to the outside. As she walked the 200 yards to the VOQ, she grinned broadly and said, "Gotcha!"

Chapter
18

Katie snapped the book shut and placed it on the end table. She stood and stretched from head to toe, side to side, and front to back. "Man, I had better get in some exercise before I turn into a big blob. Maybe I should go out for a run...I could even hit the convenience store on my way back. Hmm, if I do an extra couple of miles I could even get a container of Ben & Jerry's. Oh, yeah, Cherry Garcia!" Now that she had the incentive to run, Katie changed into her long, black spandex pants, a long sleeved t-shirt, and burnt orange sweatshirt. She tied her Reeboks, did a few stretches, slipped the chain holding her room key over her head, and headed out the door, locking it behind her. On her fourth lap around the running trail, as she came up to the path where she'd seen Dr. Prokov earlier that morning, she slowed her pace as she remembered the look on the psychologist's face, and the chill made a return visit down her spine.

"I wonder where she was coming from this morning?" Katie considered, as she looked down the path to the roadway. As she peered down the trail, she was surprised to see a local cab idling at the curb.

"Now what's that cab doing there?" she whispered to herself.

Curious, she decided to check it out. She slipped into the woods and quietly but carefully made her way down. When she got about ten yards from the vehicle, she hid behind a short evergreen bush and strained to pick up any conversation. There was none to be heard since the vehicle had all of its windows up, and the sound of the idling motor was all she could discern. It was dark enough to keep her hidden even with the fairly light colored sweatshirt, and also dark enough to make it difficult to see inside the cab since it was sitting in the shadows between two streetlights. As she continued her stakeout, her eyes adjusted to the point where she could barely pick out the silhouette of two passengers from the subtle glow of the dashboard. She gasped as she recognized Dr. Prokov in the passenger seat.

Out for another tête-à-tête? Katie wondered as she continued watching. The conversation turned heated, and soon, Dr. Prokov opened the door to exit the cab. The dome light had been turned off, so she still could not recognize the driver, but the words that followed, although benign, raised the hair on her neck from the fury with which they were spoken.

"Take care of it tonight!" Meisha spat as she got out. She shut the cab door quietly, and watched as the vehicle pulled away from the curb. Once the cab was out of view, she turned and started up the path. At that instant, Katie's cell phone decided to begin vibrating. When Dr. Prokov came abreast of where Katie was hiding, she slowed, looked around, and was about to walk into the woods when a squirrel bounded from the bush, startling the doctor and headed up the tree on the opposite side of the path. Katie had been holding her breath as she realized that the woman in front of her was about to come her way, obviously alerted by the vibrating phone. When the squirrel jumped out of the evergreen, she about lost it. She had been so intent on watching the cab, that she never noticed the critter sitting on the limb of the bush. As Meisha watched the animal scamper up the tree to her right, she shook her head and turned back to the path, heading up it without looking back. A dull flash of gunmetal caught Katie's attention as Meisha slipped the gun she had been holding in her good hand back into her coat pocket. When the psychologist was far enough out of earshot, Katie slowly let out her breath. When she flipped her phone open, she saw that the call had come from Dean.

Phew! That was close. Reflecting on the glimpse of the gun, Katie thought, *I wonder why she feels she needs to carry that around here? Surely she can't think these grounds are unsafe. I wonder what a cabbie has to take care of tonight? Just who was that guy...or...was it another woman?* Shaking her head, the blonde decided there were just too many questions, and her initial assessment of Dr. Meisha Prokov was in need of a review in light of her strange behavior. *But, was her behavior really strange? Or is it just because I've never been exposed to this side of her? C'mon, Katie. Why would a world-renowned profiler have clandestine meetings with cabbies? Whoa! Where did that come from? Damn, Dean, why'd you have to be gone right now?*

Sighing, Katie slipped out from her hiding place, deciding to take the longer route back to her room, and headed down to the road, picking up her pace as her muscles re-warmed. Her mind raced with questions and how she might get some answers. After another fifteen minutes of jogging and a quick shower when she got back to her room, a very tired Katie crept into bed without even missing her self-promised reward of Cherry Garcia ice cream. Before she turned off the light, she dialed Dean's cell phone.

* * * * *

Dean closed the phone and wondered where Katie was at that hour without her phone. *She's probably in the shower,* Dean thought as she placed the phone on her nightstand and checked her watch one more time, mentally calculating the five-hour difference in time. *Guess I'll give her a call tomorrow.* Dean pulled the blanket back and sat on the side of the bed. Scrubbing her face with her hands, she inhaled deeply then slowly let out the breath, centering her thoughts. She reached down and slipped off her wool socks before sliding her long body under the covers. Finding a comfortable position on her back, Dean stared at the ceiling and started running down her mental checklist.

One...the rape pushed Gunter into joining the neo-Nazi's. Two...my bet for who committed the rape goes on Hans or his brother and not one of our soldiers. Three...why was it so important to get Gunter into the group? Four...how am I going to convince him that it was his own men that hurt his sister? Five...where are Hans and his brother hiding? Six...where to next? Dean closed her eyes and concentrated on her relaxation technique, easing herself into a light sleep in the process. Ten minutes later, her cell phone chirped.

Dean picked up the phone and answered, "Colonel Peterson."

"Agent O'Malley, here," Katie countered in a faux official tone.

"Hey. How are you?" Dean asked, eyes still closed.

"Tired. I ran about six miles tonight. Figured I needed a bit of exercise."

"Well, that should have done it. Didn't you have your phone with you?"

"Yep, but I couldn't pick up when you called."

Frowning, Dean asked, "Why not?"

"Um, I was hiding in a bush and didn't want to be found out."

"Okaayy. Why were you hiding in a bush?"

"Long story, but the short of it is, I happened upon a clandestine meeting between Dr. Prokov and a cabbie."

"What makes you think it was more than just being dropped off by a cab?"

"Well, for one thing, it was a weird place to be dropped off...on the back side of the housing area. The cab can go right up to her housing unit, so why there?"

"Okay, go ahead."

"For another, she didn't sound very friendly when she was getting out. The sentence was non-committal, but the tone was very aggressive."

"What'd she say?"

"Something like 'Take care of it tonight,' but with an attitude."

"Hmm, maybe she was just commenting on the condition of the cab?"

"Could be, but why in such a violent tone? Then, when she was coming up the path, she may have heard the vibrating sound when the phone went off..."

"Uh oh. What happened?"

"Well, luckily there was a squirrel in my bush, and the vibrating spooked him out and across the path to another tree. Prokov must have figured it was just the squirrel."

"Lucky you!"

"Yeah, especially when she saw it was just a squirrel, and she put her gun back in her pocket!"

Dean was not happy with this bit of information. "A gun? What's she doing carrying a gun there?"

Katie sensed the concern in her lover's voice. "Who knows? Maybe she needed it for protection wherever it was she went? Hey, love, don't worry; everything turned out okay."

"Yeah, thanks to a nervous squirrel." After a pause, Dean added, "Look, love, just be careful around her. I'm not too sure I liked that woman in the first place."

"Well, I'm beginning to do a little critical review of her myself," Katie offered.

"Maybe the less contact you have with her, the better," Dean suggested.

"Mmm, that's what I've been thinking, too. I don't want her to get curious, so I'll just try to keep minimal contact with her." *After I have lunch with her tomorrow and try to find out why she carries a gun,* Katie thought. "So, how goes it there?"

"I think we got a big break tonight. If all goes well, I'll be on my way to Fort Leavenworth by this time tomorrow."

"That's good news, then. I hope it all works out."

"Me too, love. Hey, you'd better get to sleep."

"Yeah, you too. Night."

"Goodnight." Dean closed the phone and returned it to her nightstand. She felt better being able to talk to Katie, but was concerned about the turn of events with Dr. Prokov. *Katie, Katie. Just stay out of trouble until I get home, will ya? At least at Quantico you're safe from our wacko.* Finishing that thought, Dean rolled over and went back to sleep.

* * * * *

It was now 0700 on the 13th of December. Dean was up, showered, and ready to put her plan in action. She had begun to formulate her next steps as she'd drifted off to sleep the night before, and finished her thoughts while in the shower. If the Krantz/Wertz brothers couldn't be found, she was going to take a trip to see Elsa. Her gut was telling her they were responsible for the rape, and hopefully, she would be able to get Elsa to recognize them from their pictures. Then, she would need to convince Gunter of their guilt. The big question was, why get Gunter into the neo-Nazi group in the first place. Gunter hated the fact that his only brother Erich was involved with them; he hated war, hated violence. He had always been a man of peace, so what had made him change? Elsa's rape was obviously the prod, but what was this group trying to accomplish by getting Gunter involved?

The questions continued swirling in her head while Dean jogged the short distance from the VOQ to Captain Kern's office. As soon as she entered, Corporal Jenkins called the other personnel in the office to attention as he rose from his desk. Colonel Peterson directed the group to resume their duties as she spied a fresh pot of coffee brewing behind the corporal.

"Have enough of that to share?" Dean queried as she pointed at the coffee pot.

"Yes, Ma'am!" the corporal replied, and turned to pour her a cup. "Take anything in it, Colonel?"

"Not today, Corporal. Three and a half hours of sleep calls for drastic measures."

"Excuse me, Ma'am?"

Smiling at the young soldier, Dean told him that she normally drank tea, but figured that office coffee would probably be more potent.

"That it is, Colonel. That stuff will take the rust off a WWII tank." He picked up his bottle of Pepsi and smiled at her. "This is my eye-opener."

Nodding, the colonel asked if Captain Kern was in yet, and found that the captain had come in about ten minutes earlier. Corporal Jenkins offered to tell him she was there, to which she shook her head in the negative, saying that he'd be expecting her.

"Thanks, Jenkins," she supplied as she headed into the captain's office, coffee mug in hand.

"Any time, Ma'am," he replied, resuming his seat and going back to his filing.

Colonel Peterson walked down the hallway to Captain Kern's office, conscious of the veiled looks she was getting from the rest of the staff. She knocked once, then entered the office. The captain did not look like he had gotten any more sleep after she'd dismissed him the night before. *Good. He was probably up the rest of the night trying to find the two brothers.* As soon as he saw her enter, he stood at attention.

"At ease," Dean commanded as she took a seat across from his desk. She took a healthy swig of the coffee and had to use all her self-control to keep from grimacing.

"Um, that's pretty strong stuff, Colonel. I have my own pot right here." He pointed at a coffee pot on the bookcase.

"Nope, this is just fine," she lied. "Now, tell me how the search is going. Have you found the brothers?"

"My men haven't reported in yet, Ma'am. I'm expecting them soon."

"Let's hope they found them; but just in case, I'm going to the hospital to see Elsa." She took the photos out of the file folder she had brought with her. "I'm betting that these two are the ones that raped her. If I can just get through to her, we may be able to defuse this situation."

"Will you be able to get in to see her?"

"Not a problem, but I'll need you to get me a few things before I leave."

* * * * *

By 0800, Colonel Peterson was heading to the Heidelberger Universitätskrankenhaus. She was dressed as a doctor, complete with white lab coat, stethoscope, clipboard, and a pair of black-rimmed glasses. With her hair in a bun and a no-nonsense expression, she very much looked the part of a physician. She parked the borrowed black Mercedes in a slot for visiting doctors, and walked authoritatively toward the hospital entrance. Approaching the reception area, she informed them she was there to see Elsa Krieg.

"Guten Morgen. Ich bin Doktor Schwann aus Berlin. Ich bin hier, um Elsa Krieg zu sehen. Ihr Bruder Gunter hat mich um eine Beurteilung ihres Zustands gebeten."

The receptionist looked up at Dean and replied, "Ja, Doktor Schwann. Sie ist im Westflügel, Raum 435. Hier, Sie brauchen diesen Ausweis, um Zutritt zu erhalten."

"Danke," Dean said as she accepted the proffered pass to the psychiatric wing. Smiling at the young woman, she turned and headed for the elevators. Arriving at the secure wing, she showed her pass and was allowed to enter. She nodded at the nurses at the front desk and repeated the information she'd given the reception-ist. These nurses were not as easy to fool, and they asked a few more questions before accepting Dean's story. Satisfied, they led her to Elsa's room, where they left her to do her evaluation. Once Dean verified that the nurse had returned to her station, she pulled a chair over to Elsa's bedside and looked down at the young woman, her determination reaffirmed to seek justice for the crime committed.

"Elsa," she spoke softly as she picked up the woman's hand and softly caressed it with her thumb. It was hard for Dean to believe that it had been nearly thirteen years since she'd first met Gunter's sister. Elsa was twelve at the time. At twenty-five, she had blossomed into a definite beauty. Nearly as tall as Dean, with medium length blonde hair and deep hazel eyes, her Teutonic her-itage was evident. Her body, though, showed signs of atrophy, even though she was receiving daily physical therapy to work her muscles. Looking down at her, Dean was overwhelmed with sad-ness.

"Elsa, it's Dean. Do you remember me?" There was no response, so Dean adjusted her position to be in direct view of the woman lying in the bed. "Elsa, do you remember the nickname I had for you? Munchkin...my little munchkin." She smiled down on the young woman, with fond memories of a gifted girl of twelve giggling at the Lollipop Guilders in the Wizard of Oz. Enthralled with the movie, she'd watched it over and over, until she could recite nearly all the lines by heart. Desperate to rekin-dle Elsa's memories, Dean inhaled deeply and began singing one of their favorites from the show in a nasal tone.

"We represent the Lollipop Guild, the Lollipop Guild, the Lollipop Guild..." A flicker in Elsa's eyes; Dean continued, "That's it, munchkin. C'mon, sing with me." Dean continued with the whimsical song, moving closer to Elsa's face, watching her lips begin to form around broken words. "...We wish to wel-come you to Muchkinland... Atta girl, c'mon, just a little more..." By the time she'd finished the silly song, she could have sworn that Elsa was trying to sing with her, but no voice accompanied the feeble lip movements. Not knowing what to do next, Dean stood and gently placed the hand she was holding back on the woman's chest.

Sighing heavily, she walked to the window and looked out at the hills surrounding the city. "Oh, Elsa, it's a terrible thing they've done to you. No one should have to endure that." She looked back at the quiet patient lying in the bed. "I promise you, Elsa, I will find out who did this to you and make sure they are punished for their crime." Dean turned back to the window, tears now making their way down her cheeks. She stood there for a minute longer before returning to the bedside.

Settling down in the chair next to the bed, she resumed holding Elsa's hand and began humming *Somewhere Over the Rainbow* from *The Wizard of Oz.* Her eyes closed as she started to softly sing the lyrics, tears still tracking lines on her face. She was nearing the end of the song when she noticed the hand she was holding was squeezing hers back. Opening her eyes, she gazed at Elsa's sleeping form. *Was I dreaming, or did she really squeeze my hand?* Her eyes followed the hand she was holding back to its owner, finally resting on Elsa's face. That's when she noticed the tears. Elsa was crying.

"Elsa?" Dean whispered as she took her right hand and gently brushed the tears from Elsa's face. "Elsa, it's me, Dean. Please...please open your eyes and look at me." She waited, holding her breath, hoping that Elsa was able to recognize her.

"Glinda," Elsa whispered, barely audible.

"Yes!" Dean almost shouted as she recognized Elsa's nickname for her. "Yes, Elsa. It's me." She reached down and pulled the fragile young woman into her arms, tears once again springing to her eyes. She remained holding Elsa for a bit longer, then finally, gently, laid her back on her bed. "Sweetheart, do you know where you are?"

Elsa looked around the room, taking in every card and flower. "Am I in hospital?"

"Yes. You have been here for a little over two months."

"Why?" she asked, wide-eyed.

"Elsa, this will be difficult. If you want me to stop, just tell me." The young woman nodded but was obviously confused. Dean continued, "You were attacked by some men."

Elsa looked at Dean, confusion still evident. "Who would attack me? Why?" she asked slowly. Dean was not sure if she should give her the details up front, let her work it out for herself, or a combination of both.

Opting to help her work it out, Dean led her through a series of exploratory questions, leading her to the night of the rape. A silence pervaded the hospital room as Elsa searched her memory for bits and pieces that might lead her to the horrific event. Not able to conjure up the needed memories, Dean carefully broached the topic of the Krantz brothers.

"Elsa, do you know two brothers by the name of Hans and Fritz Krantz?"

The young woman searched her memory, but shook her head, "Ich erkenne nicht die Namen. Um, no, I do not."

"How about Heinrich and Friedrich Wertz?"

Pausing, Elsa could not come up with a memory of those names either.

"Elsa, I want to show you some pictures of these men. It may help to stir your memory, but it may also be very painful. Are you willing to risk that?"

"Ja," she answered almost immediately. "I am not afraid. I have my Glinda with me," she smiled at Dean, "and she will protect me."

Dean leaned over and gave Elsa a hug, then said, "You are a very brave girl, munchkin." She released her, then stood and retrieved the folder with the pictures and returned to Elsa's side.

"I am not a little girl any more. I am a woman," Elsa said proudly as she labored to make room for Dean on her bed, her loss of strength obvious.

Nodding, Dean simply smiled at the courage shown by her young friend and took a seat next to Elsa, ready to do whatever was necessary if the reaction brought an unpleasant response. She handed the folder to Elsa, and braced herself. Elsa opened the folder and considered the pictures. At first, Dean thought her gut instincts were wrong, but then she noticed that Elsa's hands began to tremble.

"Elsa? Are you all right?" Dean moved to look directly at her, studying the reaction and trying to decide if she needed to intervene.

Elsa began nodding her head and rocking. "Ja ja ja...diese Männer...sie...sie..." Her English was completely lost as she stared at the pictures.

"Elsa. Are they...are they the men who hurt you?"

"Diese Männer...sie haben, sie haben...mir weh getan. Sie haben mich festgehalten und meine Kleider weggerissen...sie..."

Dean took the photos from her trembling hands and wrapped her arms around her, rocking with her. "Yes, Elsa, those men hurt you. But I promise you, they'll never hurt you again."

"What the hell are you doing here?" Gunter shouted as he walked into the room and saw Dean holding a crying Elsa. "Get away from her!" He stormed over to the bed and grabbed Dean violently, pulling her off the bed and nearly pulling Elsa with her.

"Gunter...Anschlag!" Elsa choked out, reaching for the hand that was headed toward Dean's face, Gunter's anger and fear overriding his affection for Dean.

"I will not stop..." he said, then did exactly that, turning to face his sister. "Elsa? Elsa, my God, Elsa...you...you're..." He released his hold on Dean and stepped closer to the bed, staring in confusion at his sister, then back to Dean. "What happened? How..." His words were lost as he pulled his sister into a gentle embrace, weeping along with her. Dean stood and watched as Gunter stroked his sister's hair, touched her face, and kissed her cheek.

"The good witch Glinda broke the spell," Elsa said, as she wiped the tears from his face.

"Glinda?" he asked, confused.

"Yes, Gunter, Dean...Glinda...my good witch from childhood. You remember?"

"Ahh." He released his sister and turned back toward Dean, who was smiling at Elsa. "I'm sorry, my dear friend. I should have known you wouldn't hurt Elsa."

"You're right, Gunter. I would never hurt her." She reached over and placed her right hand on Elsa's shoulder. "Right, munchkin?" That got a smile and a nod before Elsa's exhaustion caused her to fall back against her pillows, her brother's concern evident in his expression. "Gunter, she's had a couple of rough months, but she'll be okay. She's back with us now."

Quietly, Elsa added, "Yes, brother. I will be okay."

In the next hour, Dean filled Gunter in on how she was able
to bring Elsa out of her state of shock, and more importantly, on
whom her attackers really were and how they were going to deal
with them.

"Fritz and his brother? But why?" Gunter asked, still baffled
as to why they would have done this to his sister.

"I don't know for certain...but probably to lure you into the
fold. What's the background on these guys? Where are they
from?"

"I don't know much about them. They came just about the
time Elsa was..." He looked over at a now sleeping Elsa who had
a relaxed, peaceful look on her face. "All I know is that they came
from one of the factions up north."

"So, they're new to the area. Do you know where they are
now?"

"Yes. They are preparing for the symposium...in our camp."

"There's got to be more to this than meets the eye," Dean
shook her head. "Gunter, now that you know the truth, you have
to stop the attack on the symposium, then we'll take care of the
Krantz brothers."

"You have my word. The symposium will not be disrupted."

"Good enough for me." Dean reached into her coat pocket
and pulled out her phone and placed a call to General Carlton giving the go-ahead for the symposium. She checked her watch and
noted that it was 1300 hours. She had completed the job well
before the deadline. "Okay, Gunter, let's tie up a few loose ends,
then I've got a plane to catch back to the States tonight at 2200
hours."

Chapter
19

14 December, 1245 Hours

Katie was now standing in line at the deli section of the cafeteria, waiting for her sandwich. Her protective instincts warred with her professional instincts: she was both relieved and disappointed to see that Dr. Prokov was nowhere in sight. Relieved because she really wanted to keep at a distance, but disappointed because she wouldn't have the chance to see if she could find out more about the clandestine trips the psychologist seemed to be making at strange hours. *Hmm, maybe she ate already. Well, Dean did want me to stay away from her.* She picked up her order of corned beef on rye from the food service worker, placing it on her tray. Walking over to the milk machine, she picked up a large glass and filled it with skim milk before heading over to the dessert section. While she evaluated her choices, she did not see Dr. Prokov set her tray on the tubular tray rails next to her. Deciding on the last plate of apple cobbler, Katie reached for it just as another hand slipped her prize away from her. Disappointed, she followed the hand as it placed the cobbler on the tray next to hers. It was only as she looked up, that she noticed it was Meisha Prokov.

"Oh, hi," she said in a startled voice.

"I'm sorry, Katie. Did you want the cobbler?" Meisha knew that Katie had been reaching for the cobbler, and was just barely able to sneak it away from her grasp.

"Huh? Oh, no, go ahead. I probably should stay away from

dessert today, anyway."

"Really? With all the running you do, I would imagine you could eat just about all the dessert you want."

I wonder if she did see me last night. "Running?" Katie almost tripped over the word.

"Yes. I mean, didn't I see you running the other day?"

Uh oh. "Well, possibly, but I really don't pay much attention when I run. I'm just concentrating on putting one foot in front of the other..." Katie blurted.

Meisha just laughed as she picked up her tray and pointed at an empty table near the corner. "Want to sit by the window?"

"Uh, sure. That is, if you want company?"

"Of course. I've been looking forward to our little lunchtime chats...haven't you?" Meisha reached the table and set her tray down, chuckling internally as she saw the young agent begin to blush.

"Yes, yes, of course. It's just that, I don't want to...impose...if you would rather be alone."

"Nonsense! Now, what have you been up to?"

Oh, wow. That's a loaded question. Okay, kiddo, may as well make the most of it. Let's see what we can find out today, shall we? "Well, I've just been working on my lesson plans for after the holidays. How about you?"

The two women talked about generalities as they ate, neither divulging much information in their idle chit-chat. Finally, as Meisha rearranged her tray to place the plate of cobbler in front of her, Katie found herself staring at Meisha's deformed hand as it held the plate. Without thinking, Katie asked, "How did your hand get injured?"

Placing her spoon down, Meisha clasped her hands together, enfolding the deformity with her good hand as she pulled it to her chest.

"I'm sorry. That was rude of me." Katie spoke quickly as she saw a flicker of...something...in the doctor's eyes.

"No, it's not a problem," the psychologist replied as she stared down at her hands. "Actually, it's my little reminder of what happens when you underestimate your prey."

"Prey? I don't understand. Are you a hunter?"

"You could say that." Meisha looked up at Katie and smiled.

"I enjoy a challenge. The deadlier the prey, the more exciting the challenge."

Having tried her hand at deer hunting once with a college friend, Katie pursued the topic. "I went deer hunting once with a friend. I had my sights lined up on a doe, but just couldn't bring myself to pull the trigger. She was so peaceful looking. When her eyes met mine... Well, it was almost as though she winked at me, then dashed off into the woods." Katie recalled the scene as though it were just yesterday. "I haven't had the desire to do that again." She paused, "So what kind of game do you hunt? Deer? Turkey?"

Meisha laughed, "Oh, no. I don't bother with small game."

"Oh? Big game, then, like bear or moose?"

Meisha shook her head. "No, I hunt predators."

"Predators?"

"Yes. I hunt the hunters." She smiled at Katie, tempting her with the metaphor. "My injury occurred when I underestimated the power of a cornered predator's mate."

The look she gave Katie as she explained sent a chill up the blonde's spine, temporarily discomfiting her.

Katie had the distinct feeling that she was being baited. "Ah. Well. I guess you were lucky then to come away alive."

"Yes, I guess I am. But, I'll settle the score some day... Maybe soon."

The sentence hung in the air for a long moment, pulling Katie into her own thoughts as flashes of something familiar niggled her. "Oh, my." She looked at her watch. "I really have to go." Katie stood and picked up her tray, wanting to get away from this woman, but not knowing or understanding why. "Maybe I'll see you later."

"Oh, I'm sure you will." Meisha pushed away from the table and stood, watching Katie as the blonde headed to the tray deposit station. Softly she added, "Soon."

* * * * *

Katie was on her way to her small office when her cell phone chirped. Pulling it out of the backpack, she opened the phone and held it to her ear. "Hey, you have the best timing."

"Excuse me? Is this Agent O'Malley?" the voice asked, a bit confused at the salutation.

Realizing that it was not Dean on the other end, Katie recovered and replied, "Yes. This is Agent O'Malley."

"This is Lieutenant Green...from the Woodbridge PD."

Recognizing the name, Katie nodded in response. "Yes, Lieutenant. Sorry, I was expecting someone else to call."

"Well, I'll make this short then."

"What can I do for you?" Katie continued walking to her small office as she spoke.

"Well, I know Colonel Peterson is out of town, so I thought I would take a chance and try to call you."

"That's right, you were going to interview the night clerk. Was she able to ID our perp?" Katie cut in as she remembered what day it was.

"Yes and no. That is why I'm calling, but unfortunately, the clerk won't be able to ID anyone."

"What do you mean? Was she unable to give a description?"

"It seems as though Ms. Fitzgerald had a heart attack last night. She didn't make it."

"Oh my God," Katie replied softly as she entered her office. "I didn't realize she was elderly."

"Actually, she wasn't. She just turned thirty on Monday. She was celebrating her birthday with friends and family while on vacation."

"Was there any indication that she had heart trouble?" Katie's mind was processing possibilities as she considered this information. "Is an autopsy being done?"

"At this point, no autopsy is being ordered since there is no evidence of foul play. We're checking with her physician to see if she had a history of heart trouble." The lieutenant sighed audibly before continuing. "If anything turns up, I'll let you know; but for right now, we're back to square one."

"I understand. Thank you for calling, Lieutenant." Katie disconnected and placed the phone on top of Meisha's book, which was lying on her desktop. "Well, that just sounds a little coincidental to me," she spoke out loud. She looked down at the book and thought about the enigmatic author. "I think it's about time I try to find out a little more about you, Dr. Prokov." With that thought in mind, she picked up the book and perused the book jacket, then the inside pages for more information. Finding scant detail on the author, Katie decided to contact the publisher.

*   *   *   *   *

Meisha Prokov was pacing her small office, cell phone in hand. "What do you mean, she figured it out? Of all the incompetent." She paused, exhaling deeply, trying to control her temper. "Where is she now?...What do you mean, you don't know!...Never mind, I'll find out. She's probably on her way to Kansas City."

Irritated, Meisha stomped across her office to her desk, pulled out the chair, and sat down. "No, I don't care about the symposium. Your job was to get Krieg involved in order to make her presence necessary there and keep her there while I got things set over here, and you've botched that. Now, tell me how you escaped from Gunter." She spent another three minutes on the phone before she disconnected. "Damn," she cursed out loud. "Now I'll have to move up my timetable." She picked up her phone once more and entered a number. When the voice on the other end answered, she said in a controlled voice, "The schedule has changed. Get everything ready and wait for my call." She hung up before there could be a protest.

*   *   *   *   *

The huge cargo plane landed at the old city airport across the river from Kansas City. She had been lucky to catch the U. S. Army Reserve plane to this airport instead of having to detour to Fort Leavenworth, Kansas and then drive to Kansas City. Leavenworth was less than an hour from KC, but this worked out a lot better, even with the long delay in Rotterdam. Picking up her bag, she exited the plane from the rear ramp, along with several jeeps that were being off-loaded by the reservists returning from a two-week training mission. She inhaled deeply of the fresh air as she walked off the ramp. The weather was clear and the temperature in the mid-fifties. She spotted the commander of the reserve unit and walked over to him.

"Colonel Smith," she called, extending her hand to him. "Thanks for the lift. I really appreciate it." Colonel Mitchell Smith was the Chief Nurse for the 352nd General Hospital Unit located in Independence, Missouri. He had seen a lot of active duty and was just finishing out his last year in the reserves before retiring. He had been the charge nurse on the floor where Dean had been recovering from one of her nastier missions, so it had made the ten hour flight much more enjoyable.

Colonel Smith accepted the proffered hand and smiled back at her. "My pleasure, Colonel. The offer of a lift into the city is still on the table."

"Thanks, but I'll just get a rental. I could use a ride over to the Hertz dealer, though."

"Can do," he replied, signaling a staff sergeant who was driving off one of the jeeps. "Give my regards to Major Kidd the next time you see her." He picked up Dean's bag and placed it in the back of the open jeep, directing the sergeant to deliver the colonel to the Hertz dealer. "Good to see you again, Dean." He saluted her as she eased into the passenger seat.

Returning the salute, Dean nodded.   "Same here, Mitch. Thanks again for the lift."

The rental office was across the tarmac, on the civilian side of the airport. It only took a few minutes to traverse the distance, and ten minutes longer before Dean was loading her bag into the trunk of the Grand Am she'd rented. Checking the map the rental agent gave her, she decided to check into the Crown Center Hotel on Pershing Road first, grab a shower, and change into civvies before calling on Reverend Lewistan at the City Mission. A little voice in her head started to speak, *Yeah, that's right. Put off seeing your Dad 'til the last possible minute.* Out loud she answered the voice. "No, I just need a shower. Besides, I don't need to be showing up in my uniform." *Why? Are you ashamed of it?* "No! I'm not. I just... Damn it all! All right, let's get this over with!"

Dean turned the key, bringing the car to life. She checked her mirrors and pulled out of the parking lot, taking North Broadway across the Missouri river. Checking the street signs, she took a right on 17th and another right on Jefferson. The city mission was at the end of the block and faced the Interstates 35 and 670 interchange. The area was old and rundown with several of the buildings abandoned, but the little mission was a rose among the thorns. The building before her was a four-story red brick structure with a metal fire escape zigzagging down the side of the building facing the parking lot. It looked to her like it may have been converted from an old school building. The vicinity immediately around the structure was clean and had short evergreen shrubs surrounding it and the parking area.

Dean pulled into the parking lot, noticing a fenced playground behind the building. There were several children playing on the equipment, the sounds of their laughter mingling with the traffic sounds from the interchange. As she stepped out of the car, she checked her watch, noting that it was nearly 1430 hours. In another hour or so, it would be too dark for them to play.

Okay, let's get on with it. She stepped briskly to the side door, each step ratcheting up the queasiness in her stomach. Entering the building, she saw a directional sign for the main office and followed it to the front of the building. The office was enclosed in a wall half of plasterboard, half of glass. The glassed upper half was covered with mini-blinds that were open, allowing office staff to see out and visitors to see in. Dean scanned the interior of the office and was almost relieved that she did not recognize anyone resembling her father. Placing her right hand on the doorknob, she took a deep breath and scolded herself for the trepidation she was feeling. *C'mon, Dean. You've faced horrible things in your life. How bad can this be? You're just gonna see him. You don't have to spend a lot of time with him. Just see him and get back to Katie as fast as you can.* Steeling herself for the final time, she turned the doorknob and entered.

The young black woman sitting at the desk looked up as the door opened. "May I help you?" she asked as she took in the sight of the uniformed woman entering with her hat in hand.

Swallowing hard to gain her voice, Dean nodded. "Yes. I'm looking for Reverend Lewistan. I'm Colonel...I'm Deanna Peterson."

"Oh, yes!" the woman responded, standing quickly and smiling at her. She stepped around the desk and offered her hand to Dean. "The reverend said you would be coming by." Dean accepted the small, warm hand and shook it gently. "My name's Rhonda. Have a seat." She pointed at the old wooden pew under the front window that served as visitor seating. "She's out on the playground with the children. I'll go get her."

Before Dean could utter her thanks, the young woman was out the door. Dean sat where she was told, resting her hands on her thighs. Looking down at her combat boots and her cover still in her hand, she began to regret not going to change first. Hearing footsteps in the hall, Dean stood, looking at the office door. Reverend Martha Lewistan entered, smiling.

"Hello, Dean. Welcome to our little city mission." The petite woman walked over to the tall visitor and embraced her. She immediately picked up on the anxiety level Dean was experiencing, hugging her more tightly in response. "I'm glad you could make it." She released her and stepped back. "Come into my office, and we'll chat a bit before I take you to your father."

My father, Dean thought numbly as she followed wordlessly.

Once in the office, the older woman pointed to a guest chair next to her desk. "Have a seat." Dean sat, still speechless. "I take it that everything was cleared up in Germany?" she asked as she circled behind the desk to sit in her chair.

"Yes, yes. Everything worked out fine." Glad to be talking about anything other than her father, Dean gave a thumbnail sketch of the events in Germany without disclosing pertinent details.

"My, I'm glad it all turned out well. Will Elsa recover completely?"

"The doctor's are very optimistic. Mentally, she's still dealing with the rape; but physically, she should bounce back quickly." Silence filled the room as they each waited for the other to speak.

"Well, I suppose you would like to see your father. After all, that's why you're here." The reverend stood and walked around to the front of her desk, sitting in the chair next to Dean's. She placed her hand on Dean's arm. "It will be okay, Dean. He's very anxious to see you, but I'm afraid that he's not doing too well right now. In fact, I didn't tell him that you would be here today, so he wouldn't try to overexert himself to prepare for you."

This piece of information surprised Dean as she shifted to look at Martha. "Why? What happened?"

"Nothing unusual, dear. He had his chemo treatment on Monday, and it's taken its toll on him. It usually takes a few days for him to get back on his feet after a treatment.

"Does he live far from here?"

"Well, if you call three flights up, far... C'mon, I'm sure he's awake by now. He takes a mid-afternoon nap to cope with the effects, but he's usually awake at this time." Martha stood and took the lead toward the door, Dean following after her. They walked back toward the way Dean had come in, turning right at the back corridor. Midway down this hallway, Martha stopped and pulled open a metal expansion gate, exposing a small freight elevator. "It's not plush, but it serves the purpose," she explained as they entered. Pulling the gate closed, she hit a button simply marked "up," and the elevator slowly jerked its way upward.

"Here's the tricky part. Getting it to stop even with the floor." Martha watched as the wall in front of them, marked with a big white "3" inched past. The top of the wall ended, and Dean could see the hallway for the third floor appear. Martha waited, hand poised at the button until she decided it was the right time. She pushed the "stop" button, and the elevator chugged awkwardly to a halt. Looking at the meeting of the elevator's edge and the floor of the hallway, Dean noted a slight two-inch step up to exit the elevator. "Not bad," the reverend said as she pulled the gate open. "Watch your step."

Dean exited first and waited for Martha. The minister indicated a direction to the left. "This way." When they reached the end of that hallway, she turned left again, stopping in front of a room with a nameplate screwed to the door reading "Peterson." She knocked twice and listened.

"Come in," came an almost immediate but weak reply.

Martha looked at Dean who was now a bit paler than when they'd left the office. "It'll be okay, Dean. Just trust yourself to do the right thing." Then she opened the door.

* * * * *

It was 1530 hours, and Katie was in her office waiting for a reply from the publisher of Dr. Prokov's book, *Murder, Mayhem, and Madness*. Dr. Prokov, although a well-known criminal profiler in Europe, had never been to the United States prior to her current visit. The most Katie could find out was that the psychologist preferred to do most of her work via phone, letter, or email, and was rarely seen in public. She was hoping the email she'd sent to the publisher would answer some questions. The first one being, why had she come to the U. S. now? The second one: why to such a public venue?

Katie was becoming more alarmed that there was undoubtedly more to the professor than appearances suggested, especially after her comments at lunch. She couldn't help the feeling of dread that was crawling under her skin and making her nerves jump. And jump she did when the phone rang, startling her out of her thoughts. Taking a deep breath and letting it out slowly, Katie calmed herself enough to answer the phone that was ringing on her desk. "Agent O'Malley," she spoke evenly into the receiver.

"Katie, it's Tiny."

"Hey, Tiny. How's Tom doing?"

"Tom died about an hour ago. I've been trying to reach Dean, but her phone must be off."

"Oh, Tiny. I'm so sorry to hear that. Is there anything we can we do?"

"That's why I'm calling. Tom's originally from Niagara Falls, and he always wanted to be buried back there in the family plot. I talked with his brother just a bit ago, and we're planning a memorial service for this weekend. Do you suppose you and Dean could come to it?"

Without hesitating, Katie agreed. "I'm sure we can work it out. Dean's in Kansas City right now, but she'll want to be there." She paused, then asked, "Do you mind if I call Tracy and Colleen to let them know?"

"No, I was hoping you would. I know Bill won't be able to come, since he's still in the hospital, but if you could tell him..." Tiny's voice started to catch, and he cleared his throat a couple of times before continuing. "Sorry about that. As I was saying, if you could let Bill know, I'd appreciate it."

"Sure thing, Tiny. Just let me know where and what time." Katie reached for a note pad and pen to jot down the information as Tiny gave her the particulars. Before hanging up, she spent a bit longer on the phone trying to console Tiny. She copied the details into her Palm Pilot, returned the PDA to her backpack, grabbed her coat and left for her office totally unaware that she was being watched as she ran to the housing area.

Now what's got her in such a rush? Meisha stepped out of the shadows and entered the building where Katie had her office. Since most personnel were at dinner or home with their families, the building was quiet. The only person she encountered was the guard at the building's main entrance. She was wearing her ID badge, so she didn't have any difficulty walking by him and down the hall to Katie's office. A quick check over her shoulder to confirm her solitary presence, and she swiftly opened the door to the office and slipped inside. Meisha didn't have to turn on the light because, in her haste to leave, Katie had neglected to shut down her computer.

"My, my. She was in a hurry. Well, let's see what's on her computer." The psychologist walked behind the desk and sat in the chair, turning it to face the computer. "Hmm, nothing here." She hit a few keys to bring up the email program, scanning the mail that had been sent. "Ah, that's better. Let's see... Oh, Katie, you've been a bad girl. Contacting my publisher for information about me." Just then, a response from the publisher posted to her inbox. "Well, well. Let's see what they say." Opening the email, Meisha frowned when she read the particulars of the reply. "Guess the game is up. They found the good doctor's body a bit faster than I had anticipated. I've always said if I want a job done right, I have to do it myself." Meisha laughed and waved her hand at the computer. "Well, I was getting bored with this little game anyway. Time to move on."

She hit "reply" and typed a message thanking them for the quick response, before deleting the email. Swiveling the chair back toward the desk, she noticed the notepad with the scribbled message. "Well, at least one of my people was successful." Reading further, she found the information on the funeral arrangements. "Oh, this is perfect!" Meisha sat back in the chair and thought for a moment. "Yesss. And I know just the right spot." She promptly rose and exited the office as quietly as she had entered.

* * * * *

Dean wasn't ready for the sight that greeted her as she

entered her father's room. Although it was bright from being a corner unit with windows on two sides, the room carried an air of gloom. Medicine bottles lined the tall dresser near the door, and there was a distinctive odor she associated with illness. Her stomach, which had been queasy all day, did an immediate flip, causing her to gasp lightly. Martha caught the almost imperceptible sound and reached out, tenderly placing her hand on Dean's arm. That touch buoyed her enough to regain her composure and step fully into the room. She looked over at Martha and mouthed a "thank you."

Joshua Peterson was sitting in an old faded wing chair, intently reading his Bible in the fading daylight. "Joshua, you have a visitor," the minister said kindly as she led Dean to the small sitting area in the corner by the windows. Dean looked at the shell of the man that was her father. The man she remembered who was full of rage was nowhere in sight. Instead, she saw a different human being—one who had paid the price for his act of anger. A man that had been humbled over the years and transformed into a submissive servant of the afflicted, a frail skeleton of the man he once was.

Joshua let the book fall into his lap as he lifted his head to see who his visitor was. At first, his eyes registered confusion, then recognition, and finally tears welled up and threatened to fall. "Deanna? Ohh...Deanna, you came..." was all he was able to say before the tears fell freely down his leathery face.

All the anger Dean had carried for years in her heart dissolved in that instant, and she rushed to him. Wrapping her arms carefully around his wasted body, she hugged him and began to cry. In between sobs, Dean whispered, "Father...I...I've missed you."

Sensing that everything would be all right, Martha quietly backed out of the room, closing the door behind her.

* * * * *

Katie pulled out her keys as she reached the door of her small room. Inserting the key in the lock, she unlocked the room, entered, and flipped on the light. She immediately saw the message light blinking on her phone. Walking over to the desk, she dialed the message retrieval digits and waited. The message was from Dean and had come in at 1530 hours. She checked her watch and realized she had missed the call by twenty minutes, then she heard her lover's voice as the message played.

"Hey, love. I just got to the city mission. It's about 1430 here, and I was hoping to talk to you before I go in, so you could give me a little courage. You didn't answer your cell phone, so I thought I'd try here." She paused and exhaled loudly into the phone. "I'm going to turn my phone off for a bit when I go to see my father, so don't be alarmed if I don't answer. Just leave me a voice message, and I'll get back to you. I love you." Pause. "See you soon, love."

Katie held the phone in both hands as she listened to the message, replying out loud, "I love you, too," when it was finished. She put the receiver back in the cradle and reached into her backpack to check her cell phone. When she pulled it out, she realized that the battery had gone dead. "Damn. Well, it'll have to charge in the car." Picking up the phone once more, Katie called her supervisor to alert him that she would be leaving immediately for Niagara Falls, but would be back on Monday, or Tuesday at the latest. She was going to call Dean, but knew that she wouldn't reach her right then anyway, so she figured to wait until she got back to the house. She surveyed the room to see what she would need to take with her. Deciding that she really didn't need anything from there other than her backpack, she changed into her favorite jeans, turtleneck jersey, and a large sweatshirt, slipped on her Reeboks, and picked up her backpack and jacket before heading out. On her way to the car, she remembered that she'd forgotten about the email she'd sent to the publisher, but figured that she could check her inbox from home. Unlocking the Boxster, she tossed her backpack onto the passenger seat, slipped behind the wheel, and headed for home.

Chapter
20

14 December, 1630 Hours

The sleek Boxster idled outside the garage as the door rose slowly, her impatient driver tapping the steering wheel as she watched the door pass the height of the sports car, then quickly pulled forward and parked. Turning off the ignition and removing the keys, Katie hit the garage door control again to send it back down before picking up her backpack and exiting the car. She made her way quickly to the house, unlocking the door and turning off the security alarms. The stack of mail on the hall table caused her momentary alarm, but then she remembered that Dirk had offered to stop by and take it in.

Shaking off her coat and hanging it on the coat rack, she picked up the backpack and headed for the phone. Realizing that it had only been an hour since Dean had called, she wasn't surprised when she got the recording to leave a message. "Dean, please call as soon as you get this message. I'm at home, so call me there." Next, she dialed Bill at the hospital, filling him in on Tom's death and the memorial service in Niagara Falls.

Finally, she called Tracy and Colleen.

"Hey," she greeted as Colleen picked up the phone. Katie somberly told her about the memorial service.

"I'm sorry to hear that. I'll try to reach Tracy on her cell phone and fill her in."

"She's still at work?" Katie asked as she checked her watch.

"Sorta. She and Linna are on another trip. They just left this morning."

"Where to this time?"

"Actually, they went to Niagara Falls for the Winter Festival of Lights. They're staying at a small motel on the Canadian side. Let me give you the number there." There was a pause as Katie heard some papers being shuffled. "It's 905-222-1111. It's called the Gorge View Motel. They should be getting back from dinner about now."

"I take it her shoulder is healing okay, or she wouldn't be traveling."

"Yeah, it's doing pretty well, but she's still got to be careful. Linna will make sure she doesn't do anything outrageous."

"I bet she will," Katie chuckled at the thought of Linna playing Nurse Ratchet. Okay, I'll see you two at the service. Right now, I'd better leave the line open for Dean to call." They said their goodbyes and set up a time to meet at the motel before the memorial service.

Katie had just finished sorting the stack of mail when the phone rang. She picked up the receiver and plopped into her favorite chair at the same time, causing her voice to come out in a rush as she answered. "Dean?"

"Yeah, it's me. What's wrong? You sound strange."

"Oh, sorry. I just plopped into the chair as I answered. But there is something you need to know." She wasn't sure how to say it, so she just decided to be direct. "Tiny called a bit ago. Tom didn't make it."

There was the expected pause before Dean responded. "When I find that bitch..."

"She'll have to answer to the law," Katie cut in as she felt her partner's anger rise.

A thousand miles away, Dean nodded, calming herself as she felt Katie's words seep into her soul. "You're right. She'll answer to the law."

Changing the topic for a moment, Katie asked how the visit with her father had gone. She was not surprised to hear Dean speak of the reconnection beginning between her and her father.

Dean's words rushed out in an anguished torrent as she told Katie about the pain her dad had gone through for the previous years, describing his fall into substance abuse, and finally, his decision to turn himself in and pay for his crime.

"I guess I never tried to put myself in his shoes, to imagine how he must have felt when he faced the fact that he had taken the life of his own flesh and blood. The shame and misery, and the subsequent loss of the rest of his family devastated him. After Mom died, he couldn't bear it any longer, and he couldn't bring himself to face me." Dean paused, her emotions beginning to show in her voice. "Not that I ever gave him a chance. I carried the hate and anger so long... If it hadn't been for you...back in the Catskills...I probably would have driven myself to..."

"Dean," Katie interjected softly, "the point is, the hate and anger didn't destroy you; you were able to overcome them. And now, you and your father can both find forgiveness...and love."

"You're right, but we don't have much time. We've wasted so much of it; and now Dad is dying."

"Dean, it's not the quantity of time that's left, it's the quality of that time. We'll do everything we can to make it the best for him...and you." She paused, deciding that it was time to ease back to the memorial for Tom. "Sweetie, we need to make arrangements to meet at the memorial service on Saturday. Will you be able to catch a flight?"

Calmer now, Dean was able to concentrate on the logistics for Saturday. They agreed that Katie would fly up earlier and secure a rental car and room, while she spent another day with her father. While they talked, Katie went over to her laptop on the kitchen table to check flights from KCI to Niagara Falls International, booking herself a flight for late morning and making a reservation for Dean on the afternoon flight. Dean would leave Kansas City on the 12:15 flight to Niagara Falls, and Katie would pick her up at the airport.

Once the arrangements had been completed, Dean asked, "How're things going with Dr. Prokov?"

"I'm doing a little background check on her right now," Katie offered. "There's just something about her that's niggling at me. I haven't been able to put a finger on it yet, but I will. I was just going to check my email for a message from the publisher when you called."

"Why? What's setting off the warning bells?"

Katie went on to describe the lunchtime conversation they'd

had, and Dean also found the bit about hunting predators very interesting.

"Could be it's just an off-shoot of her professional life...hunting criminals...but it does sound a bit strange."

"That's what I thought at first, too, but I guess it was the way she said it and the way she looked right at me when she said the part about underestimating the cornered predator's mate." Katie shuddered. "It really gave me the creeps."

"Well, love, you just be careful. Have you set all the security codes?"

"No, not yet, but I will as soon as I hang up."

"Okay, then we'd better hang up now. I don't like the thought of you sitting in that house without the security measures on. I'll see you tomorrow."

"I'll be waiting. Love you."

"Love you, too. Now, go set the codes."

"Yes, Ma'am!" Katie replied smartly, then hung up and headed downstairs for the den and the main security console. She took the stairs quickly and turned the corner. She never saw them come out of the shadows, but when she felt the needle enter her arm, she knew she was in trouble. Two men held her as a third person stepped into view.

A deformed hand gently caressed Katie's cheek. "Hello, Katie. Surprised to see me?"

The Oxford accent was gone now, and the pieces that had niggled at her fell into place as Katie struggled to maintain consciousness. The face was not the same, but as the woman before her started laughing evilly, and the drug took effect, the laughter turned into an echo, playing over and over in her head. Katie's vision blurred and her knees buckled. The last thing Katie said before she blacked out was, "Natasha."

* * * * *

Opting to spend the night at the city mission in one of the vacant rooms on the third floor, Dean cancelled her reservation at the Crown Center Hotel. She ate dinner with her father and the others who stayed at the mission, and spent the evening with her father, listening to him tell of his work there. He hadn't asked her about her career in the Army, and she was grateful for that. She wasn't ready to bare her soul and her own feelings of rage and hatred just yet. They turned in early, mostly because her father needed the rest, but she figured she could use the sleep herself as she'd had precious little of it over the last few days. Her sleep, unfortunately, was restless, as her mind replayed her visit with her father and the phone call with Katie. Thoughts floated through her mind, mingling with facts and questions. Her body was still trying to decide if she was in Germany, or DC, or Kansas City. She'd barely had time to compensate for the jet lag, and now she was reeling with more emotions than she had ever experienced before. Love and hate, tenderness and anger, compassion and fear...all ran together, sending her mind and soul into a maelstrom of confusion.

Giving up, she got out of bed and slipped on her sweats and running shoes. *What I need now is a good long run. Maybe if I exhaust myself, I'll be able to get a few minutes of sleep.* She tied her hair back into a ponytail and plotted a run that would take her down to the river and, eventually, River Front Park. Dean checked her watch and noted it was 0330 hours. She took the map of downtown with her as she took the stairs down to the main entrance. Reverend Lewistan had said that the mission was open 24-7, and she found a night receptionist in the main office. Poking her head in, she whispered to the young man that she was going out for a run.

"Ma'am? At this hour? I don't think that's a good idea," he cautioned. "There's all sorts of bad people out at this time of night."

"I don't think they'll be bothering me," she replied with a wink. "I should be back in a couple of hours."

"If you say so. But if you're not back in a couple of hours, the Rev is gonna have my head!"

Dean waved at the young man and stepped out into the night air. Doing some stretches first, she started out in a slow jog, allowing her muscles to warm sufficiently before speeding up. She jogged back up Jefferson to 17th and headed back downtown on Broadway. She made a few turns through some of the streets nearer the river until she found Levee Road. Jogging along on Levee Road, she finally came to River Front Road and the park.

Running always cleared her head, and soon she was caught up in the joy of the run. She ran on, past the string of riverboat casinos on the other side of the bank. When she saw the I-435 roadway suspended above her head, she looped back the way she'd come, pushing herself through her exhaustion. Backtracking through the streets, she arrived back at the mission in a little under two hours. When she entered, she noticed the young man pacing in the office. As soon as he saw her, he looked up at the ceiling and said, "Thank you, Lord," and sat back down at his desk.

Dean took the stairs back up to her room where she grabbed a towel and her toiletries, and headed to the bathroom down the hall. *Reminds me of boot camp,* she thought as she locked the door to her stall. After a quick shower, she dried her hair and returned to her room to get dressed for breakfast, which would be served at 0730 in the dining hall. Her thoughts now clear, Dean sat at the small writing table, pen in hand. The words flew onto the paper as she began to write. She put everything out on the table: the anger and the loss she felt; the rage she'd felt over Thad's death that had been bottled up inside her for years; how she'd used that rage to fuel her actions during her covert assignments. She bared her soul, detailing all of the people that were hurt at her hands. The guilt she felt. The absolution she needed. Then she described meeting Katie. How she had filled the void in her heart and brought love back into her life. She told her father everything in that letter and ended with the hope he could accept her as Katie had. Dean read the letter over several times before signing it and sealing it in an envelope. She added her father's name to it, then set it aside, intending to leave it for him before she left. She wasn't sure how he would react, especially to the part about Katie and how much the woman meant to her. Only time would tell, and there really wasn't much of that left for him. She could only hope for the best. *I know this is the coward's way out, but I'm afraid to find out how he'll react about Katie. We're just finding our way back together, but I'll live without him before I live without her.* Her thoughts were broken by a knock on the door.

"Come in," Dean said as she slipped the envelope into her bag. Joshua Peterson opened the door and smiled brightly as he saw his daughter.

"I was afraid it was all a dream," he said as he stepped into the room. "That you really weren't here."

Dean stood and walked over to her father, gently hugging him. "Nope. I'm real. How about we go get some grub?" Father and daughter stepped out into the hall, walking arm-in-arm for the first time in many years.

Chapter
21

Katie woke for the second time, still groggy from the drug she'd been given; and she had a wicked headache. Her mouth felt dry, and she noted a distinctive taste—similar to iodine—as she swallowed. *Yuck! Remind me not to swallow!* She tried to sit up, but realized she was tied up pretty tightly. *Hmpf, not taking any chances, eh, Natasha.* Wherever she was, it was very dark and very confining. She tried rolling to the side, and hit a wooden wall. She tried the other side and hit another wooden wall, her shoulder brushing something above her. Trying to shout, she realized she had tape across her mouth. *Damn, I think they have me in a box. This isn't good. Nope, this is definitely not good at all.* Katie decided to remain quiet in hopes of hearing something from outside the box. She dozed on and off as she waited in the silence for something, anything, to happen. She was hoping someone would come soon, because she really had to pee. Just then, she heard voices, and the next thing she knew the top of her box was being pried open. When the lid came off, she was nearly blinded by the lights overhead. She squinted as she watched four powerful arms reach in and pick her up like a rag doll. They roughly set her down on the cold floor and walked out of the room. Scanning her new quarters, Katie was puzzled. The room looked like a huge locker room, but without lockers. The walls were all finished in a putty colored tile, and there were rows of benches. Along the walls were coat hooks. A variety of locked tool boxes were scattered about, and she saw a sign that said, "Pardon our dust as we work to improve your view." At the far end, she saw what she really needed, a restroom. As she tried to figure out how she could manage getting over to the toilet, she heard footsteps approaching from somewhere around the wall to her right. Looking in that direction, she saw Natasha walk in, dressed in a long yellow raincoat with a hood.

Tossing back the hood, Natasha looked down at Katie. "Ah, the sleeping princess is awake. Have a nice nap, hmm?" The woman reached down and violently ripped the duct tape off Katie face.

"Owww!" Katie screamed before she could stop herself.

"Oh, did that hurt?" Natasha bent down to see the redness that had resulted from the tape's abrupt removal. "Hmm, well, in a few hours, you'll be wishing that was all that was hurting. So, what do you think of the new me?" she said as she spun in a tight circle. "The plastic surgeon was a real artist. Add a little hair color, the Oxford accent...I was able to change everything about my appearance except for this damn hand!"

"Natasha," Katie implored, "I really need to go to the toilet. What say you let me do that, and then we can discuss whatever you want."

"The toilet! That's all you're worried about? Going to the toilet?" She began to laugh uncontrollably, tears running down her cheeks. "You know, Katie, you've got guts. I'll hand that to you." She wiped the tears from her eyes, still laughing. "Okay, you get to go to the toilet, and then we'll have a little chat...some girl talk...a little catching up, okay?" She called for her goons, Pavel and Aleksei. When they came into the room, she told them to untie Katie while she took off her raincoat.

"Now, don't try anything stupid. I'm in no hurry to kill you, but if you give me an excuse, it'll just speed up the process." She pointed at the restroom and followed after the blonde.

When Katie came out, she was immediately trussed up, but this time in a chair. The tape wasn't put back across her mouth, for which she was very thankful. "You know Dean will find me," Katie said confidently. "When I'm not at the airport to pick her up, she'll figure it out and find me."

"That's exactly what I'm counting on, dear. Your lover and I have a little confrontation we need to finish. Of course, I would have finished her off back at the UN, but I just didn't count on you being there." Natasha put a finger to her lips. "Guess that's what happens when you leave an important job to someone else. That won't happen this time, though. When she and I have our little chat, she won't be able to get to you in time. I'll make sure of that! Besides, I owe you for this!" she said angrily as she thrust her gnarled hand in Katie's face.

"Well, I'd have to say that getting a bullet in your hand is a small price to pay for trying to kill off all of the UN delegates, the President of the United States...and, oh, how about all those innocent children? Katie looked at her captor without the least bit of fear. "I guess you deserved what you got."

The comment nearly threw Natasha off balance. She stomped over to Katie, grabbing her around the throat and pushing her head back violently. "It's your fault, you know," she said in a slow guttural voice. "Those imbeciles in Siberia didn't have a proper doctor to take care of it...so, now I have you to thank for this." She released Katie's throat and pulled her hand to her chest, caressing it with her good hand. "I can't tell you what an inspiration it's been. Just the thought of exacting my revenge on you and killing your lover, kept me going through that long, cold winter."

"How'd you get out of Siberia?" Katie asked, trying to find anything that might help her.

"That was easy!" She began laughing again. "Let's just say that the guards lacked female companionship. Only I was a bit more woman than they could handle. Isn't that right, boys?" The two guards beamed at their boss, even though they did not understand much of what Natasha had said in English.

"What happened to the real Dr. Prokov?"

"Oh, the poor old dear slipped and hit her head on something really sharp. If these boys," she looked at Pavel and Aleksei, "had done what I told them to do, her body never would have been found." She smiled at Katie, "Yes, your inquiry to the publisher was finally answered. I thanked them for the response they sent." Natasha looked at her watch. "My, how time flies! Your sweetie will be landing in about six hours, and I have so much to do."

"We're in Niagara Falls?" Katie asked incredulously.

"Oh, Katie, we're not only here in Niagara Falls, we're under them! Right on the other side of that wall, in fact."

"How did you know she was coming here?"

"I've known everything you two were doing for a very long time now. I'm surprised you never found my little bug in the book I gave you. Tsk, tsk. Dean wasn't very careful was she?"

Katie closed her eyes, thinking of all the conversations they'd had in the presence of that book...and all the other things they'd done with the book lying there on the bedside table... A blush of anger started creeping up her face.

"Yes, even those intimate little moments were captured on tape. My, my, you two are worse than dogs in heat...just can't get enough of each other, can you?" She laughed again as Katie turned her face away. Natasha turned very serious, tired of toying with the blonde for the moment, "Well, enough chit-chat for now... We have work to do." She motioned to the two men as she donned her raincoat. "Go ahead and scream if you want to. No one will hear you." Then she turned and left, followed by her two goons.

* * * * *

Dean had spent the entire morning with her father as he told her about the work he was involved with at the mission. He took her around to the different areas in the building where people were putting their lives back together. Former drug addicts, homeless people, and runaways were all working together at simple tasks: sewing, cooking, some doing craft projects, even working in a shop where small engines were rebuilt and then resold. Everyone pitched in at mealtimes to set the tables, serve the food, and clean up afterwards. The afternoons were spent in therapy sessions, and since Joshua had to lead some of them, Dean didn't feel bad about leaving on the 12:15 flight. She had just finished packing her bag when there was a knock on her door. "Come in," she said as she placed the last item in the bag.

"Dean, I'm so sorry you have to leave already," Reverend Lewistan began, "but I know it's something you need to do."

Dean zipped her bag closed and turned toward her visitor. "Yes, it is. I...we, didn't get to know Tom for long, but the time we shared was very intense, and we all learned a lot about each other and learned to depend on one another." The emotional roller coaster she had been on for the past few days caused a tear to fall, but Dean turned away from the minister and recovered her normally stoic composure. "His death was senseless, a cowardly act aimed at hurting me. He was just a pawn in a game being played by a mad person. And when I find her..."

Martha walked over to Dean and put a hand on her shoulder. The visions that suddenly burst into her mind caused her to lose her balance and sent her into a semi-conscious state. She would have hit the floor except for Dean's quick reaction as she caught the minister and helped her to the bed. "Martha, what's wrong?" Dean uttered softly as she noted the fluttering eyelids on the older woman. After covering Martha with the light blanket from her bed, she ran into the hall and shouted for help. The first person to reach the room was Dean's father.

Joshua went to the bed and knelt by the minister. "What happened?"

"I don't know. We were talking, and she just keeled over."

"What were you talking about?" he demanded, looking up into his daughter's eyes.

"About the funeral I'm going to." Confused and shaken at the tone of accusation in her father's voice, Dean backed away. "We...I was just telling her how senseless Tom's death was. That he was killed by a madwoman in an attempt to hurt me."

"Then what?"

"Um, she reached out and touched my shoulder, then...just started to fall. I caught her and laid her down on the bed." Dean looked at the woman who seemed to be having a petit mal seizure. "What happened? Is she going to be okay?"

Joshua nodded and focused back on Martha. He reached up and felt her pulse. It was erratic, and her eyelids were still fluttering. Joshua looked up at Dean, worry obvious in his eyes. "Whatever she saw did this to her."

"What do you mean? She didn't *see* anything," Dean countered defensively.

"Deanna," he said in a softer tone, "Martha has a gift...or sometimes, a curse, like now." He shook his head, returning his attention to the minister. "She has visions. Sometimes when she touches someone, she can see things in our past, and occasionally, in our futures. When she touched you, she must have seen something that caused this."

Dean reeled with the information, trying to remember what she was thinking when Martha touched her. *Oh, my God. I was thinking of that lunatic. Thinking of what I want to do to her. Of the pain she has inflicted on my friends...and Katie.* Dean stumbled backward, groping for the desk chair, sitting heavily on its seat. She put her elbows on her knees and brought her hands up to hold her head. "I did this?"

"Inadvertently, yes." He reached out, putting a hand on Dean's head. "It's not your fault, Deanna. Martha never knows when she'll have a vision. But, I've never seen a reaction as strong as this one."

They heard footsteps running down the hall toward them. Rhonda was the first to enter, followed by James, the night receptionist, and a couple of other mission workers from the kitchen.

"Oh, Lord!" Rhonda exclaimed as she saw the reverend lying on the bed. "She had another one of them visions, didn't she?"

"Yes," Joshua replied. "And she hasn't come out of it yet. We need to get her to her room by the office."

Dean looked at the helpers that came in, and quickly evaluated their ability to move Martha without harming her further. "I'll carry her down. You folks go get the elevator for me." They balked momentarily until they saw Dean stand and gently lift the minister in her arms. Rhonda realized that the reverend was in the best hands possible and shooed the cooks back to the kitchen. She and James hurried to the elevator, opening the gate just in time for Dean to step in. There was only room for one more person in the small space, and Joshua commandeered it. As he closed the gate and pushed the down button, Rhonda and James took to the stairs, bound and determined to beat the elevator, which really wasn't much of a contest. They were waiting by the gate as the elevator reached the first floor. Joshua opened the gate and stepped out, leading Dean to the small room next to Martha's office. Rhonda sent James to the kitchen for some strong tea before she went into the reverend's bathroom to get a cool washcloth.

Dean gently placed Martha on her bed, covering her with the

colorful afghan that was at the foot of it.

"Should we call an ambulance?" Dean asked as Rhonda reentered the room, washcloth in hand.

"No, hon, she'll be okay. She just needs to rest." Rhonda folded the washcloth and placed it on the woman's forehead, humming *Amazing Grace* as she stroked Martha's hair.

"Are you sure there's nothing else to be done?" Dean asked again.

"No, no. She'll be fine." She gave Dean's hand a squeeze. "I've seen a lot of these here spells, and she'll come out of it. Of course, I've only seen one other that lasted this long. That was a hard one on her. Really took the wind out of her sails for a while." She looked up at Dean. "Now, don't you be blaming yourself for this. It ain't your fault." Rhonda picked up the washcloth and turned it over, placing the cooler side down. Humming again, she kept watch; Dean paced, and Joshua prayed.

Dean walked over to her father and bent down. "Dad, I'm going to call the airport and try to get a flight out first thing in the morning."

Joshua put his prayer book down and shook his head. "You don't have to do that, but if it'll make you feel..."

Martha moaned, and they both turned toward the bed. Her eyes were blinking open, and she was trying to sit up. Rhonda was encouraging her to stay down.

"No...no, have to warn..." she mumbled.

"Warn? Warn who?" Rhonda asked softly, bending closer to Martha so she could make out her words.

"Dean...hurry. Water...everywhere...over and under...swirling. Natasha...danger..." The last word was spoken so softly, Rhonda couldn't make it out as the minister collapsed back on the bed, out cold.

"What did she say?" Joshua and Dean said simultaneously.

"I dunno. Don't make no sense." Rhonda shook her head. "Somethin' 'bout water, swirling and stuff like that."

Dean moved closer to the bed and spoke in a low, almost growling voice. "Tell me exactly the words she used."

"Um, she said 'Dean,' then 'hurry.'" Rhonda looked up at the tall woman standing over her and gulped unconsciously. "Uh, then she said 'water' and 'over and under' then 'swirling.' Don't make no sense at all."

"Is that all she said?" Fierce sapphire eyes penetrated Rhonda's brown ones.

"She...she said somebody's name. Uh, it sounded like 'Natasha' or somethin' like that, and then mumbled something else I didn't understand." Rhonda looked away from the piercing stare and back down at the sleeping minister. "Oh, she also said she had to 'warn her.' I think she was meaning you, Deanna."

Natasha! The color in Dean's face drained. She turned to her father and asked, "Just how accurate are these visions?"

"As far as I know, she's never been wrong." Alarmed at the look on his daughter's face, he added, "Deanna?"

Dean looked at her watch and realized she had only forty-five minutes to catch her flight, and Kansas City International was at least thirty minutes away. "Dad, I've got to go. I can't explain, but I'll call as soon as I can." Dean rushed out of the room and ran up the stairs, taking them two at a time. She flew into her room, grabbing the bag she had just finished packing when Martha had come into the room. When she slipped her leather jacket on, the letter to her father fell out of the pocket, fluttering to the floor. She stooped to pick it up and slid it under her father's door on her way to the stairs.

The traffic lights were with her as she sped toward the airport. She managed to grab James on her way out of the mission so he could drop off the rental car for her. When she screeched to a halt in front of the terminal, she grabbed her bag and handed James a hundred dollar bill. "Here, you'll need this for cab fare back to the mission."

"God bless you, Deanna. Be careful now."

"I will, James. Thank you for returning the car." She shut the door and ran into the terminal, checking the flight monitors as she ran. The gate she needed was fairly close, and she got there just as they were finalizing the boarding. Taking her seat in first class, her thoughts turned once again to the minister's warning. *Natasha! I should have figured...I just hope I get to Katie before she does.* Dean's thoughts were interrupted as the flight attendant began her safety speech. As she checked her seat belt, Dean realized this was going to be the longest flight she had ever taken. Once in the air, she tried to reach Katie on her cell phone, but kept getting the message that the customer she was trying to reach was not available. She left a message on Katie's voice mail anyway, and then called Lieutenant Green to fill him in, hoping he could locate Natasha before she found Katie. He offered to call in some markers with a friend in the Niagara Falls Police Department just in case she was headed Dean's way. Figuring there was nothing else she could do 'til she landed, Dean tried to settle herself for the three-hour flight.

* * * * *

Linna was relaxing on the bed, reading the brochures she'd picked up in the front lobby. "Hey, Tracy! Did you know that the Dome Jet goes 65 mph? And that it makes the trip to the whirlpool and back in thirty minutes?"

"I hear it's a heck of ride through all those rapids." Tracy replied, as she read the brochure on the Spanish Aero Car. "Get a load of this. The Aero Car has been in operation since 1916, travels the 3,600 foot round trip in 10 minutes, and is at a height of 250 feet over the whirlpool. The whole car is suspended over the gorge by only six cables."

"I certainly hope they've updated that puppy since 1916," Linna chortled, "or, I'm not going on it."

"Relax. According to the brochure, it had design and function upgrades in 1961, 1967, and 1984."

"Oh, well, that doesn't comfort me. It's been...sixteen...seventeen years since its last update!" They both started giggling as Linna pretended to be falling from an imaginary cable car. "Help...help...I'm falling, and I can't swim!"

Tracy waved at Linna and said, "That's okay. From that height, you'd break your neck on impact anyway!"

Linna shot her boss a look, then picked up her pillow and threw it at her. "Ya mean ya wouldn't jump in and save me?"

"Nope. You know me. I'm a warm water swimmer." They both laughed again, enjoying the comfortable camaraderie they shared.

"Are you about ready to pick up Colleen?" Linna asked after Tracy threw her pillow back to her. "The rental car is out front."

"Just about. All the arrangements for the funeral have been

made. It's going to be at St. Gabriel's Memorial Chapel in Niagara Falls, at 4:00 p.m. tomorrow. Tiny's flight has already come in, and he's on his way to the chapel with the casket." Tears began forming in her eyes as she remembered the many years she had known the ex-SEAL and the good times she and Colleen had had with Nick, Tom, and Tiny during their vacations in the Bahamas.

"Katie is picking up Dean, right?" Linna said hurriedly to redirect Tracy's thoughts.

"Yes, at least that was the plan she gave to Colleen last night. If it's any different, we'll find out when we pick up Col."

"Are you still going to make it for the Whirlpool Dome Jet ride?" Linna knew her boss really wanted to go on the jet boat ride down the Niagara Gorge.

Tracy checked her watch, noting that it was almost 1:00 p.m. The jet boat ride was scheduled for 3:00 p.m. "I'll probably just miss you guys, but I'll catch up to you at the Spanish Aero Car for the ride over the whirlpool. If I miss that, I'll just wait 'til the cable car comes back and I'll join you for the rest of the tour." Tracy knew the airport wasn't far, but they were on the Canadian side, which meant having to twice go through the security at the bridges. "I'd better get going. It's a nice day and the tourists will be out in force, making the lines at the bridges too long for my liking. But, I think I can beat some of the traffic by going over the Whirlpool Bridge and then cutting over to Niagara Falls Boulevard."

"Okay, I'll see you at the Aero Car. Tell Colleen I made room for her at dinner. She'll love the German restaurant we're going to." Linna tossed Tracy the keys to the rental car that had been delivered an hour earlier.

"Got it. Catch ya later!" Tracy commented as she caught the keys and left the motel room.

Chapter 22

Katie still had a monster headache, and the quiet of the room she was in just made it seem that much worse. She had managed to doze off again, but the pounding in her head wouldn't let her sleep too long. *Damn, I could really use some aspirin... Of course, if Dean doesn't find me in time, I think a headache will be the least of my worries.* In the interim since Natasha and her Siberian huskies had left, Katie had tried to remember everything she could about Niagara Falls. If they were "under them" as Natasha had told her, it meant they were on the Canadian side. She remembered coming here with her parents as a small child. She also remembered all the yellow raincoats, and that they smelled musty and nearly made her sick, but Mom and Dad had been so excited about walking under the falls. *Hmm, I think they were called the Scenic Tunnels, or something like that.* She paused, scanning her memory, picking up bits and pieces. *I remember reading somewhere that these tunnels were renovated, and they changed the name. Yeah, now I remember, they call it* Journey Behind the Falls. She looked around the disheveled space. *This must be one of the changing rooms. They must not be open in the winter months. Hmm, looks like they're doing some kind of maintenance, though, with all those tools lying about.* She was still contemplating her situation when she heard Natasha and the boys returning.

"Hi, honey, we're home," Natasha chimed cheerily. "Miss us?"

"Not hardly," Katie retorted. "Why don't you and your boys go for a swim? I hear the water is real refreshing this time of year."

"Oh no, sweetie. I'm saving that little pleasure for you." Natasha walked over to where Katie was tied, and squatted down next to her. She put her lips right next to Katie's ear, blowing a warm breath as she spoke. "You do know how to swim, don't you?" Katie jerked her head away from the woman, causing Natasha to laugh. Abruptly terminating her laughter, Natasha reached up and grabbed a handful of Katie's blonde hair, pulling violently. "Don't worry, the power of that water will crush your body against the rocks before you could even do one stroke." Releasing her hold, she smiled again at the blonde. "And then it will probably carry you down all the way to the bottom." She looked Katie in the eye. "Do you know how deep it is at the base of the falls?" Not getting a response, she answered her own question. "Only about 150 feet. By the time they find your body...if they find your body...there won't be anything recognizable to identify." Natasha stood and motioned to the two men. "C'mon boys, time to take Katie to see the falls, up close and personal." Pavel and Aleksei ambled over and untied the blonde. Even though she struggled, Katie was no match for their huge bulk as they carried her off, following Natasha down the corridor. They entered the elevator and descended the 125 feet to the tunnels. Exiting the elevator, they took the right turn that led 150 feet behind Niagara Falls.

Katie couldn't decide if the roar in her head was from the headache or the sound of the water thundering down. *I don't think it matters much at this point,* she thought, as the group passed two observation cutouts directly under the water. Even though she was still in her sweats, it was cold and damp in the tunnel, and it was starting to make her very uncomfortable. *Okay, Dean, any time now,* she was thinking as they passed a makeshift chain link barricade that led to the third and final observation cut-out.

"End of the line, Katie." Natasha said as she led the way to the railing.

Katie looked around and noticed there were fresh drill holes in the rock surrounding the railing. Each pencil-thin hole had a wire coming out of it. She counted six holes, two on each side and two in the floor. The wires came together and entered a strange looking junction box closer to the main tunnel. Natasha smiled at her as the men moved past her and lifted Katie up over the first railing. Katie looked back at Natasha, who smiled and waved at her.

"In case you hadn't noticed, those little holes each have a bit of C4 explosive in them. Not enough to do too much damage, but enough to release the railing and let you tumble forward into the falls. The box has a timer on it, and will trigger the charge at precisely 6:00 p.m. And, just in case your lover wins our little challenge today, it's also set with a series of laser beams that will trigger the charge if interrupted. If she takes one step into this observation tunnel, her last sight will be to see you drop out into the falls." Natasha stopped for a moment putting her finger to her lips in thought, "Hmm, I wonder if she'll just run out after you? I should have put in a video camera, I'd love to see her face!"

Katie renewed her efforts to get away from the two men, only to be lifted over the final safety railing. The men then put a set of handcuffs on each wrist, pulled her arms out, and clamped the other end of each cuff to the railing. Her feet were on a very narrow ledge that was slick with years of water splashing on its surface. She looked back over her shoulder as Pavel and Aleksei cleared the railing. Not wanting to show fear, Katie smiled at Natasha. "She *will* beat you, Natasha. I don't doubt that for a minute. And, she *will* figure out how to get me out of here!"

"We'll see...but, I've got to run now." She looked at her watch. "Time for your lover to land. Oh, and just for fun, I'm leaving the boys here to keep an eye out until I get back."

Kate watched as the three of them backed out of the short tunnel, stopping long enough to activate the black box with a remote control Natasha had. She turned back to face the thundering water that was now only six feet in front of her, and began to pray she was right about her imminent rescue.

* * * * *

Dean's flight landed ten minutes early. Once out of the aircraft, she bolted toward the terminal where arriving passengers were being greeted by friends and family. She scanned the area looking for Katie and started to worry when she didn't see her. Checking her watch, she hoped Katie was just held up in traffic or maybe running a bit late. Pulling out her cell phone to call, she was surprised when it rang in her hand. Relief poured over her as she flipped it open and quickly spoke, "Hey. Stuck in traffic somewhere?"

"Hello, Colonel." Natasha spoke in her normal voice, knowing that Dean would recognize it instantly.

"Hello, bitch," Dean replied casually, as she correctly identified the caller.

"Now, now, that's not nice. And if you're not nice to me, I won't tell you where your little blonde tart is."

The words cut straight through to Dean's heart as she gripped the phone tightly and spoke through clenched teeth. "You better not have harmed her."

"Oh, she's just fine...but she won't be in a couple of hours." Natasha entered the terminal and looked for Dean, spotting her easily. "Now, about that little challenge we talked about. Are you up for it now?"

"What's on your mind?" Dean replied, starting toward the exit nearest her.

"How about a little game of tag? Right now, you're it, and you've got to tag me to win the prize."

"What's the prize?" Dean asked as she stepped outside.

Natasha retreated through the door she had come in, being careful that Dean wouldn't see her just yet. "Not so fast, Colonel. First we get to finish our little fight. You know, the one your bitch broke up by shooting my hand? Well, winner gets the blonde. Interested?"

"Hardly seems fair, with you being handicapped and all," Dean answered evenly.

"Oh, I don't know. I still have an advantage."

"Yeah? What?"

"I know where Katie is!" Natasha laughed evilly. "Tag...you're it. Catch me if you can!" She shut off the phone and headed for her car. Opening the door, she looked back at Dean, who appeared to be shouting into the phone. Smiling, Natasha whistled loudly and waved to get Dean's attention.

"Son of a bitch!" Dean growled as she caught sight of her nemesis waving at her. A second later, Natasha was behind the wheel and pulling away from the curb. Dean looked around her, finally settling her focus on a couple stepping out of a cab. She ran to the cab, jumped into the front seat next to the driver, and said the most famous cliché line of all chase scenes: "Follow that car!"

The cab driver looked at her in disbelief and said, "You're kidding, right?" One look into the steely sapphire eyes was enough for him to realize she was deadly serious. "Right. But I'm not breaking any traffic rules," he said cautiously, as he pulled out into the flow of traffic.

Dean watched as Natasha's car pulled out into traffic. "Look, if you don't get this bucket moving, I'm going to drive it myself. Now, move!" The low growl and the feral look she gave him were all the incentive he needed. He put the accelerator to the floor and managed to slide into traffic a scant ten cars behind Natasha's black Audi. Dean watched the Audi weave through the traffic and called out instructions to the driver as Natasha sharply turned corners. Miraculously, the police never took notice of either car's speed or erratic driving. They raced down Niagara Falls Boulevard, narrowly missing a tour bus pulling into the outlet mall. By the time they approached Military Road, the cab was two cars back, and the light turned red just after Natasha entered the intersection. The cabbie started to break, but Dean slipped her foot over the transmission hump and pressed the cab driver's foot down on the accelerator while grabbing the steering wheel to pull around the cars in front of them. They bounced over the right hand curb, slipped behind the SUV that was turning left onto the boulevard, and blasted through the intersection unscathed. Natasha had a good block and a half lead, but Dean was still accelerating the cab to catch up.

"Lady! You trying to get us killed?" the cabbie screamed as Dean relinquished control of the steering wheel.

"Just catch up to that car," Dean growled, her eyes never leaving the back bumper of the Audi.

As they came to the underpass for Interstate 190, a cement mixer was pulling out from the exit ramp. The Audi's brake lights lit, then slid to the left of the big truck, nearly had a head on colli-

sion with a school bus, and then accelerated past the cement
truck. The cab driver managed to brake fast enough to avoid a
collision, but now they couldn't see around the truck to keep a
visual on the Audi. At the next intersection, they had a choice of
going either right on Pine, or left on Walnut. They slowed as the
truck took the right curve onto Pine. Dean searched the small
view she now had in front of the truck and did not see the Audi.
When she looked down the left curve, she spotted the Audi at a
stoplight. There was a charcoal Cadillac now between them.

"Go left!" she screamed at the driver. In reflex, he jerked the
cab left, heading down Walnut. They were fifty feet from the
Cadillac when the light changed. Traffic was now getting heavier,
making it impossible for the cab to pass. The Audi was in the
same boat, following behind a line of cars heading to Main Street.
All three vehicles managed to turn left at the intersection of Main
Street, and then right onto Whirlpool. When they got to Bridge
Street, two more cars muscled their way between the Audi and the
cab. Natasha made a last minute turn onto Bridge Street, nearly
causing a collision in the intersection. By the time the cab was
able to round the corner, Dean could see the Audi pulled up to the
U.S. Customs booth at the bridge. They were now four cars back.
Dean was about to leave the cab and try to catch the Audi on foot,
but quickly changed her mind as Natasha pulled out to cross the
bridge. As they were waiting their turn, a customs agent opened
another booth and the cab driver quickly slipped into the opening.
It seemed as though time was standing still, but in fact, the agent
passed them through in less than a minute. Dean's eyes never left
the Audi, watching as it turned right onto Niagara Parkway.

"Get over to the right. Turn here." She pointed as they came
to the intersection. Traffic was almost at a crawl as cars slowed
for pedestrians or to catch a glimpse of the Niagara Gorge. Dean
had lost sight of the Audi after it turned the corner, and now she
was desperately searching for it. She checked every turn and
parking space as they slowly moved down the parkway. They were
passing the parking lot for the Niagara Spanish Aero Car attraction when she spotted it in the parking lot. It was empty.
"STOP!" she commanded. The driver hit the brakes so fast, the
car behind them nearly collided with the rear bumper. Dean
grabbed her bag and flipped a hundred dollar bill at the driver.

She said a simple, "Thanks," and dashed out of the cab. The roadway was higher than the parking lot, giving Dean a valuable advantage as she searched for Natasha among the tourists. She spotted her standing at the door of the gift shop, watching Dean. Natasha waved at her and crooked her finger at Dean, enticing her to follow. Dean vaulted the guardrail and ran down the slight slope into the parking lot, watching as Natasha disappeared into the gift shop.

Conscious of all the tourists, Dean ran as fast as she could without physically harming any bystanders. When she entered the gift shop, she saw Natasha exiting it through the far door. Mumbling, "Excuse me... Sorry... Pardon me," she bobbed, weaved, and as gently as possible, pushed through the throng of mostly senior citizens and out the far door.

Natasha checked over her shoulder, impressed at how close Dean actually was. Turning to the line of tourists for the Aero Car, she hopped the railings until she was at the front of the line. Shouts arose from those waiting their turn, angered by the rudeness of the woman. The car attendant was helping the last person out of the car when she jumped inside.

"Ma'am, you can't..." His words were cut off when he saw the gun in her hand.

"Lock it and move it!" she told the attendant.

"Yes, ma'am," he replied shakily as he closed the gates to the car and put it in motion.

The Aero Car was like a huge open gondola. The sides were made from a heavy mesh of steel that extended from the floor of the car up about 30 inches. The rest of the railing was composed of two steel rails—the first one set about six inches from the mesh guard, and the heavier top railing six inches from that one. There were six steel beam supports extending from the base of the car to the roof and the superstructure for the cabling system, two at each end and two in the middle. The end result was a huge expanse of open viewing of the Niagara Gorge and the whirlpool below.

The tourists just leaving the car, as well as the ones waiting in line, had started screaming and backing away when they saw the glint of gunmetal. Dean had to push harder to make her way to the car. She got to the gate as the car started to pull away. The colonel didn't even hesitate as she tossed her bag to the still shaking attendant, stepped up on the railing, and jumped for the car. As her hands caught the overhanging roof, she lifted her feet and swung into the car, causing it to sway a bit. Screams from the tourists on land filled the air as Natasha backed her way to the opposite end.

* * * * *

Two of the tourists left at the gate stood watching in disbelief at the scene that had unfolded before them.

"Did you see what I think I saw?" Tracy asked, still transfixed on the Aero Car and its two passengers.

"Uh huh," Linna answered, nodding her head. "I think we both saw the same thing. But who is that she's chasing?"

"Got me. It's obviously someone she wants really bad." Tracy thought for a minute as the light dawned in her head. "Bet it's the bitch that's been causing all the trouble. The one that had Tom killed."

"Shit! We should help her, but how?" Linna asked as the cable car crept out into the gorge.

"We'll think of something." Tracy paused, looking around at the gawking crowd. "Where's Katie? She was supposed to pick up Dean at the airport. She's got to be around here somewhere." Tracy started searching the crowd in earnest, moving through the mass of humanity as they watched the scene in the aero car unfold. *I'm getting a really bad feeling about this*, she thought as she exited the gift shop and searched the parking lot. Finding no indication of Katie, she hurried back to Linna, squeezing her way through the crowd. When she stood next to Linna once more, she said in a low voice, "No sign of Katie anywhere. My gut's telling me that bitch out there has done something to her, and Dean's going to find out just what."

Linna looked at her boss, then back out at the gondola and said, "Fuck a duck."

* * * * *

Dean steadied herself against the railing as she landed, then stood to her full height as she moved away from the rail. "What have you done to Katie?" she snarled, taking another step forward.

"Now, now, Colonel, don't you remember my challenge? Only the winner gets Katie," the ex-KGB agent said with alacrity.

Dean motioned at the gun still in Natasha's hand, "Doesn't look like it'll be a fair fight to me."

"You mean this?" She held up the gun. "Oh, okay," she sighed, tossing it over the side. "There, is that better?"

"Fine," Dean responded quickly, then both rushed together, with Dean sending the first blow of the fight toward the woman's abdomen. Natasha went with the movement, absorbing most of the impact easily and bringing the two combatants into close contact.

"My, my, you're losing your touch. That little blonde has really done a number on you."

Not waiting for the next blow to be initiated, Natasha raised her right elbow into Dean's ribs, and then stepped to the side. Dean spun with the contact, but kept the motion going, leveling a hard kick to Natasha's head, snapping it back fiercely and following through with another shot to Natasha's abs with her elbow. This time, the double blow made her adversary fall to her knees. Dean moved behind her and wrapped her left arm around the woman's throat, pulling her back up to a standing position.

"Where is she?" Dean shouted in Natasha's ear.

The ex-KGB agent reached up with both arms, pulling down on the colonel's left arm as she bent over forcefully. Since she was nearly as tall as Dean, she was able to leverage Dean over her shoulder and onto the deck of the car. Natasha leapt on Dean, but not before Dean was able to get her feet up to repel the onslaught. The strength of her legs caused Natasha to fly backwards, crashing into the side railing. Dean stood and charged at the blonde, grabbing her by the throat with both hands.

"Tell me, bitch! Before I break your neck!"

It took all of the self-control she could muster to just smile at Dean and choke out, "Haven't...won...yet." Then Natasha clapped both palms hard against Dean's ears, causing her to loosen her grip just enough to break free.

The pain was overwhelming, but Dean managed to grab Natasha's shirt and spin her back around to deliver a right hook straight to her jaw. The blow sent Natasha over the railing of the car. Only Dean's quick reaction saved her from falling into the fast approaching whirlpool. Hanging on to the woman with one hand, Dean managed to wrap her leg around the center beam so she could reach over the side with her other hand, but the angle of her body kept her from making contact with Natasha.

"C'mon, Natasha. Give me your other hand." The blow Dean delivered still had the dangling woman dazed as she looked down then back up at her arch enemy. Dean's grip was beginning to slip from the gnarled hand that barely held on to hers. "Hurry, Natasha. Give me your other hand." Dean felt the Aero Car jerk to a halt, causing her grip to slip a little more.

Recovering from the blow, Natasha looked up at Dean and laughed. "Guess you win."

"Yeah, now tell me where she is while you give me your other hand!" Dean groaned as she tried to get a better grip.

Natasha laughed harder, only it was more evil this time. She looked down at the water, back up at Dean, then smiled. "No, I don't think so...but, I'll give you a hint: she'll be with me soon," she crooned, then winked at Dean and released what little grip she had left on Dean's hand, making it almost impossible for Dean to hold on much longer.

Panicked, Dean tried to lunge for her, but Natasha wriggled her body harder, then the cable car jerked back to life, reversing its direction back to the waiting onlookers. The jerking motion of the car, coupled with Natasha's wiggling, were too much for Dean to overcome. The gnarled hand slipped from her fingers, and she watched in horror as Natasha fell the 250 feet into the middle of the whirlpool. "NOOOooooo!" Dean shouted, watching as the water swirled violently, swallowing the offering it received. By the time the Aero Car returned to its station, Natasha's body had not surfaced and, in all probability, never would.

Chapter
23

As the cable car docked, Dean's expression was hardened, but determined. She spotted the attendant she had given her bag to and looked for it. "Where's my bag?" she grunted.

The young man shook his head and pointed into the crowd, "They have it."

Dean followed the direction of his hand and was not surprised to see Tracy and Linna approaching, carrying her bag. "Good," she stated simply and walked to meet them. She took the bag from Linna. "C'mon, we've got to find Katie."

Linna and Tracy had the presence of mind to send the seniors back on tour, with one of the "regulars" put in charge, indicating they would meet them back at the motel and to possibly not expect them until later that night. They also asked the driver to contact Colleen, who had gone back to the motel after dropping Tracy off at the Spanish Aero Car.

"What now?" Tracy asked, as they left the crowd behind. The young attendant had recovered and was chasing after them, trying to get them to wait for the Provincial Police. The trio ignored his pleas and headed for the roadway.

"I don't know for sure, but I've got to make a phone call." She reached into her jacket pocket and pulled out her cell phone. It was badly battered, but she tried it anyway. "Damn thing's busted!" she cursed. Linna pulled her cell phone out of her backpack and handed it to Dean. Dean nodded gratefully and punched in some numbers. When the voice answered on the other end, she closed her eyes, praying that it would be able to help her.

"Martha, this is Dean. I need your help." Dean gave a succinct synopsis of the events of the last hour, indicating what she hoped Martha could provide...a clue to where Katie was.

"Dean, I don't know how I can help. The vision was overwhelming. All I saw was this stranger, and water. It was over me, and under me, swirling everywhere. And it was loud, so loud it filled all my senses to overload."

"Can't you just, I don't know, recall it...see if there's more to it...some kind of clue?" Dean beseeched the minister.

"My visions can't be conjured up like that. I can't just force them," the minister explained softly.

"Martha, this is Katie's life we're talking about. You saw something and knew you had to warn me. Please, please, try." Tears were now forming in her eyes. "I can't lose her, Martha. She's my life."

Hearing the strain in Dean's voice, Martha went on, "Dean, my visions have only come when I touch the person, or touch their belongings."

"I don't have time to come back there," she groaned. "Natasha said she only had a couple of hours, and that was over an hour ago."

Martha thought quietly on the other end. "Dean, did you leave anything here? A piece of clothing, book, anything?"

Dean shook her head, "No, nothing." Tears were falling freely now, and she was pacing back and forth on the roadway. Tracy and Linna listened intently to this side of the conversation. Linna slung her backpack over her shoulder, exposing several postcards in the net pocket to Dean's view. "Wait!" she said excitedly. "I left a letter for my father. I slipped it under his door before I left!"

Martha sighed hopefully on the other end, and then gave instructions for James to run up to Joshua's room and retrieve the letter. The dead silence on the line seemed to go on interminably while both parties waited. Dean could hear James running into the room.

"Dean, I can't promise anything. You know that, don't you?"

"Yes, just try. Please try!"

Martha reached out and took the letter from James and began

praying silently as she did so. Tracy and Linna held their breath waiting for Martha's response. Dean checked her watch, closed her eyes, and waited. A thousand miles away, Martha, too, closed her eyes, waiting for a vision to appear. She was just about to set the letter down when she started to get a strange feeling...she was cold...and wet. The thunderous roar came back, causing her to sway. She saw a shadow, blurred by a veil of water, heard a muffled cry of Dean's name, then it was gone. Martha opened her eyes wide, still swaying from the vision.

"Dean, Katie's in trouble. She's somewhere where it's cold, and she's wet. I couldn't see her, but the thunderous noise was there. There was a veil of water obstructing the view, but she was calling your name. You must hurry!"

Dean's head lowered, thankful for the bits of information no matter how small. "Thank you, Martha. We'll find her."

"Hurry, Dean. She doesn't have much time."

Dean returned the phone to Linna and faced her friends. "Okay, this is what we've got. Katie is someplace wet and cold. Martha couldn't see her, but could hear a loud roar and there was water...lots of it."

Linna looked at Dean, shook her head and pointed toward the gorge. "Dean, look around you. There's lots of water; and if you go back up the gorge three miles, there's a lot of roar, too. Where do we start?"

Tracy looked at the two women as they stared at each other. "Did she say anything else, Dean?"

Dean turned to Tracy. "She said she couldn't see Katie. She was obscured by a veil of water."

"That's it, then!" Tracy said as she flagged down a cab.

Linna and Dean looked at Tracy, simultaneously saying. "What's it?"

"Guys, I grew up in this neck of the woods. I've been to the falls a zillion times, and seen just about everything on both sides of the border." She looked back at the aero car. "Well, just about everything." A cab pulled up and the three of them piled in. Tracy told the driver to take them to Niagara Helicopters on Victoria Avenue. In the cab, she went on. "The answer has to be the Scenic Tunnels or whatever they're called now. They take you *behind* the falls. The view is awesome, and the roar of the water is thunderous. And...they're closed for the winter. No one would know she's there."

Linna looked at the direction they were traveling and said, "But aren't they back there?" She pointed over her shoulder in the opposite direction.

Tracy nodded, "Yeah, but trust me. We'll never get there in time if we try to drive there. There's way too much traffic now that it's getting dark and the lights will be on shortly, drawing out even more visitors." The driver pulled up to the helicopter office. Tracy handed him $10 for the $5 fare. "C'mon. We have to get up in the air."

The trio ran to the office and explained their urgent need to get to Table Rock House. The helicopter pilot that was sitting in the office looked up as Tracy was explaining to the reservations clerk. He looked the group over and decided to check things out himself. The first thing he asked for was Dean's military ID to prove she was indeed a colonel in the U. S. Army. Satisfied with the ID, he told the clerk he'd take care of it and led the group to one of the helicopters.

"I served with the Canadian Air Force for twenty years; this is the least I can do to help a fellow officer." He opened the cockpit door and instructed them to fasten their seatbelts while he geared everything up. Tracy took the co-pilot seat, anxious to observe his flying skill. In three minutes, they were off the ground and on their way. In another two, they were hovering near the bus parking area, waiting for a bus to move so they could put down. One more minute, and they were down. The women shouted their thanks over the whomp of the blades, and jumped out. They hit the pavement running, with Tracy leading the way. By the time they made it to the side door, the 'copter had lifted off and headed back to its base.

Table Rock House not only housed the entrance to the tunnels, but also a huge gift shop, restaurant, and the only restroom facilities for this part of the falls. They plunged into the building and bullied their way to the Journey Behind the Falls attraction, stopping short as they came up to a locked folding gate across the entrance. A sign on the gate said, "Closed for the winter. See you in the spring."

"Now what?" Tracy asked, looking at her friends.

Dean reached out and tugged at the gate. It moved away from the locking mechanism, obviously left open by Natasha in anticipation of her return. Dean looked around the crowd in Table Rock House, deciding that no one was paying attention to them, and slid the gate back far enough for them to slip in. "Go...quick," she said as she kept watch on the crowd before slipping in and pulling the gate back to a closed position. They headed down the stairs, taking them two at a time to the first landing. Dean looked over her shoulder to see if anyone had followed them. Whispering that the coast was clear, she held two fingers to her lips, indicating for them to continue down the stairway as quietly as possible. They continued down cautiously, passing two more landings before they came to the bottom. Tracy went first, followed by Linna, and finally Dean. Quietly, they walked through the tiled room, eyeing the scattered tools. Linna pointed to a chair that had ropes loosely wrapped around it. Dean nodded in acknowledgement that they were on the right track. Suddenly, the noise of a toilet flushing froze them in their tracks. Linna was right in front of the stall door that opened, exposing a very surprised Pavel.

"Who are..." he began in his broken English as he lifted the Pm84 Glauberyt he was carrying, but never completed the sentence as Linna whipped around, landing a combination of jabs, thrusts, and kicks on the stunned man and grabbing the submachine gun from his hand as he fell. He hit the floor like a ton of bricks, making a loud thump as his head hit the toilet, insuring he would be out of commission for a while.

Tracy and Dean both looked at Linna, their eyebrows raised nearly to their hairlines. The secretary looked back at them and whispered, "What?" and shrugged her shoulders. Linna then checked out the weapon, finding the safety was in the "off" position. She gripped the handle, nodding approvingly at the weight and balance of the gun, flicked the safety to "on," and looked up at the two women.

"We'll talk about this later," Tracy whispered back as she shook her head in disbelief.

Dean also shook her head, "If there's one, there's bound to be more," she said softly. "Let's go, but be careful." Looking back at Linna, she said, "You know how to use that? It's a new, Polish made weapon...top of the line too."

Linna quietly replied, "You've seen one gun, you've seen them all. They're basically all the same—pull the trigger and bang."

This time Dean was in the lead as they walked around the wall to the corridor that led to the elevator. When they got there, Dean asked Tracy, "Is there a stairway down?"

"I'm sure there has to be, but I have no idea where. It's 125 feet down to the tunnels."

Dean looked around, then checked her watch. It was 1730 hours. Not knowing what they would find at the bottom, Dean decided to take the elevator. "We don't have time to look. We'll take the elevator. Hopefully, whoever is down there will just think it's Linna's friend coming back from the john."

"Hey, he's not my friend!" Linna bantered back softly.

Dean pushed the elevator button, and the doors hissed open. It was a large elevator, meant to transport at least twenty tourists down at a time. "Okay, when we get to the bottom, keep your-selves plastered against the side closest to the door just in case there's someone at the bottom." The two women looked at Dean and nodded, entering the elevator and pressing themselves to the sides as Dean pushed the button for the tunnels. The ride down was quick, but the hum of the elevator was louder than they'd expected. When the car stopped, the women got in position as the doors slid open. Dean edged her head toward the opening and checked out the room before motioning for them to leave the ele-vator and hug the wall on the right side of the room. It was a fairly large area, capable of handling a substantial number of tour-ists. As they edged toward the opening at the opposite end, they realized that if anyone else was down there, they'd never hear them coming due to the roar of the water as it echoed down the tunnel.

At the opening, Tracy informed them that the tunnel straight ahead led to an outside observation area, while the tunnel to the right led to the porticoes directly behind the Horseshoe Falls. There were three of them.

"Well, Martha said she couldn't see Katie because of a veil of water, so my guess is that she's in one of the porticoes." Tracy and Linna nodded in agreement, and the three of them readied themselves. Dean once again edged around the corner to check for another guard. Whipping her head back, she whispered, "It's all clear. Maybe there was just one guard."

Tracy added, "Or maybe he's in one of the porticoes?"

They stepped quickly into the tunnel, crossing over to hug the left wall. Inching their way to the first opening, Dean squatted and peeked around the corner. She stood and shook her head and moved forward, followed by her companions. The same was true at the next opening. As they moved to cross the second portico, they heard a shout from behind, followed by gunfire. All three women threw themselves into the second observation point as bullets ricocheted off the tunnel walls.

Dean yelled over the gunfire, "Everyone okay?" Getting two nods, she made her way over to Linna and was going to ask for the submachine gun, when Linna slipped off the safety and headed for the tunnel. She took a deep breath, then dove into the tunnel, twisting onto her back and sliding across the floor as she leveled the gun at the man coming at her. Two short bursts and he fell backward, bouncing off the wall and landing on his back. The gun skidded from his hand and stopped in front of the opening where Tracy and Dean watched in amazement as they held their hands over their ears for protection from the noise. Linna rolled over and got into a squatting position, waiting for another attacker to materialize. When none appeared, she stood, walked over to the second guard, set her weapon down, and checked for a pulse.

Tracy came out first, grabbing the weapon by the opening as she went. "Is he dead?" Linna nodded in affirmation and turned towards the last portico.

Dean looked at the calm secretary, "Nice shooting," she commented, still amazed. She froze as she heard her name coming from that direction.

"*Katie!*" Dean yelled, and ran the last twenty-five feet.

* * * * *

Suffering from exposure, Katie was quickly losing her optimism. *C'mon, Dean, I can't hold on much longer. Please hurry.* She was mentally chanting, *Hurry, love, hurry,* when she heard the first burst of gunfire. The sound rallied her spirits as she waited for the noise to stop. Then she heard the second round, followed by silence. "No, no, she's all right!" she admonished herself out loud. "Dean...Dean...*Dean*!" she began shouting, and her spirit soared as she heard her lover call her name back. Suddenly she remembered the black box and the laser beam triggers. *"Dean, stop! Don't come in here. It's boobytrapped!"*

Dean had just reached the opening when she heard the warning and came to a sliding stop barely an inch inside the opening. She saw the black box and held her arms out to the side to stop Tracy or Linna from entering.

"Katie! Are you all right?" Dean visually examined the small chamber, then fixed on the wiring from the box to the holes. "Okay, tell me what she did."

Katie looked over her shoulder and was buoyed by the sight of the three women. "Natasha has set small charges in the walls and floor. Not enough to cause a cave-in, but enough to set this railing free and send me into the falls. The charge is set for 6 o'clock. The box also has a series of laser beams that will trigger the charges ahead of the timer if the beam is interrupted." Realizing the futility of the situation, compounded by her prolonged exposure to the elements, Katie began to cry.

Seeing the tears falling from her lover's eyes steeled Dean's resolve. "Hang in there, love, we'll figure a way around this. You'll be okay."

"I will be if you can figure out a way to get me out of here. We're running out of time."

Dean checked her watch and turned to her companions. "Can't go in from here, so we'll have to get her from out there." Dean hooked her thumb towards the thundering falls.

"You have a plan?" Tracy asked doubtfully.

"Maybe. Linna, go back upstairs and grab the rope we saw in the changing room and see if there's any more laying around." She hesitated, then added, "Better take the gun, in case your friend wakes up."

"Right!" Linna answered, taking the weapon from Tracy's hands before running back down the tunnel to the elevators.

"You're coming with me," Dean said as she grabbed Tracy's coat. They ran the twenty-five feet back to the middle chamber. Dean vaulted the first railing, stopping on the other side to help

Tracy over it. She spoke as she took off her belt and wrapped one end over her fist, handing the other end to Tracy. "Okay, I'm going to see what it looks like between here and Katie. Grab hold of my belt and don't let go!" Before Tracy could comment, Dean climbed gingerly over the safety railing and stretched around the corner.

The water coming down was occasionally whipping in toward the opening in sheets of spray, soaking Dean quickly. In between the bursts of spray, Dean was able to take stock of the wall of rock between her and Katie. The water thundering down did not run against the wall. In fact, the wall almost bowed inward at what looked to be a 75 to 80 degree angle. Just enough to let her body rest against it as she found holds for her hands and feet. It would be an almost impossible journey, but she had to try. Katie's life...and her soul...depended on it. When she inched her way back to the safety railing, Linna was there with the rope and some quarter inch cable that had loops on both ends.

"I found some plastic cable ties, too, and trussed up my friend good and tight." She smiled at Dean and held out a couple of extra items. "I thought you might need these, too." She handed Dean a pair of insulated work gloves and a rock pick. Linna reached into her back pocket and pulled out a small bolt cutter. "This may come in handy, too."

"Great. Thanks." It took another couple of minutes to get the rope and cable ready and securely fastened around her waist. Dean put her belt back on, and slipped the rock pick into it, the bolt cutters into her back pocket, put on the gloves and hopped back over the railing. "Don't let go," she commanded as she winked at them before edging around the corner. The first few hand and foot holds were easy to find, but the whipping spray made it hard to see too far ahead. Blindly reaching forward, she felt a piece of metal jutting out from the rock wall. Squinting, she was able to make out a large metal hook. "Now that's handy." She pulled herself closer and slipped some of the rope slack over the hook. The mist eased a bit and Dean spotted another hook, but it was just out of her reach. Searching for another handhold, she came up blank. "Guess I'll have to make my own," she mumbled as she pulled out the rock pick with her left hand and spied a likely spot. She was thankful that the wall of stone was not perfectly vertical. In fact, it was angled enough that she could rest her body against the wall as she chipped away at the limestone. It only took about a minute to get it deep enough, but a minute per handhold was going to be too long if she had to do this often. Slipping the pick back into her belt, Dean inched forward again, then once more and she was at the next hook. She caught her breath while searching the rocks. "Aha, there you are. I'm sure glad someone stuck these here ahead of time." She reached for the next hook. It was just slightly out of reach, but she tried again and was able to get her fingertips on it. Mentally crossing her fingers, she released the hold she had with her right hand, and lunged a bit toward the new hook. Relief swept over her as she wrapped her left hand tightly against the hook. Finding purchase for her feet, she swiftly moved forward again. This time she was able to see Katie's outline through the blowing mist.

"I'm almost there, love. Hang on," she shouted over the roar.

Hearing Dean's voice coming from the outside startled Katie. "Where are you?"

"Just about eight feet away from you. I'll be there in a sec."

Not seeing another hook, Dean explored the wall for a good spot. Luck? God? Skill? Something was with her, and she found a nice niche for her left hand. Now she just needed one for her foot, but the constant spray of water against the rock made it hard to keep her feet from sliding off. She carried most of her weight on her hands and only relied on her feet to transfer her hand grips.

This last bit of distance was the toughest as she hung on dearly with just the fingertips on her left hand and the grip on the hook with her right. Finally, her left toe struck something sticking out just a wee bit as she nearly did the splits to get more of her foot on the small ledge. Pressing her body against the wall, she released her right hand and started to creep ever-so-slowly to her left, hanging on to whatever little grip she could find with her right hand. "Okay, one more set of hand and foot holds and we've got it made." Dean explored the wall and found a good foot hold, but came up empty once more for her hand. She quickly pulled out the pick and began whacking at the rock. This time it took a bit longer before she was satisfied with the grip. Reaching, stretching, changing her position and shifting her weight, she was now able to reach the very end of the railing and pulled herself next to Katie.

"Okay, let's get you out of these manacles. She pulled out the bolt cutters and went to work on the set, holding Katie's left wrist and making short work of the chain to free that hand. "Now, let's get over this railing before I do the next one."

"You think it's safe?" Katie asked as she wrapped her left arm around Dean's neck.

"We'll soon find out. Try to stay close to the railing, though," Dean instructed as she helped lift her exhausted mate over the rail, glad to see there was no reaction. "Good. Now, let's get the other one off." Dean snuck a peek at her watch as she tackled the cuffs on Katie's right hand. *Four minutes to spare*, she thought as she snapped through the chain easily. She looked at the charges and figured they were set to blow outward toward the falls. Deciding that their best bet was to run right at the black box, she looked at her lover, "Katie, do you think you can run?"

Her legs were weak and she was shivering violently, but Katie nodded her head in affirmation. "I won't set any records, but I'll give it my best shot."

"Natasha was right when she said the charges would just loosen the railing. It even looks like they're set to blow out toward the falls. My guess is, if we run toward the tunnel, the blast will be focused out, and we should be in the clear." Again, she mentally crossed her fingers. "I'm also guessing that the laser beams are concentrated on the opening by the tunnel, so we should be able to get over the next railing without setting anything off. Once I get you over, stay close to the wall." Dean pulled Katie to her, kissing her forehead softly. "Ready?"

"I'm ready," Katie chattered.

"Slowly, to the next railing," she said as she held Katie tightly around the waist. The two women moved the eight feet toward the next railing. Dean helped Katie over and waited. *No blast. That's good. Now it's my turn. Guess I'd better take this rope off now.* As she reached down to untie the rope, the explosives blew, sending a shower of rock chips inward while the main blast went out. Dean fell toward the remaining railing with the force of the small blast. Just as she started to recover, she felt herself being pulled toward the falls. *What the heck?* She hung on to the railing with both hands as she looked over her shoulder to see a part of the blasted railing caught on her rope. The iron railing had to weight at least three hundred pounds. Between the force of the blast and its sheer weight, it was beginning to win the battle. "Katie, quick. Get the bolt cutters out of my back pocket and cut this damn rope before it drags me over the side."

* * * * *

Tracy and Linna had been feeding out the rope, and now the cable as Dean made progress across the rock face.

"Looking good," Linna told Tracy as they let out some more cable. "She should be there by now."

"Let's hope so."

They waited for a long time, before the cable tugged once more, cueing them to relax their grip and let out more cable. They were nearly to the end of the cable, and they looked at each other with concern.

"I would have thought we had plenty of rope and cable," Linna said.

"Maybe she had to alter course to get handholds?

"Well, I hope she doesn't need much more," Linna commented, tightening her grip once more just as the charges went off.

"Shit! Hold on tight!" Tracy shouted as they pulled on the rope when it tugged violently.

* * * * *

"Hurry!" Dean shouted, and Katie's numb fingers groped for the tool. Dean felt a second jerk on the rope and almost lost her grip.

"Got it," Katie said as she pulled them free and went to work on the rope. Not able to fit the cutter on the piece of rope around Dean's waist, she opted to lean out over Dean's body to reach the rope extending out. "Almost there." Finally, the rope snapped in two and whipped over the edge, freeing Dean at last.

"Damn, that was close," Dean commented as she slumped with relief on the floor of the chamber.

* * * * *

Unbeknownst to Tracy and Linna, they were feverishly adding to the strain on Dean's waist and her grip on the railing. When Katie cut through the rope, it whipped through the railing, releasing the heavy weight and setting the rope free to backlash toward Tracy and Linna. Without the weight at the other end, the two women promptly fell on their butts.

"*No!*" they shouted in unison as they crashed to the floor. Releasing the cable they still held in their hands, they jumped up and ran to the safety railing, their eyes trailing down the freely dangling cable, no sign of Dean at the other end.

"Oh, my God...she's gone!" They stood there staring out at the torrent of water, tears mixing with the spray of Niagara Falls on their faces.

Linna was the first to speak. "Do you suppose they both went?"

"Went where?" the voice behind them asked.

Turning their heads, they saw Dean holding Katie against her tightly, and then they looked back over the railing at the raging water. "We thought..." Linna and Tracy looked at each other and grinned, before hugging each other with everything they had. Hopping over the railing, they ran up and hugged their two very alive, very safe, friends.

"Let's get out of here," Dean croaked as Linna bear hugged her one more time.

Chapter
24

16 December, 0800 Hours

Dean tried to roll over onto her side in the warm bed, but found her movement impeded by her lover's body wrapped tightly around her torso. Closing her eyes, she replayed the events of the evening from when they took the elevator back to the changing room. When they got there, they found several Provincial Police officers, a police officer from the American side, and the helicopter pilot from Niagara Helicopters coming down the stairs. Thanks to the intervention of the pilot and the heads-up from Lieutenant Green, they were spared much of the questioning at the site and were escorted instead to the local hospital, where Katie was examined for her exposure and given warm, dry clothing and a good dose of medicine to ward off the ill effects of her ordeal. Dean, too, was examined for possible soft tissue damage from the rope that had tried to cut her in two, and was also given a change of clothes. The rest of the evening was spent explaining what happened to Colleen, Martha and Joshua, a busload of very excited seniors, Tiny, and their new friend Luke the helicopter pilot, who treated them to several rum toddies, swearing that would protect them from catching a cold. The police were even considerate enough to postpone their statement until the next morning, indicating that Lieutenant Green would be present via speaker phone during that interview. A police car would be sent around to pick them up at noon. Tracy and Linna were going to have to report to the police station with them, but right now, Dean was perfectly happy to be where she was.

Looking down at the blonde head nestled in the crook of her shoulder, she smiled at the contented feeling she was experiencing. She bent her head, gently placing a kiss on Katie's forehead. "Well, I certainly hope I don't have to face a challenge like that again anytime soon," Dean mumbled softly to herself.

"Urf, me too," Katie groaned as she stretched her sore muscles. "Is it morning already?"

"Mmhm. But there's no rush to get up." Dean reached over with her free hand and brushed the hair out of Katie's eyes.

"Good, because I'm really warm and comfortable right here," the blonde confessed, tightening the grip she had on her partner.

Dean wiggled down further under the comforter, getting a bit more comfortable before closing her eyes again.

At ten in the morning, they were awakened by a soft knock on the door. Dean checked the clock on the bedside table, before letting her head fall back on her pillow.

"Hey, love, guess we'd better get up. It's ten o'clock already." The knock came again, only this time a bit louder. "That's probably Tracy." Dean called out, "Just a minute," before pulling off the covers. She padded over to the chair where she had placed her duffle, rummaging in it for her sweat pants and a t-shirt. Slipping them on, she waited until Katie was in the bathroom before she opened the door.

"Hey," Tracy said as Dean opened the door. "Are you two just getting out of the feathers?"

"Yep," Dean replied as she waved her visitors in. "We woke up earlier, but decided to just mellow out for a bit. We must have been more tired than we thought."

"Well, from what I heard about your little adventure, I'd say you had a good reason to stay in bed," Colleen said as she took a seat on the couch. "In fact, I tried to get these two to leave y'all alone until at least noon." She looked over at her two companions as they both just hung their heads and stared at the floor.

Dean looked at them, her brows knitting together, "Aren't you two supposed to be with your group this morning?"

"Yes and no," Tracy hedged. "They went over to the Botanical Gardens today with a local tour guide. After the events of yesterday, a couple of our regulars offered to take over for the morning tour. This afternoon, they're going to the casino, so we'll be free for the memorial service."

Linna lifted her head, a chagrined look on her face, "Besides, we thought you might be hungry...or at least, Katie might be hungry."

Dean smiled at her and nodded. "Now that you mention it, food does sound like a good idea about now. Does this place have a good restaurant?"

It took a few minutes for Dean and Katie to get ready, but they were off to the restaurant in no time flat. After ordering, Tracy looked over at Linna and said, "So, Linna, are you going to explain that little show you put on for us yesterday?"

Linna blushed as four sets of eyes looked at her questioningly. "Hey, he just took me by surprise, and I reacted."

"Where did you learn those moves?" Tracy inquired earnestly. "Did your son teach you that stuff?" She looked at Dean and Katie to explain. "Linna's eldest son is a Tang Soo Do instructor, and quite a good one, too. National champ and all."

The embarrassed secretary nodded, "Yeah, he did. I've been messing with that stuff for quite a while now. I just never had to use it before. Guess it's nice to know I can do it for real."

"And what about the way you handled that Polish Pm84? He teach you that, too?" Dean asked seriously.

"Nah! Just a lot of target practice and deer hunting," Linna chuckled.

Dean raised an eyebrow and, grinning at Linna, said, "Hmm, interesting hunting style you have there, my friend," which was followed by hearty laughter from everyone.

* * * * *

When they exited the chapel, a glorious setting sun greeted them. Vivid purples and pinks, with a tinge of gold, played on the puffy clouds overhead. The sight renewed their hearts and souls after the sorrow of saying final goodbyes to Tom. The service was short, but very moving, as friends and relatives came up to speak about the Tom they'd known. It was obvious to Dean and Katie that there was much more to the man than they had gotten to know, and it saddened them that they would never have the opportunity to explore that friendship further.

Tiny came up behind Dean and Katie and gave them a gentle hug. As they stared at the beautiful sunset, he spoke softly, "Tom was a good man. I'm going to miss him."

"I'm so sorry, Tiny. Natasha took her revenge on so many innocent people," Dean said, leaning into the hug.

"Are you going to go back to the island?" Katie asked, looking into the sad eyes.

"Nope. I think I'll head back to Texas. See what kind of trouble I can get into there." He smiled at his friends. "Nick's offered me a new job. It'll be a challenge, but he needs to beef up security at his new refinery...all high-tech stuff. He's working on a new product there. It's all hush hush."

"Well, there's nothing like a challenge to keep you on your toes," Katie said, giving his arm a squeeze.

"Katie, Tiny, please...if I hear the word 'challenge' again..." Dean drawled, shaking her head.

Katie smiled at her lover, wrapping her arm firmly around Dean's waist. She looked up into the beautiful sapphire eyes and said, "We'll be together to face the next one."

Epilogue

24 December, 1900 Hours

The holiday season was in full swing and Dean was looking forward to the surprise party she'd arranged with all their friends tonight on Christmas Eve. Dean had called everyone on the sly, swearing them all to secrecy to surprise Katie. She knew how much Katie wanted to be around family and friends on this special day, and she'd even arranged for Martha and her father to join them. The surprise was going to be perfect. No one had spilled the beans, and Dean couldn't wait to see Katie's face.

They had spent the entire weekend putting the finishing touches on the holiday decorations and hiding from each other as they wrapped their gifts. Katie placed the last present beneath the tree before heading to the kitchen to fix mugs of hot chocolate with peppermint schnapps. Dean was just finishing tending to the fire in the fireplace. Satisfied with the way the flames were progressing, the tall woman stood and stretched. She looked around the living room, smiling at the festive atmosphere. *It's been so long since I've celebrated Christmas at all, and soon we'll have a houseful of family and friends to enjoy this with us,* Dean thought as she grinned happily at the thought of everyone opening the gifts she'd bought. *I can't wait 'til Katie tackles the box with the tickets in it.* Dean had managed to arrange for a four-day vacation to St. Croix over the New Year's holiday. The resort was one of those with individual bungalows nestled on the hillside overlooking the bay. Each one was completely self-contained, and they even had their own little pool on the patio. She had requested that the management stock the small kitchen with all sorts of goodies so they wouldn't have to leave for anything unless they really wanted to. *Ah, peace and quiet after the holidays, with nothing to do but be with my sweetie...I can't wait!*

Katie came out of the kitchen, mugs in hand, catching the sight of Dean grinning. "You look like the cat that ate the canary, love. What's got you in such a good mood?"

"Ohh, nothing. Just enjoying the Christmas spirit."

"Mmhmm," Katie added wisely, grinning to herself at the thought of Dean seeing her shiny, new, black Boxster when it got delivered later that night. *Bill and Dirk will be here shortly, and Tracy and Colleen should be here right after that with Linna and her hubby. Ohhh, and wait 'til her Dad and Martha arrive. She has absolutely no idea they're coming. Uh oh,...I sure hope she doesn't get upset with my impromptu party. I can't believe no one slipped and let the cat out of the bag.*

Dean walked over to her lover and wrapped her arms around her, giving her a big hug. "Our first Christmas in our new house." She looked down into Katie's eyes, and the love she saw there filled her heart and her soul. "I love you," she said softly, bending to seal her statement with a kiss. Katie's lips welcomed the touch of Dean's, and answered the love and passion that was given and taken so freely between them. The kiss lingered on until they finally broke contact, breathless and much warmer than they had been a moment before. "Mmm, how about we move this to a more comfortable spot. I think the rug in front of the fireplace is calling our names."

"I've always wanted to make love in front of a fireplace," Katie responded tenderly, placing a hand against Dean's cheek, "But, um..." The doorbell chimed at that moment, a harbinger of the many friends that were expected that night.

Dean feigned a sigh, "Maybe if we ignore them, they'll go away," she suggested.

Katie placed both hands on Dean's chest and bowed her forehead into them. "Honey, I don't think they'll go away...not when they're invited."

Two dark eyebrows rose in question, "And that would mean...what?"

"It would mean that I planned a little surprise for you this evening." Gathering her thoughts, she quickly went on. "Christmas Eve is a time for family. I know your dad is your only *real* family, but our friends make up our extended family. And, I thought...well, I thought that it would be nice to have them here with us in our home to help celebrate." She lifted her head and looked into Dean's smiling face. "You're not upset are you?"

Before Dean could respond, the doorbell rang again. "I guess we'd better get that," Dean chuckled as they walked to the door, "It's probably Bill and Dirk."

Katie looked up at her lover. "You knew?"

"I should," she replied laughing. "I invited them."

"You...but, I..." Shaking her head, she joined in with Dean's deep laughter. "Guess the surprise is on us, huh?"

* * * * *

By 2200, everyone was assembled and having a great time. Martha and Joshua arrived shortly after Bill and Dirk, followed by Linna and her husband, Colleen and Tracy, Sergeant Major Tibbits and his wife Millie, and finally General Carlton. Things started a bit slowly, with the group not knowing how to act in Joshua's presence, but that hurdle was soon eliminated when he lifted his glass to his daughter and Katie and followed that with an acknowledgement of the love that was evident among her extended family. Soon Christmas tunes were in the air, snacks were prepared and eaten, drinks were consumed, and laughter and love were everywhere.

Katie was sitting in Dean's lap, unconsciously running her fingers through her lover's long, raven hair. They were all listening to a story Linna was telling about a trip she had chaperoned to New York City for the annual Christmas Show at Radio City Music Hall. As she told about the string of Murphy's Laws that occurred during the trip, they all laughed as Linna explained. The secretary had just finished her story when the doorbell rang once more. The timing couldn't have been more perfect.

Dean frowned as she checked her watch. "Now who could that be?"

Katie, on the other hand, was grinning fiercely. She had been waiting for this moment all evening. "Hmmm, don't know, love. Why don't you go and see?" She slid off Dean's lap and watched her get up to answer the door. When Dean was almost to the door, Katie signaled everyone to follow quietly.

Dean opened the door and found a rather rotund gentleman wearing a Santa suit standing at her doorstep. "Yes?" she inquired politely, "May I help you?"

In a deep jovial voice, the man said, "Deanna," as he pulled out a roll of paper from his pocket, allowing it to unfurl onto the sidewalk. "According to my list...and I've checked it twice you know...you have been very good girl this year!" He began a round of "ho ho ho's," grabbing his belly as he laughed. His laughter subsiding, he reached into his other pocket and brought out a little gold box and handed it to her with a wink. "Like I said, you have been a *very* good girl." He winked again, touched his nose with his index finger and turned, leaving a stunned Dean standing with the box in her hand. All of her friends and family gathered around her as she looked at the box.

"Maybe you should open it," Katie offered with a grin.

Dean nodded and opened the card on the box, reading the inscription, "With all my love, Katie." Then she opened the box, curiously eyeing the contents.

"Well?" Linna asked impatiently. "What'dya get?"

Dean held up a key ring with a set of keys on it. As she spied the logo on the keys, her eyes became round with surprise. The entire group looked up as they heard a car engine purr up the driveway and stop before them. Santa rolled down the window of the shiny black Boxster, waving at them, "ho ho's" coming freely.

Dean stood there staring at him and the car in disbelief, while Katie came up and put her arms around Dean's waist giving her a gentle squeeze. "So, ya like it?" she asked with a twinkle in her eye.

"Katie...it's...wow!" Dean stammered.

"Cool!" Linna shouted from behind them. "Can I take it for a test drive?"

"Don't you think maybe they'd like to take it out by themselves first?" her husband suggested as he poked her in the ribs.

"Yeah, take it for a spin," Bill suggested, echoed by concurring comments from the rest of their friends.

Santa opened the door and got out of the car, holding the door open for Dean who eagerly jumped in behind the wheel while Katie ran to the passenger side and slipped into her seat. The partygoers shouted whoops and yays as the engine roared to life.

Inside the car, the two women exchanged grins. Katie leaned toward the steering wheel to wave at the group, but was intercepted by Dean as she pulled her lover in for a kiss that would have steamed up the windows if the driver's window had been up. As their lips parted, a blushing Katie looked at the smiling group on the doorstep. "Um, shall we go for that ride now?" she asked as she waved at them. Dean nodded, slipped the car into gear, and purred off into the night. Santa waved at them, too, then he tipped his head and said, "Merry Christmas to all, and to all a good night!"

Other titles in this series
available from
Quest Books

Forces of Evil

Forces of Evil takes place in New York state in a small Catskills resort town. As the story unfolds, two female undercover agents from separate agencies meet, and join forces to try to decipher and stop a diabolical plot of world domination from reaching its climax. As they find themselves falling helplessly in love, adding a new dimension to their jobs, and another set of priorities, the team races to a cliffhanger conclusion.

Second Edition
ISBN: 1-930928-07-6

Blue Holes To Terror

Following in the wake of *Forces of Evil*, *Blue Holes to Terror* brings the readers another story involving Lieutenant Colonel Deanna Peterson and Special Agent Katherine O'Malley. After witnessing a near tragic "accident" on I-95, in which a retired British MI-6 agent was targeted for elimination, the pair is asked to unofficially investigate, and runs headlong into a terrorist/mercenary initiative designed to sabotage a multi-national military exercise. The action begins in Washington, DC and culminates on Grand Bahama Island in the Caribbean. Our heroines have to rely on their ingenuity, physical skills, and a little help from their growing circle of friends to succeed in stopping the terrorists from achieving their goals.

ISBN: 1-930928-61-0

Other titles from
Quest Books

For readers interested in more information on Niagara Falls, I suggest the following websites: (The teacher in me just wants folks to learn more!)

http://www.infoniagara.com/gateway.html

http://www.iaw.com/~falls/origins.html

http://www.niagarafallslive.com/Facts_about_Niagara_Falls.htm

http://www.city.niagarafalls.on.ca/fallscam.html
(This one will give you a real-time view of the Horseshoe and American Falls)

The Cover

The picture for the cover for Deadly Challenge was taken by the author at the *Journey Behind the Falls* attraction. It is located on the Canadian side in Table Rock House and gives visitors the most up close view of this spectacular natural wonder.

Trish Kocialski resides outside of Albany, New York. Although she is a New Yorker by birth, she also claims the states of Missouri and Kansas as her "other home" having lived in the greater Kansas City area for twenty-two years. Trish taught school for eighteen years and worked as an advocate for comprehensive school health education and wellness for another nine years. She wrote her first novel while working as the Director of Parks and Recreation for the Town of Liberty in the beautiful Catskills of New York. Trish has now returned to work in the field of education.

Trish can be reached at tkocialski@catskill.net or through visiting her website at http://xenamultimedia.com/trish/

Printed in the United States
31204LVS00007B/22